THE HERRON HOUSE

RANDOLPH CASEY HORROR THRILLERS
BOOK 4

ROCKWELL SCOTT

THE HERRON HOUSE

PROLOGUE

The man heard his name whispered from the shadows.

He didn't turn around. Refused to. He'd done that too many times before, only to find no one there.

Instead, he refocused his attention on what was in front of him—a chess board, the pieces arranged in mid-game. The whisper had broken his concentration, but he found his train of thought again. He advanced his white rook up a few squares to cut off the black, attacking queen that threatened his king.

The man lifted his eyes to the chair across the table. It was empty. He'd almost forgotten he'd been playing alone, making moves for both white and black. He found it quite amusing that he was beating himself.

Another whisper came from somewhere in the large home office. The man clenched his eyes, willing the voice to leave him alone.

He'd lost track of how long he'd been holed up inside

his home office—days, perhaps. But locking himself away from his family and the rest of the outside world was for the best.

He could not articulate exactly what was wrong with him, but he knew he was unwell. In the last couple weeks, a dark heaviness had come—a powerful dread that had settled upon his shoulders. It was debilitating. He could hardly think clearly. Sometimes, he felt as if he'd lost control of his own body. He'd suddenly snap back into awareness to find himself doing something he didn't remember starting... such as the game of chess he was currently playing.

And, of course, the imagined whispers in the corners of the room persisted.

With it all came an uncharacteristic rage that he took out on his wife and son. The man had enough clarity remaining to know they didn't deserve it; it was best for him to keep away until whatever was wrong with him resolved itself.

There came a knock on the door, startling him.

"James?" came his wife's voice, soft and trepidatious.

There was a time when his wife hadn't feared him, but he could scarcely remember those days now.

"Please talk to me."

The anger shot through him like electricity. "Go away!" He glared at the door, *daring* her to speak again. Why couldn't she understand he needed to be alone? Hadn't he explained that his isolation was best for everyone? Perhaps not. But she should've figured it out by now.

She said nothing. The only sound was her footsteps fading away from the locked office door.

He buried his face in his hands. He had no idea why

he'd screamed at her. He'd never been that kind of person. Why now? What had changed?

James.

"What do you want?"

At first he thought that his wife had returned, but this time the voice had come from behind him, in the office.

He couldn't help himself as he whirled in his chair and scanned the room. As always, no one was there.

The man slapped himself on the side of his head, over and over, chastising himself for reacting. He'd been doing so well ignoring the imploring whispers.

You must keep building.

"No. I won't." The man turned his attention back to the chess board. The game was the lone distraction he had left. He made the move for his opponent, the only one that would've made sense if he'd been playing a real person. The black queen captured the white rook, leaving the white king in checkmate.

Randolph Casey must die and this house is his tomb.

It wasn't the first time the voice had mentioned that name. The man had no idea who Randolph Casey was, nor did he want to find out.

Yet he felt his resistance slipping. What was the point of fighting it any longer? Deep inside, he knew he had no choice. Whatever held sway over him, whatever kept calling his name from the shadows... it would not go away.

Go to your desk.

But... maybe the voice would leave him alone if he complied.

The man stood from the chess board and went to his desk in the center of his sizable home office.

Open the drawer.

When he did, he found a sketchbook inside. The man was confused—he didn't remember how it had gotten there. He'd never had the desire to draw anything in his entire life.

But now that he'd relented and obeyed *just* a little, everything else was like water rushing downstream. His arms and hands moved without conscious effort, like a mere puppet.

He opened the sketchbook to the first blank page, picked up his pen, and began to draw.

1

A man came into Rand Casey's class with only a few minutes remaining in the lesson. He eased in and stood at the top of the stadium-style classroom, arms folded across his chest. A slight grin lit up his face, as if expecting to be amused.

Rand lost his train of thought. Visitors to his class were rarely a good thing. It meant he either had a prospective client seeking him out, or his class was once again being audited by the university to determine if Intro to Supernatural Studies was still a vital part of their Religious Studies curriculum.

The classroom was large enough to accommodate two hundred students, but only about thirty filled the seats. Although the spring semester had just begun, Rand's class had already seen a larger-than-average number of drops. He was accustomed to students dropping his class—almost all said the subject matter was too frightening—but the decreasing number of students enrolled in his course did not bode well for his job security.

"As I was saying," Rand continued as he shifted his attention away from the newcomer, "negative entities quite frequently attach themselves to objects. Dolls seem to be popular choices for them."

The projector screen behind Rand displayed a picture of a doll dressed in a blue shirt and white shorts. It had big eyes and a smile that seemed more ghastly than friendly.

"He's *really* creepy," said a girl sitting a few rows away from the front of the classroom.

"This doll is from a case I handled personally," Rand explained. "My client's young daughter said she'd been given the doll as a gift from a stranger. It wasn't long before the daughter started claiming that the doll would speak to her at night." The student shrank back in her seat. "At first my client didn't believe her daughter, which is how these scenarios normally go. It was only when *she* heard the voices coming from her daughter's bedroom at night that she got in touch with me."

Rand clicked his remote and the slide transitioned to the next, which was embedded with a video of the doll that he'd filmed himself. Rand went to his laptop and clicked to play the video.

Rand's hand entered the frame, holding a silver cross dangling from a chain. He brought it near the doll, which sat upright on a table.

"*Take it away!*" a terse, snarling voice shot from the doll. Many of the students cringed.

"But why dolls?" asked the girl who'd spoken up earlier.

"One of the primary goals of these evil entities is possession," Rand explained. "They possess humans, as we've talked about in prior lessons, but if they don't find an opportunity to do that, that'll happily take over an object that resembles a human, such as the situation here." He gestured toward the doll on the screen. "From the object, they can continue tormenting the living. In this case, it was the little girl who played with the doll."

Rand clicked his remote again, and the doll was replaced by a picture of a gold pendant attached to a chain. It was laid on a table covered in a black tablecloth.

"This is another situation I've personally dealt with. In my experience, there are two types of cursed objects— ones that actually have an entity within them, like we just discussed with the doll, and ones that don't have an entity in them, but still emit negative energy that affects the person who owns it, which was the case with this neck-lace. These objects curse the person who owns them, and the curse often manifests as a pattern of very bad luck which usually becomes exponentially worse over time. If the person doesn't recognize they've been cursed and quickly do something about it, then it usually ends with their untimely death."

A student at the back of the class raised his hand. "Which kind of cursed object is worse?"

"In my opinion, something like the necklace is worse. Objects like that are very unassuming and most people won't recognize that their misfortune began soon after they purchased the object or received it as a gift. Even if I were to point this out to them, they might not even believe me if they tend to be more skeptical of supernat-ural things. When it comes to talking dolls, however, as soon as you hear them speak you *know* you have a problem."

The same girl raised her hand. "You said an object could be given as a gift. Why would anyone want to give someone a cursed object?" she asked, seeming genuine upset.

"Usually it's an honest mistake," Rand said. "Someone will go shopping in an old thrift store and spot a necklace like this one here. They'll have a friend or relative who they think will like it and buy it for them. Other times, the curse is… very intentional. A person will take an object they know their target will like and invest the time to learn *how* to curse it, and then actually do it." Rand shook his head. "There are some very bad people out there, unfortunately. It's harrowing to think about, but I've learned by now that there seems to be no limit to the evil some people are willing to inflict onto others."

The man at the back of the classroom was not smirking anymore. He stood with folded arms, listening to Rand intently. He was also no longer alone. He'd been joined by a woman and a young girl who looked about nine or ten years old.

He's not here to audit, Rand thought. *If he's brought his family, then he's here for my help.*

"We'll leave it there for today," Rand told the class as he glanced at his watch. "Have a good evening, everyone."

The students began filing out of the classroom. The couple at the back of the room stood aside to allow the crowd to leave. When they were the only ones who remained, the man turned to face Rand. "Interesting stuff," he called down with a smile.

"That's one word for it," Rand said. He wished he had a dime for every time someone referred to his subject matter as mere "interesting stuff."

"I was hoping for a moment of your time."

"Sure."

The man descended the stadium-style steps. The woman instructed the young girl to sit in one of the seats near the door, where she took out some coloring books from her backpack to occupy herself.

The man reached the bottom of the steps and extended his hand. "Jackson Herron."

"Randolph Casey. Friends call me Rand."

Jackson's grip was a bit too firm. He had youthful face, with a close-trimmed beard framing his flawless smile. He wore dark blue jeans, brown shoes, and a blazer over a white button-up shirt with an open collar. His brown hair was gelled messily, a style that seemed a bit too young for his probable age—perhaps a few years younger than Rand —but he pulled it off regardless.

"This is my wife, Miranda."

Miranda joined them at the front of the classroom. The blonde woman offered Rand her limp right hand for him to shake. She wore light-blue, hight-waisted jeans and a loose-fitting white blouse. Rand could already tell she was uneasy about being there.

"You're an easy man to track down," Jackson said, smirk returning to his face. "That's a good thing."

Rand assumed that meant Jackson looked him up on the university website. "What can I do for you?"

Jackson's smile faltered just a bit. He tried to exchange a glance with his wife, but her eyes were glued to the tile floor.

"We have a… little problem," Jackson said, clearing his throat.

2

client, Rand thought. Just as he'd suspected.

It had been almost three months since his last case, where Rand had faced off against a pair of black-eyed kids on Halloween night. He'd cautiously enjoyed Thanksgiving and Christmas, yet was unable to fully relax, feeling as if his next supernatural battle was just around the corner.

"I see," Rand said. "Why don't we go—"

He'd been about to suggest they go to his office to talk, but Jackson had already helped himself to a desk on the front row. Miranda quickly sat on her husband's left side.

Seeing as they'd already made themselves comfortable, Rand pulled up a navy-blue chair that he rarely sat in—he preferred to teach while standing. He placed the chair about five feet from the couple and sat facing them.

"Tell me about the problem," Rand said.

Miranda glanced at her husband, looking nervous. Jackson met her eyes briefly. "It's quite the odd story," he told Rand.

"I'm guessing you've been experiencing paranormal activity," Rand said. "Perhaps a haunting, and you're coming to me to fix it."

Miranda's face tightened as if Rand's words had triggered a negative memory. Even Jackson, despite his pleasant demeanor when he'd arrived, shifted nervously in his seat. Rand figured it was the first time the couple had had their situation verbalized so bluntly.

"Yes, I... believe that's what's happening," Jackson said slowly.

"Do you mind if I record our conversation?" Without waiting for a response, Rand stood and went to his leather work bag, which lay on a table near the classroom's podium. He took his digital recorder from the smaller pocket and scooped up the four-legged stool from behind the podium. He put the stool halfway between his chair and the Herrons, with the recorder on top. He clicked the red button and it began recording. "Standard operating procedure."

"By all means," Jackson said, although the way he suspiciously eyed the recorder suggested to Rand that perhaps Jackson *wasn't* fully comfortable with the idea.

"January fourteenth, three-fifteen in the afternoon," Rand said for the recorder. "This is Jackson and Miranda Herron." He sat back down. "Now, tell me about the experiences that you two have been having."

"Our experiences..." Jackson slowing shook his head. "Where do we even begin?"

"At the beginning," Rand said.

"Right." Jackson chuckled. "Well, in that case..." He leaned forward and pursed his lips while he gathered his thoughts. "My father's house allegedly has some… strange and unpleasant things happening inside."

"Allegedly?" Rand asked.

"What I mean is—" Jackson straightened in his seat. "When it started, I was skeptical. Now I'm… less skeptical."

"So you believe there's paranormal activity in your father's home," Rand said. Jackson nodded. "Does your father live there alone?"

"He passed," Jackson said. "Last year."

"James suffered from dementia in his final years," Miranda added.

"I'm sorry for your loss," Rand said. "Who lives in James's home now?"

"No one."

"Do you own the home?" Rand asked.

"Yes."

"If no one lives there, then how did you learn about the paranormal activity?"

"The caretakers," Jackson said. "We've been through a few dozen over the years. Even though I pay them well and give them free housing on the property, they all eventually quit on me."

"Free housing on the property?" Rand asked.

"My father's home is…" Jackson wagged his head as he considered. "…fairly large."

"Come on, Jack," Miranda said pointedly.

Jackson seemed to relent. "My father lived in a mansion on a huge piece of land. There's a cottage on the property that he built specifically for the caretaker."

There was no shortage of large houses in town, but

Rand couldn't think of any that would be considered a mansion. "Where is your father's home?"

"In Beau Ridge," Jackson said. "About an hour north of here. " Rand had heard of the small town, but had never been there. "I've been told that over the last couple years or so, the locals have begun referring to the mansion as the Herron House."

"Has a nice ring to it, I suppose," Rand said. "What do these caretakers report?"

Jackson blew out his breath through puffed cheeks. "Well. That's where it gets weird. They all say pretty much the exact same thing."

"Which is?" Rand knew that if multiple people reported the same incidents, it was very likely that the mansion did, in fact, have a supernatural presence.

"They see people inside the house, even when they thought they were alone."

"Ghosts," Rand said. He could tell Jackson had been trying to avoid the word.

"That's what they say, yes," Jackson relented.

"Did any of the caretakers ever describe the ghosts?" Rand asked.

When Jackson hesitated, Miranda spoke up. "Some see a woman and others see an old man. One or two of the caretakers saw both."

"I see," Rand said. "And the woman and the old man were reported by your caretakers multiple times?"

"Yes," Miranda said.

"How long has this been going on?"

Jackson and Miranda looked at each other, each considering.

"I'd estimate five years," Jackson said.

"You said your father passed last year," Rand said. "Did *he* experience any paranormal activity?"

"We actually put him in a nursing home in four years ago," Jackson explained. "He lived alone in the mansion for a long time after my mother passed, but when his dementia worsened we had to relocate him. He never mentioned anything of the sort, but then again, he wasn't entirely himself toward the end."

"You mentioned you were skeptical," Rand said to Jackson. "Do you not believe what these caretakers reported?"

Jackson hesitated, as if interpreting Rand's words as an accusation. Rand figured the man struggled to balance his skepticism with not wanting to outright dismiss the experiences of his caretakers.

"One of the ghosts comes to our own home now," Miranda said.

Jackson nodded, lips pressed together. A hint of fear had risen in his eyes.

"Oh." To Rand, that was an interesting point. It was common for entities to remain within a single location. But when they ventured outside of that location, that could mean they were attached to a person rather than a place.

In Rand's experience, that was almost always worse. He'd had clients in the past who thought they could solve their paranormal problems simply by moving out of their home—only to have the haunting entity follow them.

"Which ghost do you see?"

"The old man," Jackson and Miranda said at the same time.

"Do you also live in Beau Ridge?"

"No. We live in the country club here in town," Jackson said.

That was the wealthiest neighborhood in the city. Rand's ex, Tessa, also lived there with her fiancé, Bill.

I wonder if Bill knows these two, Rand thought. Living in the country club meant the Herrons were quite well-off. They and Bill might run in the same circles.

"Can you describe what happens when the old man appears?" Rand asked.

Jackson looked to his wife.

"Well…" Miranda said, taking a breath. Rand could tell she didn't like to think about it. He didn't blame her. "He always comes late at night. I'll be asleep, and then suddenly I'm wide awake. And I just get this feeling that I'm… being watched. I know he's there. I try not to look, but I can't help it. It's like he *makes* me look." Miranda kept her gaze on the floor as she spoke. Jackson laid a comforting hand on her thigh. "He's always standing in the corner. Even though the room's dark, I can still see him clearly. His body is like a shadow, and his eyes glow white…"

Rand didn't like the sound of that at all. He knew what he needed to ask next. "What time of night does he come?"

Miranda met Rand's eyes. With a wary expression, she replied, "Always around three o'clock in the morning. Why?"

3

I t was just as Rand suspected. *This entity is most likely demonic.*

A demon was *very* different from a ghost. A ghost was a spirit that had once been human and hadn't yet moved on after they'd died. A demon, however, was an inhuman spirit with one goal: to torment the living.

Demons were most active at three o'clock in the morning, and most of what they did was associated with the number three. It was their way of mocking the Holy Trinity.

"How long has the old man been appearing in your house?" Rand asked. He planned to hold off on diagnosing a demonic infestation for the moment; he didn't want to frighten the couple before he had all the information.

"I'd say about a year now," Jackson said.

"Around the same time your father passed?" Rand asked.

Jackson looked up and away as he thought about that.

"Yeah, I suppose you're right. I never put two and two together."

"Does the old man *resemble* your father?" Rand asked.

Jackson looked at Miranda.

"No," Miranda finally said after some hesitation.

"And have you ever seen the old man?" Rand asked Jackson.

"No."

That also checked out. In Rand's experience, demonic entities usually only revealed themselves to one member of the family. When that person kept seeing a terrifying apparition over and over again, yet the rest of the family refused to believe them because they'd never seen it themselves, it caused arguments, discord, and distrust—which was precisely a demon's goal.

Rand glanced to the young girl at the back of the classroom, oblivious to their conversation as she worked on her coloring book. "Is that your daughter?"

"Yes," Miranda said. "Carmen. She's nine."

"Has she seen or experienced anything unusual?"

Jackson and Miranda exchanged a glance.

"No," Jackson said.

"Hmm," Rand said. "That's atypical."

This demon is bypassing the child and choosing to appear to Miranda, Rand thought. *But why?*

"Atypical?" Jackson asked.

"Entities in the home usually reveal themselves to children before anyone else in the family," Rand explained. "Young kids are easier targets for these spirits, because they don't yet have a full understanding of what's real and what's paranormal. I can't tell you how many cases I've had that began when a client's young child suddenly met an 'imaginary friend.' "

"Oh." Jackson's brow furrowed, as if struggling to digest what Rand had just told him. "Well, so far she hasn't complained to us about anything."

"That's a good thing," Rand said. "Most children in these types of situations aren't as lucky." While that was true, Rand couldn't recall a single case he'd worked when a demonic entity had chosen *not* to reveal himself to the child. It was very unusual behavior. "Other than the old man appearing, has there been anything else out of the ordinary going on?"

Both Jackson and Miranda thought for a moment before they both shook their heads.

"Do personal belongings in your home disappear and reappear in different places?"

"No," Jackson said.

"Do you ever notice objects levitating?"

"Definitely not." Jackson seemed quite put off by that idea.

"What about pets? Do your animals start growling or barking at things you can't see? Particularly in the corners of rooms?"

"We don't have any pets."

"Has there been anything physical? Have you ever felt followed, or shoved, or scratched?"

"No."

Usually Rand's clients had suffered some, if not all of those common signs of a haunting.

"Is it a good thing if we haven't experienced any of that stuff?" Jackson asked.

"Yes. You've come to me a lot sooner than most of my clients tend to. Your situation doesn't seem to have escalated yet."

"That's encouraging, I guess," Jackson said. "What do you suggest we do?"

Rand leaned back in his chair. "It sounds to me like this spirit—the old man—is primarily drawn to your father's house. He needs to be removed from there. Once that's done, he should stop appearing in your bedroom as well. I can also get rid of any other spirits that are in the home, such as the ghost of the woman your caretakers reported."

"That sounds exactly like what we're looking for," Jackson said, exchanging a look with his wife. "You can do that for us?"

"Yes."

For the first time since they'd arrived in the classroom, the Herrons seemed to lose some of the tension they'd been holding.

"What does all this entail?" Jackson asked.

"I'll perform a cleansing in your father's home," Rand explained. "It's best if I do it at night, since that's when spirits are most active, and therefore more susceptible to being removed. I'll cleanse and bless every single room until the spirits have no place else to go. At that point, they'll be forced to leave."

Whatever momentary relief Jackson and Miranda had experienced seemed to evaporate. Both gave Rand a troubled look.

"What's wrong?" Rand asked.

"*Every* single room?" Jackson asked.

"Yes..." Then it struck Rand. "How many rooms does the place have?"

Jackson swallowed. "At present... two hundred and thirteen."

4

---

oly shit, Rand thought. A cleansing on a house that big would take all night. Perhaps even *multiple* nights. That was an issue because, once begun, a cleansing should be completed in a single session without any breaks.

"Yeah, I know," Jackson muttered. Rand figured his reaction must've been clearly written across his face.

"What do you mean by 'at present'?" Rand asked.

Jackson squirmed in his seat. "Dad became quite... *eccentric* in his later years."

Rand didn't like the sound of that at all. "How so?"

"When his dementia started getting worse, he became obsessed with remodeling and redesigning the house. Over and over and over again."

"Okay..." Rand waited for Jackson to elaborate.

"He drew blueprints by hand, then hired contractors. He told them to follow his designs exactly."

"Had your father studied architecture?" Rand asked. "Did his designs actually make sense?"

Jackson's shoulders rose in a long, exaggerated shrug. "He must've taught himself at some point, because the workers he hired did as he said. They tore down walls and demolished entire rooms, and then built new ones exactly like Dad wanted."

"Where were you when all this was going on?" Rand asked.

"I was living here in town by that point," Jackson said. "I'd drive up to check on Dad every so often, try to talk him out of this insanity, but he never listened to me. The place became a twenty-four-seven construction zone. He wound up having three teams that worked in shifts around the clock."

"Seems a bit… excessive," Rand said.

"I once overheard the foreman talking to a few of his workers. Apparently Dad was paying them three times their usual rate."

"Why did he suddenly decide to do this?" Rand asked.

"To this day I still don't know. I just figured it had to do with his dementia."

That explanation didn't sit right with Rand. From his limited experience with people suffering from dementia, their declining condition usually brought their overall activity level *down*. They didn't usually become committed to extensive, complex projects.

Maybe James Herron had been influenced by the entity in his home, Rand thought.

"Did your father ever show an interest in the super-natural?" Rand asked. "Rituals, séances, fortune telling… anything like that?"

Jackson thought for a moment before shaking his

head. "Not that I know of. But then again, there's no telling what he got up to when he was living there alone for all those years." Jackson perked up. "Oh, he became obsessed with astrology toward the end of his life. Does that count?"

"Eh, not really," Rand said. He'd been wondering if perhaps James Herron had done something that had either purposely or inadvertently invited the demonic spirit into his home. He probably had, even if Jackson didn't know about it.

But it probably didn't have anything to do with astrology, Rand thought. His ex Tessa had recently become interested in astrology. If Rand thought it had the potential to invite negative spirits, he'd have warned her away from it. But so far, in all his supernatural cases, he'd never found any evidence that it did.

Rand realized that his original question hadn't been answered yet. "Did your father not finish his renovations? You said 'at present.'"

"I don't think the house was ever *meant* to be finished," Jackson said.

"Why do you think that?"

"Because Dad just kept going. He drew more and more blueprints and handed them to his workers. He was always changing his mind, too. No sooner would one of his room designs be completed than he would order it torn down. The men were furious every time they spent a month building a room, only to have Dad demand it be torn down and redone. But the bosses complied because, again, Dad was willing to pay.

"Sometimes he'd want the same thing rebuilt following

the same design, as if he thought it would somehow turn out differently the second time around. Other times he ordered a replacement design built in its place. Sometimes he combined two rooms. There were instances where he wanted two rooms separated and the contractors had to improvise some zig-zagged hallways between them.

"Although most of Dad's blueprints made sense, sometimes they didn't; those times, the builders warned him that what he wanted wasn't structurally sound. He didn't care. He just told them he was paying them to build, so they should stop asking questions and get to work. Sure enough, every couple weeks a room would collapse in on itself, just as the builders had warned. That usually happened when Dad wanted a second story on top of an unstable section of the first."

"That sounds… dangerous," Rand said.

"It was. Some of the builders quit, but most stayed. They eventually figured out that they could ask Dad for even more money by claiming the project had become unsafe, and he agreed to pay them whatever they wanted." Jackson looked away as a wave of sadness seemed to envelop him. "Then there was Mom."

Miranda's eyes softened. "Oh. Mrs. Kendra."

"What about her?" Rand asked. "You mentioned earlier that she'd also passed."

"As Dad declined, he began to treat her worse and worse. Yelled at her. Ignored her. Refused to speak to her for days at a time. I tried to move her out of the house but she refused to leave him, no matter how bad he got." As he spoke, his sadness seemed to turn to spite. "She forced herself to stay in that mansion, surrounded by strangers who kept tearing down her walls and ripping up her floors." Jackson took a steadying breath. "She died in that house. One of Dad's unstable rooms collapsed in on top of her."

Rand frowned. "I'm very sorry to hear that."

"Dad refused to take responsibility for it. Refused to apologize. Hardly even wanted to acknowledge it. He even tried to get away with not telling me at all—I'm still not sure how he thought he could do that, even in the state he was in. When I finally got him to admit it, he said he'd already handled everything. There hadn't been a funeral and he wouldn't even tell me where he'd had her buried."

Rand wondered how a mentally declining James Herron had managed the logistics of a deceased spouse— arranging burials and death certificates and all the rest. Rand wanted to question Jackson about it, but he could see the topic upset the man.

Another thought came to Rand, and he felt he had to ask, "Did the builders know what happened to your mother?"

A darkness had settled over Jackson. "I never got a straight answer from them. I suspect they did, though I presume Dad bought their silence."

I'm pretty sure James Herron was demonically oppressed, Rand thought. From what Jackson was saying, this was far more than mere dementia. Although people who suffered from actual dementia could become irate toward their loved ones, people who were demonically oppressed rapidly turned against their friends and families in the most horrific ways. If what Jackson was saying was true, it just wasn't normal for James Herron to hardly care that his wife had died. This was the behavior of someone who was being influenced by something truly evil.

"What's the house like today?" Rand asked, eager to steer the discussion back to business.

"Many parts of the home aren't structurally sound, even though they still stand," Jackson said. "And I completely lost track of the remodeling. I grew up in the house, but I don't think I could find my way around today. It's too different now, almost like a giant maze." Jackson paused and stiffened. "Does hearing all of this change your mind about helping us?"

Rand had to think about that for a few moments before answering. Never before had he performed a cleansing in such a dangerous home. He could see Jackson growing more nervous with each silent second that passed.

"I'll still help you," Rand said, "but I'll need a guide. Someone who knows the house and can tell me which areas are unsafe. I'll also need help visiting all the rooms so we don't miss any."

Jackson chewed his lip as he digested that request. "I'm not sure there's anyone who knows all of that."

Rand was afraid that'd be Jackson's response.

The man seemed to deflate. "If the solution is doing your ceremony in every room… then I can't ask you to do that. It's just too dangerous." He looked at his wife, but Miranda's expression was unreadable. "I'll just have to go with my plan B, which was to demolish the place altogether and just be done with it."

While venturing into the mansion *did* sound dangerous, Rand felt compelled to give Jackson the honest truth. "I don't think that's a very good idea."

Jackson frowned. "Why not?"

"From what you've told me, this entity seems attached to your family *and* the Herron House. We know that because he's appearing in your home, not just in your father's mansion. Demolishing it won't remove the spirit, and might only make him angry."

That was especially true if this same demonic entity was the one who compelled James Herron to keep redesigning the house in the first place, as Rand suspected.

Jackson sucked in a deep breath. "I'll do it with you." Miranda shot her husband a sharp look, but Jackson ignored it. "I may not know my way around the home anymore after all the renovations Dad made, but hopefully I can figure it out."

"Fair enough," Rand said.

"When are you available to get started?" Jackson asked.

"I'll have to check my schedule and get back to you," Rand said. There were certain preparations he always needed to handle before committing to a firm time. Before anything else, he'd need to speak with his friend Miller Landingham about the case. Rand already knew he'd *definitely* need Miller's help cleansing such a massive place.

"Sure." Jackson stood and took a business card from his blazer interior pocket, which he handed to Rand. It had his name, cell number, and email address. "Call me anytime. We're eager to resolve this."

"I will," Rand said, standing as well.

"It was good to meet you." Jackson once again offered his hand, with a grip just as firm as before.

"And you," Rand said.

"Thank you so much," Miranda said, though her voice was almost a whisper.

Jackson turned and began climbing the classroom's stadium steps toward the exit. Miranda followed, then went to their daughter Carmen and helped her pack up her coloring books.

"Mr. Herron," Rand called when the man had reached the top. Jackson turned and looked down at Rand. "How exactly did you hear about me?"

"Are you kidding?" Jackson said. "Everyone knows about you. Word of mouth is a great thing, my friend. In my experience, it's the best kind of marketing there is. It's free as well. Have a good evening."

With that, the Herrons were gone.

Rand chewed on the man's response for a few minutes. It was true that most of his clients came to him after he'd been recommended by someone else who he'd also helped, but they always told him who'd referred them.

Rand shook his head, clearing his mind. The good news was that the Herrons seemed to have come to him earlier than most of his clients. The demonic entity's activity level still seemed to be low, which meant he likely didn't have a strong presence. If Rand could successfully navigate James Herron's complex mansion, he had a good chance of removing the demon for good.

A quick case, Rand thought. *In and out.*

But first things first—he'd speak to Miller. Ever since Rand had helped the man with his own haunting situation years ago, Miller had become a stalwart friend and a partner in these cases.

It was Tuesday, which meant Rand knew exactly where to find his friend—Marie's Southern Fry restaurant, indulging in the Tuesday-night discount menu. He'd head there now.

Rand pocketed Jackson's business card and pressed the red button on his device to stop the recording.

5

Later that evening, Rand arrived at Marie's Southern Fry restaurant and, as he'd expected, found the parking lot crammed with cars. He sighed.

Not in the mood for all this, he thought.

Rand was always overwhelmed by the crowds packed into Marie's on Tuesday nights. Tuesdays meant five-dollar fried shrimp po-boys, and Miller *never* missed. Of course, Miller's yellow truck was parked right up front, meaning he'd closed his bookshop early and beaten the dinner-time rush.

Rand understood Miller's and everyone else's enthusiasm—the shrimp po-boys *were* great—but the chaos was a bit much for Rand, especially after a long day of teaching.

On top of that, a new case always gave Rand a sense of stoic focus. He wanted to be totally present with the matter until it was resolved, and a busy restaurant was definitely not the place for him at the moment. But Rand's case briefings were conversations that needed to be had face-to-face, and no hurricane or flood would separate Miller Landingham from five-dollar po-boy night. This wouldn't be the first time Rand had briefed Miller over baskets of fried food.

Rand parked his Jeep in one of the few remaining spots at the rear of the lot. He walked briskly to the restaurant, hands shoved in his zipped-up jacket's pockets and scarf tight around his neck, with the end of it tucked into his jacket. Despite Louisiana's infamous heat and humidity, January could be bitterly cold.

Rand entered the restaurant to a burst of warmth and blaring pop country music from the overhead speakers. A crowd had accumulated by the door, waiting to be seated.

Rand shouldered his way through the people to the young hostess at the podium. She studied a laminated seating chart, brow furrowed in stressed concentration. But when she looked up and saw Rand, her expression softened.

"Oh. Hey, Rand."

"Hey, Sydney." Despite his sporadic presence, Rand was always shocked how the staff at Marie's remembered him. He figured they associated him with Miller, their dedicated regular. "Po-boy night—always seems like so much drama over a sandwich." He nodded his head toward all the people waiting to be seated as he loosened his scarf.

"It's always insane," Sydney said. "But at least the tips are good."

"Fair enough." Rand remembered well how lucrative the tips could be when he used to wait tables.

"Miller's in his usual spot," Sydney said. "You can go on back."

"Thanks."

Rand bypassed the "Wait To Be Seated" sign, ignoring the confused glares of the people in the waiting area who'd arrived before him.

Despite the crowds, Miller Landingham had a booth to himself, which he always managed to secure by arriving early. His po-boy was long gone with only a few shreds of lettuce and breadcrumbs remaining in the basket alongside a few surviving fries. He was now chowing down on some buffalo wings, his usual side.

Rand approached Miller from behind and slid into the booth bench opposite him. Miller at first appeared alarmed someone would dare invade his private booth, but his expression softened when he saw who'd come.

"Ah, Rando's arrived. Every week you say you're never coming back because of the crowds, but not even you can resist the siren song of fried food."

Rand had to chuckle—his friend was right. He *hated* the crowds that Marie's could attract. "No food for me tonight. I needed to speak with you about something."

"You could've just called," Miller said.

"I know you don't touch your phone when buffalo wings are involved."

Miller followed Rand's gaze to his fingertips, which were covered in honey barbecue sauce. Miller dug some white paper napkins out of the metal dispenser at the end of the table and began wiping his hands.

Rand hated talking on the phone, but he hated texting even more. His daughter Libby regularly poked fun at him for that, telling him he needed to get with the times.

"Don't know if you saw her when you came in, but your daughter's here," Miller said, as if he'd read Rand's mind. He nodded his head as he twisted a soiled napkin around his ring finger.

Rand looked over his shoulder. He spotted Libby at a table full of high school kids. He recognized two or three of her friends.

Libby caught his eye and she waved, and Rand returned it.

"Is she still full-time with Tessa?" Miller asked cautiously, as if knowing the question could stir up some hard emotions.

"Yeah," Rand said.

Rand's last three cases had been the most treacherous he'd ever worked. His daughter Libby had even gotten roped into his previous two. Rand and Tessa had decided together that it would be best if Libby lived exclusively with Tessa and her fiancé Bill for a while.

Rand had wanted to protest, to assure Tessa that Libby spending time with him did not affect the cases that came to him. He missed having his daughter around in the evening—his house could be a silent and lonely place. But Libby *had* been in serious danger because of his work, so he'd reluctantly agreed so Tessa would feel more comfortable.

Rand still spoke to his daughter often on the phone and, begrudgingly, over text. But to him, it wasn't the same.

"Have you seen *him* lately?" Miller asked.

"No." Rand hadn't seen his shadowy nemesis Shindael in quite a while. "That's the weirdest part. He usually pops up around corners or in my peripheral vision, just to let me know he's there. But I haven't seen him since Halloween night."

"Maybe he's moved on," Miller said. "Realized he can't beat you."

"That'd be nice, but I don't think so."

The cynical side of Rand figured the demon was merely biding his time, preparing something especially sinister.

Miller eyed Rand for a short moment. "I'm guessing you're here because your quiet streak has finally come to an end."

"You're right."

Miller rubbed the bundle of napkins at the edges of his mouth. Even after that, some brown sauce remained in his beard scruff around his lips.

The waiter, Derrick, appeared. He wore the same black uniform shirt as Sydney the hostess. He carried a tray with a single glass of whiskey on it—a double.

"Sydney told me you came in, Mr. Rand," Derrick said as he set the drink down in front of Rand. "Haven't seen you in a while. This one's on the house."

Rand couldn't help remembering what Jackson Herron had said about word of mouth.

"I appreciate this very much," Rand said, taking a sip. The stiff drink's bite was incredibly pleasant.

Derrick held the tray in both hands in front of his body. "Anything else I can get you guys?" He looked to Miller. "Another round of wings, Miller?"

"Not tonight," Miller said.

Derrick raised an eyebrow. "You sure? You've only had one so far."

"Rando and I need to discuss something. Maybe afterward I'll change my mind."

Derrick seemed to sense the tension at the table. "Sure. Just let me know."

"Good kid," Rand said after Derrick left. "He's going to LSU next year. Last time I was here he told me he was planning to take my class as an elective, and I tried to talk him out of it. Pretty sure he listened to me, but who knows."

"Why not let him take your class if he wants?" Miller said. "You get less people enrolled every semester and even more who drop it. Soon you'll be out of a job."

Miller was right. It was a problem Rand saw coming, but until he received a grim email invitation to meet with the head of the Religious Studies department to discuss the shaky viability of his class, he didn't want to worry about it.

"I could always work here." Rand looked around the restaurant. Tables that were meant to seat four had extra chairs shoved under the corners to accommodate the large groups. Even though the booths had long benches, they were so packed that the person on the end had to let one leg hang out from under the table. On Tuesdays, Sydney the hostess often put two different couples sitting in one booth just to make room for everyone.

Miller's private booth was a testament to how much Marie valued his dedicated patronage.

Miller adjusted himself on the hard, wooden bench— his only oft-repeated complaint about Marie's. "So what's the case?"

Right, Rand thought. *Daydreaming about working at Marie's means I'm procrastinating.*

He pulled Jackson Herron's business card from his jacket pocket. He set it face up on the table and pushed it toward Miller. Miller wiped his hands on his shirt one final time before sliding the card closer toward him.

"Jackson Herron," Miller read.

"He and his family showed up after my class today. They told me their story."

"A haunted house?" Miller asked.

"A haunted *mansion*," Rand said.

"That ride at Disney isn't so bad," Miller said.

"This one's apparently called 'the Herron House' by the locals in town." Rand took another sip of whiskey. It was half gone now, and a pleasant wave of tipsiness had begun taking away the edge he'd arrived with.

"First, let's see who we're dealing with." Miller slid his laptop from the carrying case that rested on the bench next to his thigh. He used his forearm to swipe the empty baskets in front of him to the side to make room for his computer. "If he has a business card, then he should be searchable." Miller opened the screen and began typing. "Have you looked him up online yet?"

"I leave the hacking to you," Rand said.

"Not so much hacking as it is doing basic research," Miller muttered as he hit the return key and scrolled the results. The white screen reflected in the lenses of his glasses. "Yeah, he comes right up."

"Weird that his business card doesn't have his employer on there," Rand said. Maybe Herron had different sets for different situations, although Rand couldn't imagine why.

"He's the CEO of HOI—Herron Offshore Incorporated," Miller said.

"Sounds like oil," Rand said. "Figures. It was pretty clear he and his family have money."

Miller started typing again, then scrolled and read some more. "Okay, says here HOI was founded by *James* Herron, not Jackson."

"That's the father," Rand said.

Miller traced the pad of his finger along the screen as he read. "James Herron was born in 1935 and founded the company in 1964, here in Louisiana. Blah blah blah…" Miller's eyes darted back and forth as head. "Yeah, you're right, Rando. Oil and oil wells. Says here that although there're no official records, it's assumed James Herron was the state of Louisiana's first billionaire. Is this Jackson?"

Miller spun the computer around. On the screen was the picture of the man who'd visited Rand's classroom. It was a posed photograph, his body facing off to the side while he looked directly at the camera. He flashed the same easy smile that Rand had seen earlier. Underneath the picture was an article that had been written about him.

"That's him."

"So what's Mr. Jackson Herron's problem?"

"His father's old mansion is haunted. They've run through a bunch of caretakers who spot apparitions, get scared, and quit. They all report seeing a woman and an old man. I believe the old man is actually a demonic entity."

"Oh," Miller said, grimacing.

"He's now been appearing at Jackson's home here in town. His wife Miranda has been waking up at three in the morning and she sees the old man watching her from the corner."

"Definitely *sounds* demonic."

"All he's done so far is appear. Activity hasn't escalated yet. There's been nothing physical, and no one's been harmed."

"That's good news," Miller said. "That means he should be easier for you to remove."

"I thought the same thing, but here's where it gets tricky…"

Rand relayed to Miller what Jackson had told him about his father's mansion and all the bizarre renovations, it's size, and current condition. After he finished, Miller took a few seconds to consider the story.

"Very odd behavior," Miller said. "Not to mention the place sounds extremely dangerous."

"I suspect James Herron was *oppressed* by the demon, and that's why he behaved the way he did," Rand said. "I think that demon was telling him what all to do to the house."

"But why?" Miller asked.

"I don't know." In a few of Rand's previous cases, he hadn't been able to uncover a demon's reasoning behind the things they did. But from what he'd learned over the years, they generally had one primary goal—to create chaos and fear. "If I can find out, then I will. I think Jackson's still carrying some baggage around about what happened to his father, so I if I can dig up any answers for him, then maybe that'll bring him some closure."

"Going above and beyond, as usual," Miller said. "I think that would be a nice thing for you to do."

"I'm going to need your help with this one," Rand said.

"Even though Herron agreed to come with me, I'll need you with me inside the mansion too. I'll need a support person who knows how cleansing ceremonies work."

Miller let out a long breath through his nostrils, but seemed to accept without much resistance. Rand knew that his friend—while always willing to help with his cases—usually preferred to provide support from the sidelines. He was often too afraid to face demons in the field.

"I understand," he muttered. "Plus, someone needs to watch your back and make sure the ceiling doesn't come down on top of you."

"That too," Rand said. *It seems there's a strong possibility of that happening,* he thought.

"I'll call Herron and make a plan for a night this week."

"Seems like you're moving pretty fast," Miller said.

"I'd like to get this over with."

Miller picked up the business card and studied it closer. For the first time, Rand saw that there was something written on the back of it. He leaned across the table and snatched it out of Miller's hand to examine the writing closer.

It looked like a sideways letter A, partially circled. It had been drawn by hand.

"What is it?" Miller asked. Rand handed the card back to Miller, who adjusted his glasses as he studied it. "Looks like some kind of symbol. You just now noticed it?"

"Yes. Does it mean anything to you?" Rand asked.

Miller shook his head. He used his phone to take a picture of the symbol. "I'll do some more research when I get home. See if I can find anything. Maybe it has something to do with his situation?"

"Then why not tell me about it when he came to me?" Rand asked. "If it was relevant, surely he wouldn't have just *forgotten* about it."

"Ask him about it when you call him," Miller said. "Or maybe you're overthinking it. Maybe it's just a mindless doodle that doesn't mean anything at all."

"Maybe," Rand said... but somehow he doubted that. "When are you free to make the trip up to Beau Ridge?"

"Whenever. Just let me know."

Rand should've known. Outside of Tuesday-night dinner specials, his friend had never been known for his robust social calendar.

"Okay. I'll call him and set up a time on the way back to the car. It's way too noisy in here right now."

"Sure you won't stick around and eat?" Miller asked.

Rand finished the remainder of his whiskey, savoring the final burn.

"Or have another drink?"

"Not tonight. I can't focus on anything else until this done. You know how it is." Rand pulled his recorder from his pocket, then placed it on the table in front of Miller. "You can listen to this to get all the details."

"Will do." Miller put the recorder in his laptop carrying case.

6

_____

As he left Marie's, Rand caught Libby's eye again and waved goodbye. They'd speak later—he didn't want to interrupt her while she was with her friends. Usually he informed his daughter whenever he took on a new case, but given his and Tessa's current effort to shield her from his work, he figured he'd have to keep this one a secret. He hated to do it, but it was for her wellbeing.

Rand walked from the restaurant to his Jeep. Many of the other cars had cleared out now that it was later in the evening. He dialed the number from Jackson Herron's business card.

"Dad."

Rand turned to find that Libby had followed him out of the restaurant.

Rand shoved his phone and the business card back into his jacket pocket. "Oh. I didn't want to bother you when you were with your friends." It was only then that Rand saw the concerned look on his daughter's face.

"Do you finally have a new case?"

Rand was caught off guard. He was bad at these kinds of situations, since his daughter could almost always see straight through him. "I came to have dinner with Miller."

"You never come here on Tuesday—you hate the crowds. And the way y'all were talking the whole time... I don't know. It just seemed very serious."

"Just figured it'd been a while since I've seen Miller."

"You're really going to do this, Dad?" Libby grew more upset. "You've never kept your work from me before. Why now?"

A young couple passed them as they approached their car. The man gave them a side eye, likely sensing the conflict. Rand took a few steps closer to his daughter. "Look, your mother and I explained all this to you," he said, lowering his voice so they wouldn't draw any more attention.

"So I get kidnapped *one* time and all of a sudden I'm a huge liability?"

She was referring to the time Rand had gone head-to-head with a demonically possessed preacher who'd planned to marry Libby off to one of his underlings.

"Libby, can't you see it's weird that you even have to say that? Most high school girls don't get kidnapped *at all.*"

"Yeah, and that really lit a fire under my ass. Now I understand the kind of spirits and people you deal with, and what they're willing to do. I want to *help* you. You shouldn't be doing all this alone."

"There isn't much you can do. And I always have Miller."

"You wouldn't have made it through your last case

without my help."

"Still…" Rand's words trailed off. His daughter had a point.

"This is all Mom's idea. Come on, you never agree with her about *anything*."

"I agree with her about this."

That was the truth. Perhaps Libby had saved his last case, but it was his own fault for letting it get that far out of hand to the point where he'd needed to involve her.

Rand was thankful this new case would be little more than a simple cleansing—albeit of an oversized mansion.

"I hate living with Mom and Bill full-time," she went on. "I miss you, and I worry about you when you do this kind of work. I just want to help."

"I understand," Rand said. "But this is just one of those things…"

Libby only shook her head at him, looking like she might cry. Rand hated the expression of betrayal she wore, but he could only hope that this would be one of those things that she'd understand better when she was older.

"Whatever, Dad."

With that, she turned around and returned to the restaurant, leaving him alone in the parking lot.

He watched her go until she was out sight. He hated to make his daughter feel that way, but he reminded himself that this was all for her protection.

He took his phone and the business card out of his pocket once again, then dialed the number. As it rang, Rand couldn't help but flip the card over and once again study the symbol on the back.

"This is Jackson." Although long after business hours,

the man still sounded upbeat and full of energy.

"Jackson, this is Rand Casey."

"Ah, good. I was hoping you'd call soon."

"I'm free Thursday night. We should meet at your father's house in the afternoon so my partner and I can get our bearings. Then once the sun sets, we can begin the cleansing."

There was silence on the other end of the line. *Maybe the CEO of HOI isn't used to being told what to do,* Rand thought. He didn't care. He was a professional in his own right, and he had a certain way of doing things to ensure the safety of everyone involved.

"That can be arranged," Jackson finally replied, and honestly Rand was surprised the man hadn't come back with some kind of counteroffer.

"Good. Let's meet there around four in the afternoon."

"That works."

"Excellent. Text me the address."

"Sure."

Rand briefly considered asking about the symbol, but held himself back. He preferred to ask Jackson in person so he could see the man's face when he did. If it was meaningful in some way, Rand had a feeling the man's reaction would tell him more about the symbol than the actual words of his response.

"I'll see you then."

Rand hung up.

"In and out," Rand whispered to himself as he opened his Jeep's driver-side door. His breath frosted. "Then it's case closed."

After all the chaos of his previous cases, Rand hoped he'd finally gotten something simple.

7

Rand's black gym bag was on his desk in his home office, unzipped. Inside was a flashlight, a pair of two-way radios, a pocket-sized Bible, and a regular-sized one. He gazed at the supplies, knowing he was forgetting something.

Holy water, he finally remembered. *Can't do a cleansing without it.*

He opened the doors of the standing wardrobe in the corner of his office. Rand lifted the lid off the wooden box that contained his supply of holy water. The glass vials were neatly arranged within. He studied his supply. Usually, Rand only brought a few vials with him to a cleansing, but the enormity of the mansion needed to be taken into account. He closed the lid, picked up the entire box, and set it carefully into his black bag.

He was about to zip it up when something else caught his eye—a simple wooden cross, which was propped up against a line of books on his shelf. Rand went to the shelf and took the cross down. He held it gingerly even though it wasn't fragile.

It was the cross he'd used on his last case. It had been broken in half, but when an angel of the Lord had appeared to him, she'd fused it back together. To Rand, the cross represented the moment God had finally sent help in his time of need to aid him in fighting the demons of hell. Every time he saw the cross, it strengthened his resolve that his life mission was to help those who were tormented by these creatures—and that God was watching over him.

He heard his front door open. He looked up from the cross, a spike of fear shooting through him. He knew he'd locked it earlier.

"It's only me," called Tessa from the other side of his small house, which brought Rand relief.

"And me." Libby.

Both Tessa and Libby had a key to Rand's house, and it wasn't uncommon for them to let themselves in.

Rand returned the cross to his bookshelf and stepped out of his office and into the hall. He closed the door behind him to hide his packing. "What are y'all doing here?"

Libby was already down the hall and entering her bedroom. "I just need to grab a dress. Then I'll be out of your hair so you can keep pretending like I don't exist." She proceeded to her closet, where she rifled through the hanging clothes.

She's still pissed, Rand thought.

He went down the short hallway and into the living room. Tessa lingered by the front door, waiting for Libby.

"She insisted we stop by to get a dress she needs for the weekend," Tessa explained as Rand neared.

"That's fine," Rand said.

"Apparently you two had quite the fight last night." She raised her eyebrows.

Rand sensed some exaggeration from his ex. "Libby just reminded me that she isn't in favor of this new arrangement."

"Forcing me to only live with Mom is really throwing off my routine, you know," Libby called from her bedroom. "I keep certain outfits here with the assumption I'll be staying here regularly."

Rand and Tessa's eyes met. She knew just as well as he that Libby was just being petty.

"Grab a bunch of stuff and bring it with you," Tessa called.

"No! That feels too much like moving out."

She muttered something else under her breath, but Rand wasn't able to make out what she'd said.

"Libby has it in her head that you're on a case," Tessa said, keeping her voice low. "Is that true?"

Rand reluctantly nodded.

Tessa's face stiffened. "Really? After all this time? I thought they were done."

Rand found that to be some extreme wishful thinking on Tessa's part. She'd known him back when he'd first started doing this kind of work. She should understand that the cases would likely never end. "It's a simple house cleansing. In and out."

"You say 'in and out' every time."

She had a point. His cases had become a lot more complex—and dangerous—lately. "I mean it."

Tessa rolled her eyes. "Now that I know what's going on, this makes a lot more sense." She dug into the Gucci purse that hung in the crook of her elbow. Tessa's lifestyle had upgraded ever since she'd started seeing Bill, and it was hard to miss.

"What makes a lot more sense?" Rand asked.

"I brought you something."

"A gift?" Rand smirked. "Is that to make up for you not getting me anything for Christmas?"

"You can consider it a gift if you want," Tessa said flatly. She withdrew a large, folded-up piece of paper and handed it Rand.

"I hope it's a treasure map," he said as he unfolded it.

"Almost."

It was a circular diagram split into twelve sections by lines, while other colored lines zig-zagged through it. There were a lot of symbols he didn't recognize. Rand rotated the paper, wondering if maybe he was holding it sideways.

"I had your star chart done."

Rand eyed his ex. *Astrology.* It was incredible how many new hobbies one could find when they were about to marry into money and didn't have to worry about working anymore.

He didn't consider astrology dangerous, but he'd warned Tessa to not get too carried away and start seeing psychics or fortune tellers. That could stir up some supernatural stuff that neither of them wanted.

"How thoughtful," he said, voice flat. "Wish you hadn't folded it. I could've had it framed." He recalled something else. "My client mentioned his father had also become interested astrology in his later years."

"I know you think it's nonsense, but you should look into it more."

"Is *this* why you texted me to ask when I was born?" Rand had thought at the time that the message was strange. It had come just before he'd begun teaching his class, though he'd forgotten to ask Tessa about it afterward. She already knew his birthday, of course, but she'd wanted to know his birth time down to the minute.

"I think it's interesting to go through the charts of people in my life and see why we were drawn together."

"I'm sure this is very illuminating," Rand said. "You said this makes a lot more sense now. Why?"

"My astrologer says you're about to go through a period of significant change," Tessa said.

"Let me guess, you have to pay extra to learn exactly *what* that significant change is."

Tessa shot him a biting look. "Actually, the positions of your planets say you're about to go through a period of significant change, not my astrologer. He couldn't tell me exactly what the change will be, only to be on the lookout for it."

"I'll make sure to keep my eyes peeled," Rand said, refolding the paper. He walked into the kitchen adjacent to the living room and set the star chart on his round dining room table. He wanted to end the conversation. The last thing he needed before beginning a case was for Tessa and her astrologer to plant wild ideas in his head.

Libby came into the living room carrying a dress still wrapped in plastic from the dry cleaner. Her eyes bounced between her parents. "Y'all seem tense."

"Your father didn't like his gift," Tessa said.

"*Told* you he wouldn't." She fixed Rand with a pointed

glare. "Are you ready to tell me anything about this new case you have? Or at least confirm to me that you have a new case at all, instead of treating me like a child?"

"Libby—"

"No? Fine." She stormed through the front door and out of his house.

"She'll come to her senses," Tessa assured him. "This is for the best."

"I know."

After Tessa went outside, Rand watched through the kitchen window as she backed her brand-new Lexus— also courtesy of Bill—out of his driveway.

The stillness of his home settled in around him once again. Rand's house had been so quiet since Libby had begun living away from him. He hated it. Although his daughter had been angry with him and Tessa had shoved some superstition in his face, he was still glad they'd come by. It had been a break in the monotony that had become his life over the past couple months.

Rand returned to his home office. Once again, his eyes went to the cross on the shelf, as if it were calling out for his attention, despite being simple and unassuming.

Why not? Rand thought as he took the cross from the shelf once again. He put it in his bag on top of the other supplies and zipped it closed.

8

There wasn't much to the town of Beau Ridge.

It was early evening when Rand drove past the well-kept, pink-and-yellow welcome sign. He guessed some long-term resident took it upon his or herself to make sure it was presentable to the few people, like Rand, who found themselves passing through.

As Rand cruised down the town's main thoroughfare, he passed a strip mall, a local seafood restaurant, and a small grocery store. The tallest building was the water tower, which had the town's name printed on the side.

He checked his GPS on his phone. He was looking for the Beau Ridge Rose Motel, and according to the map it was only a few minutes away.

Miller had put himself in charge of booking the motel. Since the case was likely to take all night, both he and Rand thought it was best to get a place to stay so they didn't have to drive home immediately after it was done. Rand was often quite exhausted after a cleansing.

Rand exited the GPS, then scrolled to the last page of apps, where he opened up Local King, an app that had long overstayed its welcome. It was a dumb social media app that allowed friends to see your current location and recent "check-ins." It had lost popularity years ago, but Rand knew one person who still used it, blindly adamant that it would experience a resurgence.

There was a single notification within the app. It read: *Miller Landingham has checked in at the Beau Ridge Rose Motel. He's been crowned the new king!*

When someone "checked in" using the location services in the app, the user was given a point. After enough check ins, someone could become "king" of a location, meaning they'd checked in there more times than anyone else.

"Looks like he's arrived," Rand muttered to himself. "King Miller came, saw, and conquered."

Rand drove past a church, a liquor store, then another church before taking a right turn. After that, it wasn't long before he arrived.

He groaned as soon as he saw the motel.

The building had long ago been painted white, but now the walls were covered with grime. The parking lot *badly* needed a repaving. The wooden sign out front had not received nearly the same attention as the town's welcome sign.

Miller had said that the motel he'd found was the only one in town. At the time, Rand hadn't realized that was his friend's way of warning him.

. He pulled up next to Miller's yellow truck, the only car in the lot. As soon as he did, a door on the second floor of the motel opened and Miller emerged with a bag slung over his shoulder. He closed the door behind him and locked it with the key.

Miller came downstairs, opened the trunk of Rand's Jeep, and tossed his bag in before getting into the passenger seat.

"Is it as bad on the inside as the outside?" Rand asked as he backed out of the lot, going faster than he probably should have. Probably because he wanted to get away from the run-down, shady motel as fast as possible.

"Before I forget," Miller said, "the guy in the office lied about having a twin bed setup, so we'll be sharing a double."

"I can't believe you want to spend any more time in there than you have to."

Miller had a personal rule for his life—never waste time when renting a room. To him, checking in late and checking out early was money down the drain.

"You know I always show up early to enjoy the amenities," Miller said. "But... there weren't any amenities here, as I'm sure you can imagine."

"I hope you didn't enjoy yourself too much on that bed we're sharing," Rand muttered. He reached for his phone to put in the address Jackson Herron had sent him.

"I already got it," Miller said, holding up his phone, GPS on the screen.

"How far?"

"Twenty minutes. Looks like it's a little outside of town," Miller said, studying the screen. "Actually... the so-called Herron House is in the middle of nowhere. Have you heard from Jackson yet?"

"No." Which was strange. The sun was just beginning to set and their agreed-upon meeting time was nearing. The entire day had passed without a word.

"I'm sure he'll be there," Miller said.

9

"We have to be getting close," Rand said as he drove.

Miller used his fingers to zoom in and out on the GPS on his phone. "Just a little ways farther up this road."

The sun was just beginning to set over the high trees that lined the narrow, winding highway. Thankfully, the Jeep's heater kept the evening's chill at bay.

The small town of Beau Ridge was about as rural as any Rand had ever seen, but his GPS had led him to an even-*more*-isolated area from the main town. He was surprised his cell phone still managed to find reception.

Rand picked up his own phone from the space underneath the center console, plugged into a charging cable. No message from Jackson Herron.

"Still nothing?" Miller asked.

"Nope." Rand set his phone down just in time to see the sharp curve in the road—he turned the steering wheel and took the turn a little faster than he would've liked.

"Whoa," Miller said.

"Curviest damn road I've been on in a while."

Red and blue lights flashed.

Rand groaned as he glanced into his rearview mirror. "Damn it." The police cruiser followed, seeming to have come out of nowhere. He must've been parked off to the side, nestled in some trees and waiting for speeders.

Rand checked his speedometer. "Come on. I'm only going six over."

He slowed and drifted to the right. The highway didn't have much of a shoulder, so the Jeep lurched a bit as the right side of the car went off road.

"I figured Beau Ridge was a speed trap town," Miller said, watching the police cruiser slow to a halt in his mirror. "Only way these guys can make their money is pulling people over for just about anything."

"Get my stuff out of the glove box, please," Rand said. Miller leaned forward and found the registration and insurance paperwork. "I don't care if he gives me a ticket or not. I really just need him to leave us alone."

One of Rand's personal rules was to never involve the police when he was on a case. He'd learned long ago that law enforcement and police procedure didn't mix well with supernatural situations. Fortunately, he hadn't *technically* started the case yet.

A large man in a tan police uniform approached the driver's side of the Jeep. Rand lowered the window.

"Evening." The officer's voice was loud and commanding with the hint of a southern drawl.

Rand nodded. "Officer."

"Any idea how fast you were going?"

"Forty-six miles per hour," Rand said.

The officer seemed put off by that. Rand figured he rarely received a precise answer to that question.

"License and registration."

Rand passed him the documents.

"Randolph Casey. You're not from Beau Ridge are you?"

"I'm not."

"What brings you to town?"

"Meeting up with a client," Rand said.

The officer narrowed his eyes at Rand, then glanced at Miller, as if trying to decide if he was going to probe further. "Since you're not from here, you might not know that we prioritize safe driving in our town. I'll have to give you a citation for violating the speed limit."

"Sure." Rand wished the man would hurry up and do his job and let them go on their way without the lecture. As Miller had said, "prioritizing safe driving" was just another way of saying speeding tickets were a good source of income for the small town.

The officer waited a few beats, as if he expected Rand to argue or try to talk his way out of the ticket—he seemed displeased when that didn't happen. "Y'all wait." He lumbered back to his police car, red and blue lights still flashing.

"Wish he'd move a little faster," Rand muttered as he watched the officer in his mirror.

Another car appeared around the highway's curve behind the police cruiser. It was a red Audi, driving much faster than Rand had been. The car instantly caught the officer's attention.

"Look at this guy. He's going *way* faster than I was," Rand said.

The Audi abruptly slowed as he passed, then came to a complete stop a few feet ahead of where Rand was parked.

"What's he doing?" Miller asked.

The Audi reversed on the highway and pulled over behind the police cruiser. The driver's door opened, and out stepped Jackson Herron.

"It's him," Rand said.

Jackson approached the police officer and they began speaking. Although Rand's window was down, he was too far away to hear what they were saying. Miller twisted in the passenger seat and peered through the rear window.

The conversation lasted less than two minutes. Then, the officer returned to Rand's window and handed his license and paperback back to him. "Y'all have a good night."

He got back into to his car and killed the flashing lights.

"What's going on?" Miller asked.

Jackson approached Rand's window, passing the lingering police cruiser. "Sorry about Officer Tom bothering you. He was just doing his job." He spotted Miller in the passenger seat. "Hi, there. I'm Jackson Herron."

"Miller Landingham," Miller said softly, seemingly still amazed by what Jackson had just done.

Rand was too. "How'd you talk me out of that?"

"My family's always been known around here. That tends to come with a little bit of... influence." Jackson shrugged.

Rand hadn't taken Jackson Herron for the kind of man who had pull with the police, but Rand generally assumed —particularly when he was in a cynical mood—that most wealthy people had a unique and privileged relationship with law enforcement, in some form or fashion. He just never thought that relationship would ever actually benefit him.

"Right. Well... thank you."

"Don't mention it. Look, Dad's house is just up here on the right. You can follow me the rest of the way."

After Jackson returned to his car, the Audi pulled back onto the highway and continued on. At first, Rand hesitated to follow. His eyes lingered on the police cruiser in his rearview.

"What're you waiting for?" Miller asked.

"I guess he really is just going to let me go."

Rand eased back onto the road and accelerated, and the cruiser vanished into the distance.

Rand caught up with Jackson, who'd resumed driving far faster than Rand had been when he'd gotten pulled over.

"How'd Jackson know it was me?" Rand asked. As far he knew, Jackson Herron wouldn't know what kind of car he drove.

"He probably just assumed," Miller said. "Might not be many people coming out this way."

Perhaps Miller was right, but if that was the case, then why had the police officer been staking out this stretch of highway?

Rand figured he was overthinking it. He should've been grateful that Jackson Herron had shown up when he did and helped him out.

Soon, Jackson's car slowed and his right blinker began flashing.

We're here, Rand thought.

10

———

They'd come to an unassuming, black, wrought-iron fence. It was set a little ways off the road, nestled into some leafless trees. If Rand hadn't already been on the lookout for it, he would've driven right by it. A security camera was mounted atop the brick pillar that bookended the gate. It pointed straight at Jackson's car.

"This is strange," Miller muttered. He held his phone in his left hand, head craned over the screen. He used his thumb and forefinger of his right hand to swipe around.

"What?"

"You'd think since this mansion is locally famous it'd be labeled on the GPS, but it isn't."

"What's it say?" Rand asked.

"Nothing at all. The map just makes this area look like an empty field." Miller held his phone so Rand could see.

Miller was right. The blue circle that represented their current location was right next to a black-and-white checkered flag which indicated their destination. Except for the highway, the entire surrounding area was green and empty.

"Hmm, that is a little weird," Rand said.

The gate opened and Jackson proceeded through it. Rand followed. Just beyond the gate was a dirt path that soon transitioned into pavement. It led through a canopy of trees so thick Rand couldn't make out what was beyond them. Even though their leaves had fallen, their thick branches still obscured most of his surroundings save the path ahead. It was a perfect natural privacy wall.

After a few minutes of driving, the trees opened up onto an expansive property. The Herron House was directly ahead.

It was built on a slight hill and stone steps led up to a sprawling front porch. Thick pillars supported a triangular structure above, which to Rand resembled the Pantheon in Rome, only larger.

The main part of the house was *very* square—jarringly so. It felt unnatural, like a giant box that was never meant to serve as a family home.

A single cylindrical tower sprouted from behind the main body of the mansion, looking especially phallic and reaching high into the air. It was capped with a domed ceiling. Two balconies wrapped around the upper section, one higher than the other. To Rand, the tower seemed very out of place relative to the rest of the mansion. He wondered if it had been one of James's bizarre additions. From what Rand could see, the mansion had been constructed from cold, grey stone.

Both Rand and Miller stared at the sprawling structure, necks craned awkwardly to take it all in from behind the windshield.

"That's... more than a mansion," Miller said.

"It's a fucking castle," Rand said.

Rand and Miller looked at each other.

"You think you can cleanse every room in a single night?" Miller asked.

Now that Rand had seen what he was dealing with, his confidence had crashed. Still, for the sake of his client he had to proceed. "I have to at least try." He suddenly realized that Jackson's car was no longer in front of him. "Where'd he go?"

"There." Miller pointed to the right, tapping his finger on the passenger window.

While Rand had been mesmerized by the Herron House, Jackson had parked next to a small cottage nestled against the tree line.

"That must be where the caretakers lived," Rand said. He hadn't even noticed it due to the massive structure that had commanded his attention. He parked next to Jackson's car, and he and Miller got out of the Jeep. Rand found his eyes once again drawn to the Herron House— particularly the tower that reached toward the clouds.

"Bigger than you pictured?" Jackson asked, following Rand's gaze. He placed his hands on his hips and seemed a bit nervous, as if wondering if Rand was reconsidering now that he'd seen what he was dealing with.

"Very much so," Rand said.

"Let's head in here first," Jackson said, gesturing toward the cottage. "I want to show you something I think will help us."

"Is this where the caretakers lived?" Rand asked as Jackson led the way through a squeaky screen door and into the cottage's living room.

"It is."

Two snot-colored couches faced each other in the center of the room. The set reminded Rand of something that would sit in the back of an antique store for years, forgotten about. A dark-brown wooden coffee table was between the two couches. The white paint on the walls had cracks and flakes, badly in need of a touch up. To the right was a doorway that led to a small, simple kitchen. The warmth inside was a welcome relief from the chilly evening. To Rand, it was almost *too* warm, as if the heater had been left running.

Odd to leave a heater on when no one's here, Rand thought. "Is the current caretaker here right now?"

Jackson eyed Rand strangely, as if he wasn't sure why Rand was asking. "No. I sent him away since I knew what we'd be doing here tonight." He gestured toward the ugly pair of sofas. "Make yourselves at home, gentlemen. I'll be right back." He disappeared through a doorway at the far end of the living room.

Rand sat on one couch while Miller took the other. The cushion was lumpy. Rand adjusted to get more comfortable, but he couldn't find a position that helped.

"The caretakers lived way better than I do," Miller muttered, glancing around the room.

"I prefer my house," Rand said, even though his home was definitely much smaller. However, Rand couldn't blame Miller. He'd seen the hovel his friend currently called a home.

Jackson's heavy footsteps approached from the rear of the house. They thudded heavily on the wooden floor, giving off a hollow sound. Jackson returned to the living room, holding what appeared to be a large sketchbook. He handed it to Rand. "Take a look at this."

Rand flipped the blue cover over the metal spirals that bound the sketchbook at the top. The first page beyond the cover was yellowed and marred with brown smudges, but the page's content was still clear.

"James's blueprints," Rand said.

The first drawing was for a square-shaped room. Its dimensions and square footage had been handwritten within the design. Doors were represented by breaks in the straight lines, swinging inward. Calculations had been done by hand in the corner.

"Maybe this can be used almost like a map," Rand said, looking up from the sketchbook. Jackson stood with his hands in his pockets, seeming nervous about how his gift would be received.

"We're not that lucky," Jackson said. "That book doesn't have every room in the house, but it does have some. I've given that to each caretaker I've hired, and all of them have told me it's incomplete." Thin strips of torn paper were caught in the spiral, indicating that there had indeed been some pages removed from the sketchbook. "And that's not all. Some of the past caretakers found hidden passages inside the house as well."

Rand raised his eyebrows. "Interesting…"

Jackson waved his hand. "It's just a big mess. Point being, those blueprints aren't an exact map, but they might help."

"It's better than nothing, I guess." Rand closed the

sketchbook and glanced out the window near the cottage's door. The sun was drifting toward the horizon, leaving behind only a small amount of orange light in the sky. "It's almost dark. We need to get started."

For the first time, Jackson appeared fearful. "I'll lead the way," he said with a deep sigh.

11

The three ascended the stone steps to the Herron House's porch and passed between two columns on either side that supported the overhanging, triangular roof.

The mansion's main entrance was a set of double doors twice Rand's height, made of thick, dark-brown wood and set within a decorative stone arch. Long windows flanked each side of the door, though they were covered by bars.

"What's with the windows?" Rand asked.

"Dad made sure they were all blocked," Jackson said.

"*All* the windows are barred?"

"Yes."

Rand looked at Miller, who seemed equally unsettled.

"Shall we?" Jackson took his keys from his pants pocket and singled one out from the among the rest. "Been a while since I've had to use this." He pushed the key into the lock and forcibly jiggled it with both his hands. Rand worried Jackson might break the key off. But the man apparently knew what it took to unlock the door, because a moment later, the latch gave a loud, metallic clunk. He twisted the doorknob, jiggled it a bit, then used his shoulder to shove the front door open. Specks of debris rained down from overhead.

"That was quite the battle," Rand remarked.

"As I said, it's been a while," Jackson said. "After you." He extended his arm toward the mansion's interior.

Rand walked into a home that felt more like a tomb.

The remaining sunlight streamed in from the open door and the barred windows, and when Rand's eyes adjusted, he took in the massive entrance hall.

The room was perfectly square—the interior of the block-shaped section of the mansion he'd first noticed from the outside when they'd arrived. The tile floor was a black-and-white checkered pattern. Numerous pillars lined the periphery of the room, supporting the railed landing of the second floor. The high ceiling was mostly shrouded in shadow—the only thing visible up there was a round sunroof covered in dirt and grime. A chill lingered in the air and the room smelled like old dust.

Rand turned to face Jackson. "Lights?" He had a sinking feeling he already knew what Jackson would say.

"No electricity." Jackson gave him an apologetic look.

"Good thing we came prepared," Miller said. He slung his bag off his shoulder and onto the ground. It kicked up a plume of dust when it landed. He unzipped it and took out a heavy-duty flashlight, which he clicked on before handing to Rand. The bright white beam cut through the darkness of the room, illuminating the thick clouds of dust that floated throughout.

"Thanks." Rand always made it a point to pack flashlights when he knew he'd be dealing with the demonic. Evil spirits thrived in darkness, so they often shut off or destroyed light fixtures.

Though it's a little annoying to begin *in total darkness,* Rand thought.

Jackson walked past the pair and toward the center of the entrance hall. His footsteps clacked on the checkered tile and echoed off the walls, and his gaze glided smoothly around the room as he took it all in.

Rand gave the man his moment. He figured it must be overwhelming for Jackson to once again step foot into a home so laden with tragedy and regret.

He finally turned to face Rand and Miller. "Welcome to... my father's home." The words echoed off the walls.

Rand could tell Jackson was trying hard to suppress the emotions that had risen within him; even in the dim lighting, the sadness behind his eyes was apparent.

He tapped the toe of his shoe on a black tile. "My mother was furious when Dad ripped up the floor and put these tiles in."

Rand had seen the black-and-white tile in plenty of bathrooms, yet had never cared much for the pattern. He was no interior decorator, but even he didn't see the appeal of making it the first thing you saw when you entered the mansion.

"Did this pattern mean something to James?" Rand asked.

"Do you think there was meaning behind *anything* he did to this house?" Jackson said, tone suddenly thick with disgust.

If he was demonically oppressed, then most likely yes, Rand thought, but refrained from saying that out loud.

Rand's eyes drifted to the far side of the room. Two grand staircases rose from the floor on either side of the entrance hall, then turned in to meet in the middle to become one before leading up to the second floor.

"What's up those stairs?" Rand asked.

"Nothing special, just more rooms." Jackson pointed to the right side of the landing. "My bedroom was right up there. At least, it used to be. Who knows if Dad had it removed or changed into something else."

"I'm guessing the entrance to the tower is up there as well."

Jackson seemed to visibly tense. "Yes." His voice was low. "But I don't know what's inside. I've never even been up there."

"You seem afraid of it."

"Sort of. I'll just never forget how angry Dad would get when Mom and I even *looked* up those stairs. It was the only place he'd spend more time than his office."

Rand tried to be empathetic. No doubt Jackson had experienced a lot of negativity—perhaps full-blown trauma—before he'd finally moved away from the mansion.

But you're certainly going to see what's in there tonight, Rand thought. He'd need to go up there to complete the cleansing, even if Jackson was afraid.

"Maybe the tower would actually be a good place to start," Rand said, swinging his flashlight toward the second-floor landing. "You know, to get the hard part over wi—"

At the top of the stairs stood an old man.

12

———————

"**S**hit," Rand hissed, instinctively taking a large step backward and jerking his flashlight away.

"What's wrong?" Miller asked.

Rand aimed his flashlight back to the top of the stairs. The old man was gone. An icy chill crawled over his flesh.

"What is it?" Jackson asked.

"Did either of y'all see that?"

Neither man responded.

Rand eyed Jackson. "The old man. He was just standing at the top of the stairs."

The color seemed to drain from Jackson's face. "You're sure?"

Rand could tell it was less of a question and more of a denial. He looked at Miller, who seemed just as frightened as Jackson.

"It didn't take him long to show up," Miller said. "I don't think he's happy we're here."

"That's what I'm thinking," Rand said.

Usually, when Rand cleansed demonically infested

homes, the entity within remained dormant until Rand began his process. Only once the demon realized his dwelling was under attack would he begin fighting back.

"This one might turn out to be a little more aggressive than we thought," Rand told Miller.

And the two hundred and thirteen rooms don't help, he thought. *He has* plenty *of time to attack us with all he's got.*

"What does that mean for us?" Jackson asked.

Rand appreciated the question—it kept him on track. "It changes nothing. We proceed. Carefully. And we watch each other's backs at all times."

Jackson didn't seem comforted at all.

Rand was also put off by the haunting entity appearing so soon, but there was nothing that could be done about that.

Rand then realized something. "He appeared right after I suggested that the tower might be a good place to start."

"I just thought of that, too," Miller said.

Jackson gave Rand a questioning look.

"It means the tower probably *is* the best place to start," Rand explained to Jackson. "You sure you have no idea what's up there?"

Jackson shook his head.

"None of the builders told you anything, either?"

"Even after its construction was done, the builders claimed Dad made it very clear to them that no one was to ever go up there. So they didn't."

"But James spent a lot of time up there?"

"Yes."

Rand turned and looked at Miller, who seemed to read Rand's intention. "Should we go with you?"

The first hints of trepidation bloomed inside Rand's chest. He deeply sensed that there was something meaningful about the tower—both to James Herron and the entity that dwelled within his home. He wanted to know what it was before he began his cleansing, but he also didn't want to expose the other two to any potential danger. They'd likely face even more unsettling things as the night progressed, and Rand didn't want to overwhelm them right at the beginning.

"I'll go up alone first," Rand said. "Just to see what's there, then I'll come right back."

Miller tensed. Rand could tell his friend wanted to protest, but at the same time also didn't want to venture up into the tower with him. Although Miller could be brave when it was absolutely necessary, he was still scarred by his own haunting experience Rand had helped him with many years ago. He much preferred to help Rand with his cases from the background, usually by providing research and information.

"What should we do while you're up there?" Jackson asked.

"Wait for me here. I won't be long at all."

Jackson nodded. "Head up the stairs, go a little ways down the big corridor on the second floor, and the tower entrance will be on your right."

Rand took a moment to steel himself. As with all his cases, there was always a point when it came time to end the planning and conjectures and to start taking action. A familiar sense of fear washed over Rand, his instincts trying to warn him away from potential danger and harm.

As always, he mentally set that fear aside. Then, he started up the grand staircase.

13

_____

Rand kept his flashlight trained on the spot where the old man had appeared as he climbed the stairs. He couldn't help but feel that with every step he took, he was further intruding on James Herron's secrets.

Hopefully by the time this night's over, we'll have answers as to what exactly brought James to this point, Rand thought.

The stairs emerged onto a wide, dark corridor on the second floor. A plush red carpet covered most of the stone floor. Rand found the arched doorway a little ways down the corridor, just as Jackson had said.

There was no door. A spiral stone stairway led the way up.

Rand ascended, and the stairway lasted longer than Rand had thought it would. The tower seemed to grow darker as he went. The stairs terminated at another arched doorway that looked just like the one Rand had entered through.

He aimed his flashlight into the room and laid eyes on the most elaborate shrine he'd ever seen.

A large circle had been drawn onto the stone floor with a slightly smaller, concentric circle within. The space between the two circles contained symbols that Rand did not recognize. To Rand, they resembled Nordic runes. They were drawn with perfectly straight lines that intersected each other at sharp angles, as rigid and precise as their probable meanings.

Four points on the circle were labeled with the cardinal directions. Dozens of white candles surrounded the circle, all in various stages of melting with clumps of hardened wax beside the blackened wicks. A layer of dust covered the floor and thick, white cobwebs hung from the candles like veils.

A magic circle, Rand thought. His mouth had gone dry, and he noticed that his palms were slick.

A magic circle was a tool used in rituals to summon spirits. It represented a doorway to the spiritual world. Now Rand understood how the demon had likely come to infest the Herron House.

James Herron had purposely summoned him here, Rand thought. *But why?*

Rand also figured the magic circle was why James Herron had forbidden anyone from entering the tower.

"Damn it," he muttered under his breath as he realized the magnitude of the problem he had on his hands. A cleansing wasn't going to be enough. Not even close. As long as the magic circle remained, a doorway between the Herron House and the spiritual world would always be open. That door would need to be closed before he did anything else.

Rand did not have the process of properly removing a magic circle memorized, though he did have some books in his home office that explained how. There was a very specific method. You couldn't simply get down on your hands and knees and scrub away the drawings with soap and water. A magic circle was a very powerful magical tool, and it needed to be removed just as precisely and carefully as it had been created.

We'll need to call this off and come back another time, Rand thought. That might annoy Jackson, but Rand couldn't help wishing the man had found it within himself to disobey his father's orders and actually venture inside this room. Rand would've known ahead of time what he was dealing with.

Rand approached the magic circle, shining his light across the entire thing to get a better look. Two perpendicular lines had been drawn within the circle. They intersected in the middle, and that point was enclosed by the smallest circle of the three. Rand knew that center point was where the practitioner was meant to stand when conducting the ritual. Scrawled over the intersecting point was the only symbol Rand recognized.

The sideways letter A, half-circled.

Rand crouched down to get a better look, careful not to let the toe of his shoe breach the outer barrier of the circle. He removed Jackson's business card from his coat pocket and compared what had been drawn on the back to what was in the center of the circle.

It was the same.

Are you sure you've never been up here before, Jackson? Rand thought.

Rand hadn't considered that the man would intentionally lie to him. Most of his clients were too terrified and traumatized to do that. But after many years doing this kind of work, Rand had learned not to believe in coincidences.

He straightened and started for the door. He'd go downstairs and ask Jackson exactly where he'd seen the symbol he'd drawn on the card. Then he'd break the news of what he'd discovered and explain they needed to come back another time.

Rand took one step, and his toe caught on something. He stumbled, but quickly recovered. He aimed his flashlight at the floor to see what he'd tripped on. A metal clasp was embedded into the stone floor, just outside the perimeter of the magic circle. Rand traced the light around the lines and found three more just like it at even intervals around the circle.

What are those for? But then Rand refocused on what he needed to do. He strode to the door he'd entered from, keeping his light on the floor in case there was anything else for him to trip over.

The dozens of candles surrounding the circle lit themselves at the same time.

14

The flickering candlelight cast Rand's shadow, long and dancing, onto the chamber's stone wall.

I'm not alone in here.

"You have my attention," Rand said to the room. "Is there something you want to tell me?"

He received no response. Then it dawned on him what he'd need to do in order to communicate with the spirit.

Rand turned off his flashlight and set it on the floor near the arched door. He returned to the edge of the magic circle's outermost ring. Although it didn't appear like it, he knew there was a huge energetic difference between where he stood and the space just within the line. In the circle, he'd be more vulnerable to whatever entity was there with him. Never before had Rand actually *entered* a magic circle—he avoided participating in those rituals whenever he could.

I'm already here, so I may as well learn what I can, Rand told himself. If the spirit was inviting him to speak, then he could uncover some information about who he was dealing with.

He crossed the line and planted both his feet into the small circle at the middle meant for the summoner. His shoes were pressed together over the crossed lines in the center of the magic circle, covering the sideways A symbol.

Nothing came at first, and all was silent. Rand's gaze glided throughout the circular chamber, waiting for the entity to make the next move. Now that the candles burned, he could better make out the chamber. A large table covered with tools was pressed against the wall. There were two other arched doorways—one that led onto the balcony and another that opened to a second spiraled staircase that rose higher into the tower.

Rand did a double take when he noticed something that hadn't been there before.

There was a gathering of shadow near the wall opposite the northern point of the magic circle. That area of the room should've been visible by the light of the candles, but it wasn't. It resisted the light.

Two small, white dots appeared within the shadow.

Eyes.

There he is, Rand thought.

The shadow took on the apparition of the elderly man Rand had seen at the top of the stairs. Although old, he had broad, powerful shoulders and was very tall. The nearly square head almost brushed the top of the ceiling. The skin on his face was grey and mottled and deeply lined. He wore a faded grey sweater and pants.

A heavy, crawling sensation sprouted just beneath Rand's skin. It was an uncomfortable feeling but very familiar, and he knew what it meant—the entity exuded pure evil.

The demon's head dipped up and down as if scrutinizing Rand. His eyes even blinked. Never before had Rand seen that in any demon's apparition.

"Who are you?" Rand asked, and was shocked when the spirit replied.

"I am called Akhubel."

Akhubel's voice came directly from his apparition. He was not communicating telepathically like most demons did. To Rand, Akhubel looked and sounded like someone giving an interview on television while wanting to remain anonymous—the face shrouded in shadow and the voice distorted.

He just willingly gave me his name, Rand thought.

There was power in a demon's name. If you knew it, you could command him. For that reason, demons went to great lengths to conceal their identities. Never before in Rand's life had he ever had one of these creatures so boldly proclaim himself.

That put Rand on edge.

Maybe he's lying? But something in Rand's intuition told him that Akhubel had given him a real name. *But why?*

In that moment, though, that wasn't what mattered. Rand sensed that he did not have the upper hand in this encounter. The demon had enticed him to the center of the magic circle, and Rand had complied. He knew he shouldn't linger where he was vulnerable for very long.

Rand inched his hand away from where it hung by his side, moving slow, and slid his fingers into his interior jacket pocket to clutch the small vial of holy water inside.

Rand removed the vial, using his thumb and forefinger to wriggle the cork free.

Strike while I can, Rand thought.

Akhubel watched his every move, but made no attempt to stop him.

With the vial uncorked and poised in his hand, Rand was ready to take his shot.

"Akhubel, in the name of the Lord Jesus Christ, I command you to leave this place!"

Rand cast the liquid forward. It arced through the air.

Halfway between Rand and Akhubel, the water halted. It floated for a few seconds before hardening into ice, and then the frozen pebbles dropped and clattered onto the stone floor.

Oh shit, Rand thought.

Akhubel hadn't lifted a finger.

"You can't hurt me that way, Randolph. Don't waste your time."

Demons were masters of deception, especially about what their weaknesses were. *All* demons should be affected by holy water. Despite that, as with the name he'd been given, Rand believed Akhubel. He loosened his fingers and let the empty vial drop to the floor.

"Why are you here?" Rand asked. If he couldn't banish the demon using his usual methods, he figured he may as well get some information that would help him later. "What do you want with the Herron family?"

"I was summoned here long ago."

It was a vague response, but if the magic circle beneath Rand's feet was any indication, it was the truth. At least Akhubel was willing to talk. That in itself set him apart from other demons Rand had dealt with in the past.

"Do I know you?" Rand asked. That question was typically one that demons loved to answer. Over the years, Rand had sometimes encountered the same demon a second or third time. These entities always remembered him.

"We've never met," Akhubel said. "But I know you well. Many of us do."

"So I've been told," Rand said.

"Many fear you now because of what happened to Markoul," Akhubel said.

Rand blinked. "Who?"

"Markoul was the one slain by the girl."

It took Rand a couple of moments before he realized that Akhubel was referring to his most recent case with the black-eyed kids on Halloween.

Markoul must have been one of the demons from that night, Rand thought. He'd never gotten their names.

Markoul had been strong. Rand would never forget how easily the demon had seized him. At the time, Shindael had given the order for Markoul to kill Rand.

But an angelic being had come to his aid, appearing as a young girl with white eyes. Her very presence had scared Shindael away. Rand had realized just in time that if Shindael feared the girl, then Markoul did as well. Rand threw Markoul toward the girl, and when the girl touched him, he'd exploded into puddles of black slime.

Although terrifying and the closest to death Rand had ever come, that night had been a breakthrough. Before then, he'd never known it was possible to actually *kill* these demons. Rand had only ever sent them back to hell, where they were free to return to Earth whenever they wanted, and often did.

"Who are you?" Rand ventured again. While this demon had already given his name, Rand also wondered why Akhubel was choosing to be so forthright. He'd never known a demon to do that. In a way, Rand figured what he meant by asking, *Who are you?* was really, *Why are you different?*

"Although we've never met, you should already know of me," Akhubel responded calmly. Through the dark, distorted nature of his tone, Rand almost thought he detected *disappointment* that Rand didn't realize who he was speaking to.

"If we haven't met before, then how can I know you?" Rand asked.

"You've read about me."

That was possible—Rand had read about many demons over the course of his life. "Where have I read about you?"

"The Holy Bible."

Rand kept his gaze glued to the tiny white eyes in the corner of the room. His brain buzzed with adrenaline, keeping him on high alert.

"Where are you in the Bible?"

"Genesis chapter twenty-two. Verses nine through twelve."

Rand was wary of the calm way in which Akhubel spoke the name of the first book of the Bible. Demons were usually averse to *any* mention of God or Scripture. It was bizarre to hear Bible references come directly from the entity.

"Look now. You have a Bible with you."

He knows, Rand thought. *Just as he knew I had the holy water.*

Rand withdrew the Bible from his jacket's pocket. It was the one he always brought to his cases—he'd double-checked that he'd remembered it before he'd left his house earlier.

Rand kept his eyes on Akhubel. Usually, when a demon laid eyes on the Bible, they were repulsed. This one was was unaffected.

Just how powerful is he?

Rand flipped to the twenty-second chapter in Genesis. Although he'd likely read the passage several dozen times over the course of his life, he couldn't recall what it talked about, much less which particular demon was mentioned there.

"Read it to me," Akhubel said. A command, albeit a gentle one.

Rand clenched his jaw. Not only did he not want to obey this creature, but he was very bewildered by a demon who actually *requested* to hear Scripture. Reading the word of God was a go-to strategy to remove negative spirits—Rand had never met one who actually *wanted* to hear it.

By candlelight, Rand found the verses and began to read.

"When they reached the place God had told him about, Abraham built an altar there and arranged the wood on it."

Rand knew this story well.

But what does this have to do with Akhubel?

"He bound his son Isaac and laid him on the altar, on top of the wood. Then he reached out his hand and took the knife to slay his son.

"But the angel of the Lord called out to him from heaven, 'Abraham! Abraham!'

" 'Here I am,' he replied.

" 'Do not lay a hand on the boy,' he said. 'Do not do anything to him. Now I know that you fear God, because you have not withheld from me your son, your only son.' "

Rand reread the passage silently again, wondering if he'd missed something. *The angel of the Lord.*

"The girl with white eyes?" Rand asked. Akhubel did not respond—then it dawned on Rand what the demon was implying.

One way that demons perverted and mocked Scripture was to insert themselves into it. They often claimed to have been responsible for certain events in the Bible. The last time Rand had encountered this, the demon he'd been attempting to send away had identified himself as the angel of death who'd killed all the first-born children in Egypt.

Rand closed the Bible and studied Akhubel. He could only chuckle. "I think not." He'd never believed a demon before when they'd tried to insert themselves into Scripture. He certainly could not accept that Akhubel had been the one to stay the hand of Abraham.

"It matters not what you believe," Akhubel said. "Only what is true."

"No truth could ever come from you," Rand said.

"Hasn't it already?"

Rand paused. He realized that his accusation had sprung from his mouth by instinct. It was his go-to line whenever a demon tried to lie to him. But Akhubel had already told him *some* truth.

Enough of these games, Rand thought.

"You will leave this family alone," he said, mustering as much authority into his tone as he could. He was in a submissive position, having obeyed all of Akhubel's instructions, and that needed to change.

No matter how strong he might be, I'll always have the upper hand as long as God is on my side, Rand reminded himself.

"You are not here for the reason you think you are," Akhubel said.

"Then why *am* I here?" Rand asked.

"Because your time has finally come, Randolph. You must journey through the darkness."

Rand fell silent as he tried to decipher what that meant. *Journey through the darkness? What does he mean?*

On its face it sounded like a death threat, which he was used to receiving from these creatures.

"Your journey begins now," Akhubel said. "But you shouldn't linger here. Your friend is in danger."

The apparition of the old man faded, and in the next moment was gone. The candles extinguished themselves all at the same time, plunging Rand back into darkness.

"Miller," Rand whispered.

15

R and scooped up his flashlight from where he'd left it by the chamber's entrance. He then turned it on, shining the white light onto the stone steps as he barreled down them.

He's just trying to scare me, Rand thought. But he couldn't deny that Akhubel had been honest with him about other things.

He reached the bottom of the tower steps and ran to the landing that overlooked the mansion's entrance. "Miller," he called as he pointed his flashlight toward the first floor of the entrance hall. His voice echoed off the walls.

Neither Miller nor Jackson were there.

Rand went down the steps. He pointed his light to the left, then the right, checking between the columns that supported the second-floor landing. "Miller?" he shouted, louder this time.

"Rando, what's wrong?"

Rand aimed his light in the direction of the familiar

voice. Miller stood just outside the mansion's open door on the porch, looking alarmed.

"You all right?" Rand asked.

"Yeah, why? What's wrong? What did you find in the tower?"

Jackson appeared just behind Miller, looking equally startled.

Rand felt a sliver of relief. Miller seemed fine. *What danger was Akhubel talking about? Maybe he was just messing with me.* It wouldn't be the first time a demon had threatened something similar.

Rand pushed the demon's words from his mind. He needed to catch Miller up on what he'd discovered in the tower. He started walking toward where Miller and Jackson stood on the front porch. "Listen, we have a big—"

The mansion's door slammed shut.

16

"**S**hit!"

Rand sprinted to the mansion's front door, gripped the handle, and pulled. It didn't budge.

"Rando!" Miller shouted, though his voice was muffled by the thick door.

The door wasn't locked—rather, it felt as if it were being held closed by some unseen, powerful force.

Akhubel.

"What the hell happened?" Jackson asked on the other side of the door, his words barely audible.

"Hold on." Rand set the flashlight down and pulled the door's latch with both his hands. He planted his foot on the nearby wall for more leverage, but it was clear the door wasn't going to open. Not until Akhubel wanted it to open.

"The door's not moving at all," Miller said.

Rand gave up his struggle, then took some deep breaths to calm his racing heart. "It's being held closed."

"By who?"

"What do you mean the door's being held closed?" Jackson asked. "Let me try." Rand heard some brief grunting from Jackson on the other side. "Son of a bitch. That's *really* stuck."

"Rando, what's going on?" Miller asked.

"I… spoke to the demon in the tower," Rand said. He was met by a lingering silence from the other side of the door.

"So you think he's the one holding you inside, or maybe holding us out," Miller said.

"Yeah."

"What will you do?" Miller asked.

Rand had already begun to consider that question. Cleansing the mansion was out of the question, since he'd discovered the magic circle, but he'd never intended to be trapped alone inside the Herron House. "I have to get out of here."

"I was hoping you'd say that," Miller said. "I agree."

"This one… this one is different, Miller," Rand said, voice dropping. "This demon. I can feel it already."

"Demon?" Jackson asked.

"Different how?" Miller ignored Jackson's question.

"I haven't put my finger on it yet," Rand said. *Human-like. Restrained. Calculating. Patient.* Akhubel did not seem to delight in sheer chaos as most demons did. "I had an entire conversation with him. It was almost… civil."

"Sounds like Shindael," Miller said.

"You're right," Rand said. "This one must also have a high ranking."

Over the years Rand had learned that there was a clear hierarchal structure in hell. Shindael commanded several of the demons that Rand had faced in the last several months. He wondered if Akhubel was perhaps an equal to Shindael.

Or maybe even outranks him?

Given the months that had passed since Rand had last seen Shindael, perhaps Akhubel had stepped in to do what Shindael had yet to accomplish.

"Did he try to hurt you?" Miller asked.

"Not at all. But he said you were in danger. That's why I came back down so fast."

"I'm fine," Miller said. "He was probably just trying to scare you."

"Maybe," Rand said. But he also remembered how Akhubel had already told him the truth about several other things.

"Okay hold on a minute. What's all this mean?" Jackson finally asked. "I don't understand."

"It means as long as Rando's trapped inside, he's in a lot of danger," Miller told him. "We have to get him out as soon as possible."

Rand's gaze fell on the windows on either side of the mansion's door. Both sets were barred. "Jackson, what's another way I can get out of here besides this door?"

Several long seconds passed without Jackson responding. Rand's gut twisted more and more as the other man's silence stretched on.

"The front door is the only way in or out," Jackson finally said. "Dad made sure of that a long time ago."

"You're kidding."

"I'm afraid not."

"If this door is the only way in or out, then we have to *make* a way out," Rand said.

"What do you mean?" Jackson asked.

"We'll have to break down the door," Rand said.

He didn't receive an immediate response.

"I don't think we have the equipment or tools to do that," Jackson finally said.

Rand found that hard to believe. *Surely there's an axe or a chainsaw or something similar around here.* "What about in the caretaker's house?"

"I'd have to look."

"Please do," Rand said.

"Okay. Just give me some time, and I'll let you know if I find anything."

"Thank you."

"I'll help you look, Jackson," Miller added. "Rando, I have my two-way radio with me, and yours should still be in your bag. We can keep in touch with those."

Rand aimed his flashlight to where his black bag was on the floor in the middle of the entrance hall. "Excellent. Keep me updated about what y'all find at the caretaker's house."

"Will do. Hang tight. We'll have you out of there in no time."

17

Miller and Jackson's footsteps faded on the other side of the door. Once they were gone, both the silence and the darkness of the old mansion seemed to consume Rand. He remembered that his first impression of the place had been of a tomb. He quickly shook the thought from his mind.

Rand returned to the center of the entrance hall where his bag was. He knelt down and fished inside until he found the two-way radio. When he turned it on, it gave a short burst of static that pierced through the heavy silence. He straightened and clipped the radio to his belt.

Rand fished his cell phone from his pocket and checked the screen. As he'd expected, no service.

"As usual," he muttered.

That was why Rand always brought radios with him to his cases. He'd learned long ago that the negative energy from a demonic presence often interrupted signals to cell phones. Radios were far more reliable in supernatural situations, because they only connected to each other, unlike cell phones which had to go through a third point, usually a distant tower.

Rand scanned the entrance hall with his light. Beyond the two parts of the bifurcated grand staircase, the far wall of the entrance hall contained an arched doorway that led deeper into the mansion. The darkness beyond seemed to swallow the beam from the flashlight.

Rand once again found his gaze drawn upward to the second story as an idea began to take shape. Jackson had said many of the rooms had collapsed, so maybe there were some sections where the roof had caved in. If Rand could get onto the roof, then all he'd need would be a ladder to get down.

Surely there's a ladder somewhere in the caretaker's home, Rand thought.

Even though Rand fully trusted Miller to do everything possible to help him escape, he couldn't bear standing around feeling helpless, waiting for someone else to save him. He had to do *something* to try to save himself. He decided to check and see if there were any viable ways to escape from the upper floors.

Rand started ascending the stairs again. His footsteps on the stone steps echoed off the high walls of the entrance hall. When he was halfway up, he aimed his light toward the second-floor landing.

And froze.

Akhubel once again stood at the top of the stairwell, glowing white eyes fixed on Rand.

Rand's grip tightened on his flashlight. He swallowed. He was acutely aware that if the demon wanted to harm him, there was no one around to help him, or even to hear him scream.

Akhubel spoke.

"You must journey through the darkness."

That's the second time he's said that, Rand thought. *What does that mean?*

An invisible burst of energy shoved Rand up and off his feet and sent him spiraling backwards through the air.

He landed hard on his right shoulder and the flashlight spun out of his grip. His head bounced on the tile, sending a sharp pain through his skull. White light swam in his vision behind his clenched eyes.

"Fuck," he muttered through gritted teeth as the ache began to set in. He pushed himself to a sitting position. He slowly moved his right arm, working through the soreness. Nothing felt broken.

He looked around the darkness until he found a small orb of white light. Rand crawled toward his flashlight and retrieved it. The glass lens was cracked, but thankfully it still worked.

He shone the light up toward the second-floor landing where Akhubel had been. The demon was gone.

The bastard doesn't want me to go back up there, he thought.

Rand winced as he stood. His left hip and lower back ached. He limped around, forcing himself to walk off the pain.

Rand remembered the radio and his hand went to his belt—but it wasn't there. He shone his light on the checkerboard tiles until he found it on the floor nearby where he'd landed. The back cover piece had broken off and the batteries had popped out. He found one nearby, though the other had rolled quite a bit farther away.

"Please still work," Rand muttered as he shoved the

two batteries back inside. He then brought the radio to his mouth and pushed the button on the side. "Miller, can you hear me?"

Silence.

Rand's heartbeat quickened.

"Miller?"

A burst of static came, then a response. "I can hear you, Rando. You all right?"

Rand let out the breath he'd been holding. "Thank God. I thought the radio broke."

"I tried to contact you a minute ago and it wasn't working," Miller said. "What happened?"

"I tried to go back up the stairs, but Akhubel threw me off and I ate shit."

He turned the flashlight onto himself. His jeans, jacket, and black t-shirt were all covered in grey dust. Rand brushed off as much as he could.

"You sure you're all right?" Miller asked.

Although the dull aches across Rand's body lingered, he was now sure he'd avoided serious injury. "Yeah. Still hurt like hell, though."

"Who is Akhubel?" Miller asked.

Rand realized that in the commotion of getting trapped inside the mansion he hadn't yet told Miller what he'd learned in the tower.

"It's the demon's name. He straight up told me."

"Oh. That's… weird."

Rand knew Miller would appreciate how strange it was that Akhubel had willingly shared his name. "Definitely."

"That's helpful too, I guess. I'll do some searching

through my database to see if I have any information about him."

"Sounds good. What about something that can help me get out of here?"

"We just got back to the caretaker's house. Jackson's in the other room, looking for something. I'm about to check the toolshed out back."

"Thanks. Keep me updated."

"You too. Sounds like this demon has already started kicking your ass."

Rand rubbed the spot on his lower back where he'd landed. "You got that right. Listen, I'm going to try and find another way out of here, in case y'all don't find anything that can help."

"Maybe you should just stay put for now," Miller said. "It seems like Akhubel didn't like you wandering around."

"True, but I still have to try."

"Well, I can't stop you. Just be careful, Rando."

Rand clipped the radio back onto his belt.

Once again his attention fell onto the arched doorway at the far end of the entrance hall. Akhubel might not allow him to go up, but maybe Rand could travel deeper within.

You must journey through the darkness.

Rand pushed the demon's words from his mind. He told himself that if he was, in fact, going to delve into the depths of the Herron House, he would do so only in search of a way out, *not* because Akhubel wanted him to.

Rand remembered he'd brought along with him James Herron's hand-drawn blueprints. He returned to his bag and crouched beside it, his bruised lower back fighting him. Rand withdrew the sketchbook and laid it on the checkerboard floor.

He hadn't looked that closely at the drawings when Jackson had first given him the sketchbook, but now Rand studied them closer. *There's got to be some sort of indication in here for another way out,* he thought as he flipped through the pages, holding his flashlight over them while he scanned the drawings.

One page showed a room shaped like an octagon. Another denoted three oblong rooms on a single page, each connected by corridors that ran diagonally across the page in a very confusing and counterintuitive design. There were no labels as to what these rooms were meant to be, but due to the complexity of many of the drawings, Rand had a hard time believing James Herron had been planning out mere bedrooms and bathrooms. With money not being a barrier for the man, Rand could only wonder what outlandish things he'd built within the walls of his home.

Or what Akhubel told you to build, he thought.

The tower and the summoning room with the magic circle might only be the beginning.

Rand paused his page turning. One of the drawings toward the back of the sketchbook finally had a label. James Herron had written, "Office 6th Version" at the top of the page.

Rand remembered what Jackson had said earlier—besides the tower, James had spent most of his time inside his office.

Rand studied the blueprint. He inferred from the label that James Herron had his workers demolish and rebuild his office six times. Jackson had also mentioned that his father had indeed ordered some sections of the mansion torn down and reconstructed from scratch until he felt they were acceptable. Rand figured that since James had spent so much time in his office, he was likely particular about where it was located and how it was built.

The room was square, and the measurements and dimensions were precise. The calculations had been done by hand in the corner using math Rand hadn't seen since high school. Over the line that represented the office's front-wall entrance, James had scrawled a quote Rand recognized as being from the Bible.

"As for me and my house, we will serve the Lord."

Strange thing for someone suffering from demonic oppression to write, Rand thought. But then Rand remembered how Akhubel had *invited* him to read Scripture out loud.

Against both the right and left sides of the office, smaller rectangles had been drawn against the line that represented the wall. It had been labeled "bookshelves," and the dimensions and measurements were written within the rectangles.

But the shelves on the right had something else. A small section of the wall behind them was shaded darker. Next to it was a small arrow pointing off the page.

Some of the past caretakers found hidden passages inside the house as well, Jackson had said.

"It looks like his office had another way out," Rand whispered, then quickly added, "maybe." He wondered if his desperation was causing him to decipher things in the blueprints that weren't really there, only to give him hope.

I have to try, he thought.

Rand returned to the first page of the sketchbook. Although not labeled, it was clearly the blueprint for the entrance hall. James Herron had painstakingly shaded in the black squares of the checkerboard floor, and even had gone so far as to label the dimensions of each tile, causing the drawing to appear cluttered.

According to the blueprint, there were three doors to choose from to leave the entrance hall. Rand aimed his flashlight to his left and then his right, spotting arched doorways that were identical to the one on the far side of the room that he'd already seen. The doorway at the top of the drawing was labeled with an arrow at the top of the page.

Rand flipped the page. There was another arrow, this time at the bottom of the drawing, a continuation of the previous blueprint. This new area of the mansion contained dozens of crisscrossing corridors snaking in between odd-shaped rooms.

Straight ahead is probably the way to go, Rand thought. From his cursory look at the blueprints, it seemed going that way would lead him toward the heart of the Herron House, where James's office was most likely to be.

Jackson had said the blueprints weren't quite a map, but from what Rand had seen so far, he at least had the beginnings of one.

Decision made, Rand took the radio from his belt. "Miller, I think I've found a possible way out."

"What is it?"

"There might be a passage from James Herron's office."

There was a moment of silence before Miller responded. "You sure you don't want to wait on us? Jackson said the mansion was dangerous, remember?"

Miller was right. Rand had an image flash through his mind of stepping in the wrong spot and falling through the floor. Or of closing a door too hard and causing the ceiling to cave in on him. All while completely in the dark with nothing but a flashlight.

With Akhubel possibly lurking around any corner.

"I have to give it a shot," Rand said. "If y'all find a way to get the front door open, let me know and I'll come back. But until then... I can't just sit here."

"If you say so," Miller said. "Just... be careful please."

"I will."

Rand clipped the radio back onto his belt and turned his attention once again to his bag. He didn't need the supplies he'd brought for the cleansing anymore, and carrying it all would slow him down. He'd leave it behind.

But he wouldn't leave everything. He dug through the contents until he uncovered his wooden cross, which he'd packed at the last moment.

For luck, Rand thought. He slid the cross through his belt loop like a sword.

With the sketchbook of blueprints tucked under his arm, Rand shone his light toward the door at the far end of the entrance hall, the darkness beyond seeming eager to swallow him.

You must journey through the darkness.

"God, if you're listening," Rand prayed under his breath, "please give me guidance and protection."

With that, Rand walked through the threshold and ventured deeper into the mansion.

18

Miller pried opened the door of the sheet-metal toolshed that was behind the caretaker's house. He could tell it had been a long time since anyone had been inside. Touching the door had gotten his hands dirty, and he brushed them off onto his jeans.

He used the flashlight on his phone to cut through the darkness inside the shed, which was full of equipment and supplies. A lawn mower. A wheelbarrow. Weed eater. A pile of tattered and dirty work boots. On the right side was a table filled with tools. Some gasoline containers had been pushed into the far corner.

But there wasn't anything that would help Rand break out of the Herron House.

Miller sighed.

He closed the shed and shivered. Now that the sun had set completely, the only light came from inside the nearby caretaker's house, making the night seem even darker than Miller was used to. Swaths of stars were visible in the sky since they were so far from town and any light pollution.

Why is the electricity working in here but not the mansion itself? Miller couldn't help wondering.

By one of the second-floor windows, Jackson Herron paced back and forth while holding his cell phone to his ear. He paused when he saw Miller looking up at him. They watched each other for a few moments before Jackson resumed pacing.

"Are you calling for help?" Miller whispered. *He didn't say anything about that.*

Miller returned to the cottage's front porch, where he opened the squeaky screen door, then the main one. He shut both behind him as the warmth enveloped him.

Jackson's pacing footsteps were soft thuds on the ceiling. His voice was audible, yet distant as he spoke on the phone. Miller couldn't make out what he was saying.

Suddenly, Jackson stopped talking. His footsteps changed direction, then grew louder as he descended a staircase in the adjacent room. He emerged into the living room. "Did you check the toolshed?"

"Yeah. Nothing."

"Oh." He seemed to lack any real disappointment, and Miller had to wonder if Jackson had known all along that he wouldn't find anything useful in the shed.

"So… update on Rando. He thinks he's found a way out on one of your father's blueprints. Some sort of passage connected to his office."

Jackson's brow furrowed a bit. "Interesting. Wouldn't surprise me at all if there *was* some sort of secret passage in there."

"Do you know what he's talking about?"

"No. Dad never let neither me nor my mother anywhere near the office."

"Right. Who were you talking to upstairs?" Miller asked.

"Work call. I told my secretary I wasn't available tonight, but some persistent clients are still getting through."

I don't like the sound of that, Miller thought. *I need Jackson to stay focused.* "Is there anything else you can think of that can help Rand get out?"

Jackson pondered for a moment before saying, "Maybe. Let me reach out to someone I know here in town who might be able to help."

Before Miller could ask anything else, Jackson left the room again, tapping his phone screen and bringing it back to his ear.

A heavy sense of helplessness bore down on Miller's shoulders. He was in a strange place with a near-stranger, and it seemed as if his friend's fate was far out of his control. He felt like he was waiting for Jackson to find a solution, and Miller didn't like that at all. He wasn't even positive that Jackson Herron fully understood the danger of Rand's situation.

Miller crossed the living room and passed through the door Jackson had gone through. He found himself in a smaller sitting room with two couches and a stairwell that led to the cottage's second floor. Jackson had gone back upstairs.

Why does he only do his phone calls up there? Miller wondered.

His thoughts were interrupted by a name.

Akhubel.

If Rand's escape from the Herron House was out of his hands for the time being, then at least Miller could get to work doing what he did best: searching the vast amount of data he'd gathered over the years on thousands of demons. There was a strong chance he had something on Akhubel.

Miller returned to the cottage's living room. His laptop bag leaned against one the sofas, right where he'd left it. He sat down and pulled his computer from the bag and set it on the coffee table, then opened the single document that was an extensive database of demons, their names, their appearances, and their behaviors. The aged machine whirred as it loaded the massive file.

Miller brought up the search bar within the document and typed the letter *A*. Then backspaced and put *O*.

"Hmm. How's it spelled?"

He finally typed *O-K-O-B-E-L* and pressed the return key.

No results.

But he could also check the internet. Much of the information Miller had found about certain entities had come from fringe websites and forums online where people discussed their dealings with demons that had haunted their homes. Maybe someone out there had encountered Akhubel before and had written about it.

Miller's computer wasn't picking up any WiFi, so he took out his phone and activated the hotspot, which his computer automatically connected to a few seconds later.

Miller highlighted the text, then copied and pasted it into an internet search instead.

Again, the search had no relevant results.

I'm probably spelling his name wrong, Miller thought.

"Akhubel," Miller muttered under his breath, mimicking what Rand had said. "Akhubel, Akhubel, Akhubel…"

The hard *"kh"* sounded Arabic to him.

An ancient language for an ancient entity, Miller thought. Demons existed outside of the material world. They were creatures not bound by time. Many had been active throughout the ages, tormenting humans since the beginning of recorded history. It wasn't uncommon for some demons like this to be known by many different names, each name reflecting the culture and time period of the person writing about them.

Miller opened up a fresh search tab and typed in:

Ancient demon from the Middle East.

The search returned numerous results. One of them caught Miller's eye—it had the exact phrase he'd typed in. He adjusted his glasses as he clicked on it.

The link brought him to a forum that looked like it had been developed in the 90s. The site background was black, and all the text was in Times New Roman. At the top, two skull graphics spun round and round—an animation that was once ahead of its time, but now was cheesy and ridiculous.

Miller was used to these kinds of websites when he researched the paranormal and supernatural. Enthusiasts around the world had been connecting with each other online since the earliest days of the internet. For these people, the primary goal was to share information, not update their websites to the newest, most streamlined styles. Miller had also learned that the people who ran these websites preferred the outdated appearance—it warded off the people who weren't serious about discussing the content.

Miller scrolled through one of the website's forum threads. He was pleasantly surprised to find that it was still active. It had been started back in the early 2000s by a user simply named "AB," who had sporadically posted on it ever since then.

To get some context on the discussion, Miller scrolled to one of the more recent posts from AB, which had appeared a few years before. The post's heading read, "A Haunting in Rose Grove."

Miller began to read.

'This was the closest that evil has ever come to my own doorstep.

An old house here in my hometown of Rose Grove, Georgia, was haunted by a demonic entity. It took me nearly twenty years to remove it.

The problems started soon after a family with two young boys moved into the house. The demon within went after the two young boys first, as they often do. He even pushed one of the boys out of his treehouse, and the child suffered a broken arm.

The father didn't believe his sons when they told him something was wrong with the house. Over time, as the demon grew stronger from feeding off the fear and negative energy it generated, the father sank further into a paranoid depression.

It was the man's wife who reached out to me. I went to their house with my medium, and she immediately sensed a presence there. We attempted to remove the demon, but we were interrupted when the woman's husband came home early from work. He was furious and threw me out of his house before I could finish the job. I didn't hear from the family again, and as the years went on, I wondered what had happened to them.

It wasn't until twenty years later that the younger of the two brothers contacted me. He told me his brother had moved his own family back into the home, and that the hauntings had resumed. By this time I'd stopped involving myself in these kinds of situations—I'd become too old. But since it was an unfinished matter from my own past, I agreed to help him.'

Miller leaned back on the sofa, digesting what he'd just read. Whoever AB was, he sounded like he knew what he was talking about. He wasn't some careless kid trying to learn how to summon ghosts because he was bored, as Miller often encountered online.

If this story is true, then this guy sounds very similar to Rand, actually, Miller thought. Although AB hadn't stated it specifically, it sounded to Miller like he'd gone to the house to perform a cleansing, much like Rand had originally intended to do in the Herron House.

And AB mentioned he was "too old." Maybe he's been doing this even longer than Rando has.

The post titled "A Haunting in Rose Grove" was followed by many replies from the forum's other users. Someone with the username TrevorN commented: *'I was the one who moved my family back into the house. Thank you, Arthur Briggs. You helped save my life.'*

"Arthur Briggs," Miller whispered to himself. "Who exactly are you, Mr. Briggs?"

AB had not returned to the forum to respond to the replies. Miller scrolled, scanning the single posts that had appeared sporadically throughout the years which had kept the thread alive.

'I still check back here every now and then. Still nothing from Briggs?'

'What about TrevorN? Doesn't he know Briggs personally? Maybe he's heard from him.'

Miller scrolled past several more replies before TrevorN replied with a short message:

'I haven't talked to Arthur in a while, and I'm pretty sure that's how he likes it. Honestly I don't know if he still does paranormal investigations, or even if he's still alive...'

Miller scrolled faster, then stopped. AB had resurfaced a year ago with another long post.

Miller started reading, but the first line sent a spiked chill through his heart.

'I've discovered a new breed of demon. I call them the Lords of Hell.'

19

R and proceeded down an abnormally narrow corridor—if the walls were any closer together he might not have even been able to fit through. It was eventually intersected by another corridor, creating what resembled a four-way stop. Rand swung his light to the left and right. The darkness swallowed the beam in both directions as these new hallways seemed to extend forever each way.

May as well continue forward, Rand thought.

He crossed the intersection, thankful that the hallway widened a bit. So far the mansion reminded Rand of a funhouse at the fair whenever the corridors randomly transitioned from being very narrow to wide.

As Rand proceeded, the ceiling began to slope downward. Eventually, he had to get down on his hands and knees and crawl.

James made this place completely unlivable, Rand thought as he shuffled forward, digging his elbows and forearms into the floor for traction. He couldn't envision an elderly man doing what he was doing at that moment.

The ceiling started to rise again, so Rand returned to his feet, feeling like he'd just traversed an underground cavern. He had a feeling the rest of the mansion wouldn't be any better.

Rand continued down the pitch-black corridor. He could only see what his flashlight illuminated. Here, the wallpaper abruptly changed. Over a cream-colored background, green vines twisted and coiled along the walls, as if beckoning Rand forward.

He passed a spiral staircase on his right. Rand shone his light up to see where it led, but it only dead-ended into the ceiling, where a barrier of bricks had been built to wall off the stairs. Considering the magic circle Rand had seen in the tower, he could only wonder what else James Herron was hiding on the upper levels of the mansion.

Rand pressed on, his mind wandering to Akhubel. If the demon chose to suddenly appear in there with him, he'd have nowhere to run.

He's probably watching me right now, like I'm a rat in a maze, Rand thought.

Rand paused and flipped a page in the sketchbook. In the designs, the corridor he was currently in had been drawn with its varying widths, the measurements calculated by hand off to the side. Their structure had been intentional. James had also included some squiggly lines along the walls. Rand aimed his light at the vine-patterned wallpaper and compared it to the drawing.

You really knew what you wanted, James, he thought.

Numerous doors had been labeled on both sides of the

vine corridor, leading to rooms of varying shapes and sizes. One was allegedly triangular, and another was shaped like a pentagon.

Just looking at the blueprints now overwhelmed Rand. Had things gone according to plan, he would've been visiting all of these bizarre rooms as he performed the cleansing. But now Rand bypassed them all. James Herron's office was the only room he cared about now.

A loud burst of static cut through the silence of the corridor, startling Rand. He relaxed a moment later when he realized it was only his radio.

"Checking in," Miller said. "You all right?"

Rand fumbled at the radio on his belt—his hand still shook from the sudden shock. "You scared the hell out of me. It's so quiet in here."

"Sorry."

Something above caught Rand's eye. He aimed the flashlight to see a caved-in part of the ceiling. Debris had piled into the hallway and almost blocked the way forward.

"I'm going to put you on hold for a moment," Rand said into the radio. "I need my hands free to get past this part." He clipped the radio to his belt.

The ceiling had fallen on the right side of the corridor, blocking it with plaster and wood. There seemed to be *just* enough room to squeeze through on the left.

Rand flattened his back against the cracked wall and carefully crept by, though he had to suck in his gut to make it.

His shirt caught onto a piece of jutting wood and pulled it. Rand sensed the pile of debris shifting.

"*Shit!*" He darted forward just before things came

crashing down, but then lost his footing and fell. The sound of the ceiling caving in behind him was deafening. Rand covered his head, expecting to be buried and crushed.

The debris settled and silence returned.

Rand sat up and shone his light toward where he'd come from. He'd disturbed the delicate pile of rubble just enough to cause a section of the room above to fall through. The way he'd come from was now completely blocked off.

He groaned. If for some reason he needed to return to the front of the mansion, he'd have to find another way.

Still sitting, Rand took the radio from his belt. "Just survived my first ceiling collapse."

"Already?" Miller said.

"Now my way back to the entrance is blocked."

"This is why you should've just waited on us."

Rand ignored the slight scolding tone in his friend's voice. "How's your search going, by the way?" Rand leveled his light to the newly obstructed corridor. Maybe he'd be able to push through the pile of broken plaster and wood and clear a small path to the other side.

"We didn't find any tools that could break open the door," Miller said. "Jackson's upstairs now, calling for help, though he hasn't come back down yet."

That's not a good sign, Rand thought.

"This might be an odd question, Rando," Miller continued, "but have you ever heard of 'the Lords of Hell'?"

Rand had heard Miller speak but the words hadn't fully registered. Something among the rubble had caught his eye, distracting him. He quickly stood and approached, wondering if he was just seeing things. He wasn't.

Among the debris that had fallen from above was a human skeleton.

20

T he skeleton lay supine amidst the rubble, neck and skull bent backward. The lower jaw dangled open. A few strains of long hair remained on the crown of the skull, and a tattered, faded blue dress loosely hung from the torso.

"You still there?" Miller asked.

"Miller, I... just found a body." Rand hung his head, the implications of this discovery setting in.

One of Rand's biggest rules for his cases was to not get the police involved once the situation was confirmed to be supernatural. The police just didn't have a framework for dealing with supernatural situations. They were useless at best, and could cause Rand a lot of unnecessary trouble at worst.

But Rand still had to legally protect himself when necessary. If he discovered a body during a case, the police *had* to be called—that meant he'd have to explain *why* he was in the mansion in the first place.

"That's really not good," Miller said. He knew well

Rand's rules for when and when not to call the police during a case.

"No, it isn't."

"I bet Jackson can make this easier," Miller offered. "We saw how he handled the cops earlier. He's definitely got some pull with them."

Rand appreciated Miller's positive thinking, but a decomposed body on Jackson's property was a bit more serious than a speeding ticket. "Maybe."

He studied the skull. The empty eye sockets stared back at him. The gaping mouth almost made the body appear as if it were pleading with him. He wondered how many long years the corpse had been there, unknown and undiscovered.

"Hey." This time it was Jackson's voice to come through the radio.

Rand straightened and turned his back on the skeleton. "Hey. Miller told you?"

"No. What's wrong?"

"There's a body in here."

When Jackson didn't reply for a long time, Rand wondered if the man was taking it as some kind of accusation.

"I have no idea where that might've come from," he finally said.

Rand figured that would be the response. "It seems there was a lot more going on in here than you may have thought."

"Clearly. Look, I'm sorry again to put you in this situation. I should've been better prepared for this whole thing."

"Everything's going to be okay," Rand said. He hoped

his positivity didn't seem too forced, since things had gotten steadily worse for him since he'd arrived at the Herron House.

"What do we need to do?"

"We'll have to get the police involved. We still need to follow the law."

"Should I call them now?"

Rand weighed his options. He *really* didn't want the police to show up here as long as Akhubel was still lurking around. Demons were entirely willing to attack police officers, and any officer harmed within the mansion would likely be blamed on Rand. The police simply were not going to believe any supernatural explanations.

"Let me get out of here first. Then we'll do it," Rand said.

"If you think that's best."

Rand honestly couldn't tell if Jackson liked that idea or not. The man's voice now sounded tired and flat.

"That means you need to move faster, Rando." Miller had taken the radio back from Jackson. "The longer you wait to report the body, the more suspicious it'll be."

"Will do." Rand turned and shone his light on the skeleton once again. "I'll get you out of here," he said. "Just give me a little time."

With that, he continued through the darkness.

21

Miller set the radio down and sighed. The night just kept getting worse and worse.

Jackson leaned back on the sofa opposite where Miller sat. His eyes were fixed on a point on the floor, but his mind was clearly racing. Adding things up. Thinking of possibilities, explanations, or maybe even cover stories.

"Any idea about who it could be?" Miller asked.

Jackson's eyes flicked to meet Miller's gaze. "I honestly have no idea."

Miller couldn't help but wonder if that was true. *Don't get any wild ideas. I'm stuck with him for the time being, after all. Don't get paranoid.*

"Were you able to get in touch with someone who could help us?" Miller asked.

"What?"

"You said you were going to call someone…"

It took a moment before Jackson seemed to remember

what Miller was talking about. "Oh. Right, yeah. He's not answering, so I'm calling around."

As if it were a cue, Jackson stood from the couch again and took his phone from his pocket. He put his back to Miller and started scrolling on his phone again.

Miller glanced at his computer. He hadn't gotten through the entire forum post yet, and he was eager to continue, but Miller realized now that Jackson likely did not understand the gravity of their situation. The man might need some help staying on track.

Miller stood from the couch. "I feel like there's more we could be doing to help Rand."

Jackson's body tensed. He turned to face Miller again, lowering the hand that held his phone to his side. The irritation was clear in his expression. "Then by all means, *do something.*"

Miller's nerves twisted. He hadn't expected Jackson to take offense, and he hated confrontation. "Well... I would, but... it seems you know this town much better."

"Exactly. Tell me if you have any useful solutions. Until then, let me do my thing." He left the living room again and his footsteps pounded heavily on the stairs as he returned the second floor.

A bit touchy, isn't he? Miller thought.

Miller remembered that as CEO of his father's oil and gas company, Jackson Herron was likely used to being the boss at all times. That night, however, he wasn't in charge of anyone. In this particular situation, he had to defer to people he'd never met who were better able to call the shots. He probably didn't like that, or at the very least it stressed him out.

I'll give him a bit more time, Miller decided. *Then if things don't improve...*

His thoughts trailed off. He wasn't sure *what* he'd do if the night didn't get better. Never before had a case started off so badly.

Miller hoped and prayed that Rand's idea about the hidden passage in James Herron's office was correct and he'd find a way out of the mansion. Otherwise, Miller would be forced to step up and step in, and he already knew very well that he often buckled under that kind of pressure.

22

Rand felt an odd sense of guilt leaving the skeleton behind. Although they'd been dead a long time, it felt wrong to abandon them after all the decades the remains had already spent within the decrepit mansion.

But for his own wellbeing, Rand needed to proceed.

The corridor ended with a door set within yet another arch. Rand checked the sketchbook. James's floor plan verified that the narrow hallway that Rand currently occupied ended at a single doorway. He flipped the page in hopes of finding a drawing of what he might find on the other side of the door.

The room beyond was far more intricate than the oddly shaped corridors Rand had traversed so far. It was shaped like a perfect circle and divided into twelve sections with the label "30 deg" written in each. James had drawn unique patterns of dots in each of the twelve sections.

Since the ceiling collapse had blocked the way he'd

come from, this room was the only way for Rand to go; so he opened the door and passed underneath the arched frame.

The room beyond was spacious, tall and cylindrical like a silo. The ceiling was so high that the flashlight beam wasn't strong enough to see the top.

Rand counted eleven other arched doorways—one for each thirty-degree section—each identical to the door in which he'd just come through.

Too many options, he thought.

Rand checked the drawing again. The eleven other doors hadn't been labeled, so there was no indication where each one led. Rand quickly flipped through the rest of the sketchbook to see if any of the other drawings resembled where he now stood. None of them did.

"Damn it," Rand whispered. Any way he chose to go would be a complete guess.

Above each door, white candles rested within ornate sconces. They seemed to be arranged randomly. Some were higher, some lower, and others shifted to the left and right.

Probably not random, Rand reminded himself. *Akhubel guided James in all of this.*

He checked the blueprint again and compared the candle display mounted above the door he'd just come through. The positioning of the candles corresponded with the dots on the blueprint. They roughly resembled an upside-down triangle.

Rand analyzed the rest of the dot patterns on the blueprint and the candle positions above the other doors. They corresponded perfectly.

Rand unclipped the radio from his belt. "Miller."

"What's up?"

"Jackson there with you?"

"He's in the other room, but I can go get him."

"I'm in the round candle room. Ask him if he knows which way I should go."

"Round candle room?"

"He should know what I'm talking about."

Rand waited in the silence. A minute later, Jackson's voice came over the radio. "That room is in the exact center of the house. No matter what additions or removals Dad made, he was always adamant that room stayed in the middle."

"Do you know why it was so significant to him?"

If it was meaningful to James, it's because it was meaningful to Akhubel, Rand thought.

"I don't. Sorry."

"It almost looks like a clock," Rand said, although it was hard to convince himself of that. If it *were* a clock, he would've thought he'd see the numbers one through twelve somewhere.

"Miller told me you're trying to get to Dad's office, is that right?"

"Yeah."

"I never went there after the last time he rebuilt it. I don't know the way."

Rand sighed. He really didn't want to guess. If James Herron had put so much effort into designing this room, he knew the symbols and the directions that branched out from it were significant. If he could figure out what the room meant, he'd likely have a better chance of going the right way and not getting hopelessly lost.

Rand checked the drawing again. This time he focused

on the writing along the corner of the page, which he'd only glimpsed at earlier. Although they were messy, he could make out the letters, but the words made no sense.

Reverse them, Rand realized. If Akhubel *had* been guiding James as to how to modify his mansion, then there was likely to be some inversion somewhere. Demons *loved* to invert.

Rand brought his eyes closer to the writing. When he read the words backwards, he recognized the language.

He brought the radio to his mouth. "Miller, I need you to translate some Latin."

"What you got?"

Rand read the letters off one at a time. He pictured Miller typing them into his computer.

"God is dead. Pray to the stars."

Rand figured James Herron might consider God dead after being under Akhubel's influence for so long. But why would he want to pray to the stars instead?

Then, it came to him. There were eleven new doors to choose from, but including the one he'd entered from, there were twelve total. The candles above the door must've represented *stars*.

"Miller, it isn't a clock," Rand told Miller through the radio. "It's the fucking zodiac."

All of the wall-mounted candles lit up by themselves. The room flooded with dim, flickering candlelight.

Rand's mind flashed back to the chamber in the tower.

The candles there did the same thing just before... Rand clenched his jaw. *He's here.*

23

———

R and clicked off his flashlight. He no longer needed it now that the candles were burning.

A low, constant stream of static came from the radio's speaker.

Akhubel's voice cut through the static, deep and dark. The words were unintelligible to Rand, although he'd heard the language many times before on previous cases.

"Enough with the backwards Latin," Rand said. Reversed Latin was a favorite for many demons. "If you have something to say, speak so I can understand."

The radio grew hot in Rand's palm, as if it were over-heating—a side effect of Akhubel's influence on the device. Rand went to the center of the silo-shaped room and placed the radio on the floor.

"You must journey though the darkness. The correct path will lead you to the light. Everywhere else leads to death."

A threat, Rand thought. *I have to choose correctly.*

"Which door should I choose?" Rand figured there was no harm in at least trying to ask.

"Only the Lord and I know."

Rand remembered the Bible he still carried in his jacket pocket. He withdrew it and held it in his left hand.

Akhubel spoke again. "The forward path is found among those pages."

He's toying with me, isn't he? Rand thought. "You really expect me to read this whole thing just to figure out your little riddle?"

Akhubel didn't respond.

Rand laid the Bible on the floor near the radio. "Why don't you show me? I would've thought someone as powerful as you would be above these games. Maybe you *are* just a low-ranking grunt."

Demons were very prideful creatures. In the past, Rand had successfully manipulated demonic entities by calling their pride into question.

At first, nothing happened. Then the front cover of the Bible opened by itself, flattened on the floor as if someone were holding it there. The thin white pages flipped on their own, all the way to the end of the book and then back to the beginning. Rand watched as the pages danced back and forth several times.

Then, they settled. The Bible remained open somewhere near the middle.

Akhubel's voice cut through the low, constant, static that now flowed from the radio. "The Gospel according to John. Chapter fourteen, the second verse."

Again, Rand winced at hearing a demon speak about Scripture. It felt too unnatural, and it unnerved him.

Rand picked up the Bible from the floor. Sure enough,

Akhubel had turned the pages to the fourteenth chapter of John. Rand read aloud by the candlelight: "My Father's house has many rooms; if that were not so, would I have told you that I am going there to prepare a place for you?"

Yeah, he's definitely fucking with me, Rand thought.

The static faded from the radio. Silence returned to the room.

"And he's gone," he whispered. Leaving him to guess which way to go.

"Rando?" Miller sounded panicked.

Rand closed the Bible and set it on the floor again as he picked up the radio. "I'm here."

"I lost you for a minute," Miller said.

"*He* was speaking with me through the radio."

"As they love to do," Miller said. "What did he say?"

"Nothing useful. Except he heavily implied I needed to choose the right way, or I'd die."

"Sounds excessive." Maybe it was, but Rand didn't want to take any chances. "Have you decided which way you'll go?"

Rand paced the outer perimeter of the circular room as he thought about it. "I don't know. Can you ask Jackson when James's birthday was? Maybe the answer is whatever sign he was born under?"

"Sounds... too simple."

It was, but Rand really didn't have any other ideas.

Movement in his periphery caught his attention.

The Bible had opened by itself once again. The pages turned themselves slowly, one at a time.

Is he back? Rand thought. *No.* If Akhubel's presence had returned to the room, Rand would've felt it.

He took a step closer toward the Bible at the center of

the room. The pages began flipping faster. Another step. The more he closed the distance, the faster the pages went.

What's making that happen?

Rand looked around the room and found nothing that hadn't been there before. Then, his eye caught the simple wooden cross he carried in his belt loop. He'd almost forgotten he'd brought it along.

Could it be this? He took the cross in his hand and hovered it over the book. The pages flipped rapidly before settling.

"Whoa," Rand whispered. He studied the cross—it seemed there was some sort of positive energy imbued within. *But how?*

The only idea Rand could think of was that the white-eyed girl had left something of herself behind when she'd repaired the cross that night.

He'd had no idea the cross was capable of anything like that. He remembered how he'd felt compelled to put it in his bag at the last minute. Was that the energy of the white-eyed girl calling out to him?

"You still there?" Miller asked.

"Yes, but hang on."

Rand picked up the Bible to see where the cross had wanted to bring his attention. There was only one bolded heading on the page—the story of Jesus feeding the five thousand.

Rand had read the story dozens of times, but didn't know why it was significant in that moment.

The energy in the cross says it is, though, Rand thought. Then he read the passage aloud.

"Taking the five loaves and the two fish and looking

up to heaven, he gave thanks and broke them. Then he gave them to the disciples to distribute to the people. They all ate and were satisfied, and the disciples picked up twelve basketfuls of broken pieces that were left over."

Rand dwelled on the words. He knew the story was meant to demonstrate Jesus's divinity, but he didn't know why it was significant in that moment.

After a few minutes of wracking his brain, he came up with nothing. He didn't know.

He needed help, and if astrology was somehow involved, then there was only one person he could think of to ask.

"Miller," Rand said into the radio, "I… need to talk to Tessa."

"Tessa?" Miller asked.

Rand knew the request must've sounded strange to his friend. Never before had Rand purposely involved his ex with one of his cases. "Yes." Rand pulled his phone from his pocket and checked his signal, just to be sure. As he thought, there was absolutely none. "I can't call her from in here, so you'll have to."

"If you say so," Miller said. He still sounded unsure.

Calling Tessa while on a case was strange to Rand as well, but in that moment he didn't have anywhere else to turn.

24

"Who is Tessa?" Jackson asked, brow furrowed.

"Rando's ex." Miller picked up his phone from where it lay next to his open laptop on the coffee table.

Jackson lowered himself onto the sofa opposite of where Miller sat. He still seemed icy from their brief tiff earlier. "What does she have to do with this?"

"I have no idea," Miller said. One moment, Rand was saying Akhubel wanted him to guess how to proceed and that he'd die if he was wrong. In the next, Rand suddenly needed to talk to Tessa. It didn't make any sense—regardless Miller knew he needed to help his friend in any way he requested.

Miller placed his phone on the table and put it on speaker. He hoped Tessa was still awake.

When Tessa finally answered, she sounded guarded and nervous. "Hey, Miller."

"Hey, sorry to bother you. Rand needs to talk to you."

Tessa hesitated for a moment. "Are y'all still on that case?"

"Yes."

"Is everything okay?"

No, Miller thought, but he didn't have the time to get into all that right now.

Jackson watched him intently, seeming just as worried as Tessa.

"His phone doesn't work right now, so I have to relay messages between you two over the radio," Miller said, completely side-stepping Tessa's question. "I'll let him know I've got you." He brought the radio to his mouth and pressed the button. "Okay, Rando, I have her on the phone."

"Ask her what the story of Jesus feeding the five thousand has to do with astrology."

Well that's way out of left field, Miller thought.

Tessa didn't respond.

"Did you hear that?" Miller asked.

"Yes, but I don't know."

Miller exhaled deeply before breaking the bad news. "She says she doesn't know."

"Come on," Rand shot back. "How much do you pay that astrologer you meet with? You must've learned *something* by now."

Miller noted the desperation in his friend's voice. He had a feeling Rand *needed* Tessa to know something about this, otherwise...

"I mean..." Tessa sounded upset now. "I don't think the Bible and astrology have anything to do with each other. But let me think for a minute. Maybe I can call—"

Rand came over the radio again. " 'Taking the five

loaves and the two fish and looking up to heaven, he gave thanks and broke them. Then he gave them to the disciples to distribute to the people. They all ate and were satisfied, and the disciples picked up twelve basketfuls of broken pieces that were left over.' "

Miller recognized the Bible passage that Rand read from.

"The two fish is the sign of Pisces," Tessa said warily.

Jackson lifted his gaze from the phone and studied Miller as he relayed what Tessa had said.

Rand didn't respond for a long time. Miller was beginning to think they'd gotten disconnected again.

"I'll take it," Rand finally said.

"He'll take what?" Tessa asked.

"What does the Pisces constellation look like?" Rand asked.

"It sort of looks like the letter V," Tessa said.

"It sort of looks like the letter V," Miller repeated into the radio.

"I'll update you in a minute," Rand said, then his voice cut out.

Miller set his radio on the table next to his cell phone. *What was all that about?*

"Miller, what's going on?" Now Tessa seemed truly worried.

Jackson watched him intently, as if very interested in how he'd respond.

Miller picked up his phone and deactivated the speaker. He brought it to his ear. "Things have... gone a little sideways, if I'm being honest."

"What does 'a little *sideways*' even mean? How bad is it?"

"Everyone's fine. No one's hurt. Rand's just trapped somewhere right now. But don't worry, he's working on getting out."

"Trapped? Where? For how long?"

Jackson shot up from where he sat and left the room without a word. Miller watched him go, confused by his sudden departure. *Something I said?*

"I'll catch you up in a minute," Miller said. "Let me make sure Rand got what he needed."

Tessa sighed.

25

Rand located the configuration of candles that resembled the letter V. It all seemed so arbitrary, but at the moment he had literally nothing else to go on.

I guess this is what it means to have faith, he thought. *The cross led me to that passage, so I'll trust it...*

Rand clipped the radio to his belt, stuffed the Bible back into his jacket pocket, and returned the cross back through his belt loop on his waist. He picked up the flashlight from where he'd set it on the floor after the candles had lit up by themselves.

He sucked in a deep breath and, before he could overthink it, forced himself to pass through the arched doorway beneath the constellation of Pisces.

As soon as he did, he heard a clang within the walls. Double doors quickly slid from narrow slats in the arched frame, then slammed together, preventing Rand from returning to the silo-shaped room.

Once again, Akhubel wasn't lying, Rand thought. *I only get one guess.*

With the candlelight left behind, Rand was once again plunged into darkness. He clicked the flashlight on, then grabbed the radio to update Miller. "Okay, I've left that room and I'm continuing on. Thank Tessa for me."

"Glad to hear it, Rando, but... what was all that about?"

Rand understood why Miller would be confused. He didn't want to take the time to explain everything now, but there was one important thing Miller needed to know. "The cross helped me, Miller. It led me to that Bible passage."

"What do you mean?"

Rand let his hand fall to where the cross hung in his belt loop. He felt silly for putting so much significance in it, but his gut told him there was much more to the cross than he'd originally thought. "The white-eyed girl left something of herself inside this cross when she fused it back together."

"That sounds like a good thing, right?"

"I'd say so. I know I might sound crazy, so I'll just have to show you after I get out of here."

"Looking forward to it."

"Thanks again for getting in touch with Tessa." He'd have to remember to thank her as well the next time he saw her. *Her astrology kick hasn't been a* total *waste of time, after all...*

With Jesus fresh on his mind, Rand said another quick prayer for guidance and hoped he'd made the correct choice.

He then faced the new corridor ahead of him and proceeded deeper into the darkness.

26

L ibby Casey leaned against the wall, many thoughts swirling around in her head.

"Miller, what's going on?"

That question from her mother had been what had caught Libby's attention from the kitchen in Bill's house. She'd come downstairs from her bedroom to grab a snack, only to overhear her mother on the phone with Miller.

"What does 'a little *sideways*' even mean?" Tessa barked. "How bad is it?"

Libby could tell her mother wasn't able to conceal the concern behind her words as she paced around the living room—as she usually did when she was stressed—with her phone pressed against her ear. Bill observed from the couch, legs crossed with his usual business magazine open on his lap. Neither of them had heard Libby in the kitchen.

Dad lied to me and now he's in trouble, Libby thought. She'd strongly suspected that her dad had a new case when she'd seen him and Miller at the restaurant, but he was so adamant about keeping her away from his work that he'd actually *lied* to her. It stung more than she would've thought.

"Trapped? Where? For how long?" Tessa shrieked.

Libby's heart pounded. Tears came to her eyes. *This* was why Libby wanted to be involved with her dad's work. She wanted to be available to help him if he needed it—and it sounded like he needed it now.

She considered herself old enough to decide what kind of danger she was willing to risk in order to help. She'd grown up with these supernatural situations her entire life, after all, and she felt like she knew enough to be an asset.

Libby took her cell phone from her jeans pocket. The screen was filled with text messages and social media updates. She ignored them all and clicked on the one app she knew could help her—Local King. She knew only one person who still used it, and her gut told her that not even a supernatural case could distract Miller from his stupid goal of becoming "king" of as many locations as possible.

When the app loaded, there was a single notification: *Miller Landingham has checked in at the Beau Ridge Rose Motel. He's been crowned the new king!*

"You should've stopped using this stupid app a long time ago like everyone else," Libby muttered as she searched the Beau Ridge Rose Motel on her phone. It was about an hour away.

I can make it there even quicker if I drive fast, she thought.

Her mother and Bill would be going to bed soon, and Bill's house was big enough for her to sneak out of without being caught. She'd done it a few times before and had gotten away with it.

She couldn't wait to yell at her dad for lying to her, but that would have to wait. That night he needed help.

And she'd be there for him.

27

_____

The corridor Rand traversed led him straight ahead. Thick cobwebs gathered where the upper wall met the ceiling. A layer of dust lined the floor, and his shoes left prints wherever he stepped.

Doors were on either side of the corridor. Rand opened one and aimed his light inside. It was a bedroom with a broad, canopied bed. The windows on the far side had been barred.

He tried another door farther down the corridor. It appeared to have once been a library, yet the shelves were devoid of any books. Once again, the windows were barred.

A third door revealed a simple bathroom. Dirt and grime covered the tile floor.

This part seems so normal, Rand thought as he continued down the hall.

A slight ease came over him—something he hadn't felt since he'd first stepped foot inside the Herron House. He found himself peeking into the rooms not because he thought he'd discover anything valuable inside, but because he was reassured by their normalcy. After what he'd seen so far, these rooms brought a vague sense of relief.

Don't get too comfortable, Rand reminded himself. He figured what he was seeing now was the oldest part of the mansion, back when it had been a family home. This area seemed untouched by James Herron's madness.

The corridor began to narrow, and Rand realized that he was about to leave normalcy behind once again. It was as if the mansion had tried to lull him into a false sense of security just long enough before reintroducing him to the bizarre.

Rand paused and referred to the blueprints to get his bearings. One section caught his eye.

The drawings indicated a large room to the left of where Rand currently was. There were additional markings on the corridor that Rand hadn't seen anywhere else in the collection of blueprints. Arrows pointed downward, and there were precise measurements written near them. Another straight horizontal line intersected the corridor until the corridor continued on below the line.

Does this mean it's underground? Rand thought. *But how?*

In the south, it was very rare to build anything underground, since most of the terrain was already at sea level or below. Going underground usually meant you'd hit water.

Although Rand was searching solely for James Herron's office, he was also eager to learn more about the man and how he'd been guided through his descent into madness. Perhaps the best way to do that, Rand figured, was to peek his head into the rooms that were drawn with the most detail. Those were the parts of the mansion James had focused on the most.

Rand proceeded down the corridor, thankful that this one was much wider than the ones he'd traversed before. As he progressed, the floor had a notable downward incline.

It does *go underground,* he thought. Rand couldn't fathom how complicated the construction of this section of the mansion would have been.

The walls changed abruptly. The plaster and wallpaper ended and were replaced with a new building material. Rand rubbed his hand along it. The smooth, grey rock was cold against his palm.

It's like some kind of underground cavern, he thought.

Rand had visited similar places before, but those had been formed naturally from erosion over millions of years. He wondered how much James Herron had paid to achieve a similar effect.

The rock corridor terminated. Rand thought he'd hit a dead end, but then noticed a door latch. He'd almost missed it because the door had been built from the same rock as the walls, causing it to blend in. Rand pulled the latch and the door opened freely, giving way to a dark room beyond.

The moment Rand stepped in he could feel the cold, wet air hovering all around him. Now he truly felt like he'd stepped into a cave. He used his flashlight to examine his surroundings.

The room was round, with the walls of smooth rock continuing throughout the entire circumference. Seven waist-high stone pillars were arranged in a circle at the center of the room. Objects sat atop each.

What have I stumbled upon here? Rand thought.

He aimed his flashlight at the object on the nearest pillar—it was an old phonograph. An unlabeled record rested on its surface. He hadn't seen something like that since he'd cleaned out his parents' attic many years ago.

He traced his light along the other six rock pillars. They also contained identical phonographs, all armed with records. They were positioned in such a way as to project their sound toward the center of the circle.

Couldn't you have just gotten a surround-sound system, James? Rand thought. He wondered why Akhubel had put him up to this.

Rand aimed his flashlight up. The ceiling was conical and corbelled. Stone slabs overlapped each other, getting smaller and smaller as they rose, eventually terminating into a dome.

Rand checked the blueprint again. Each of the seven phonograph positions had been marked with a symbol from the same demonic language Rand had seen drawn within the magic circle in the tower.

Rand found more writing on the back of the page—which was unusual, because so far James had not written or drawn on the reverse sides of any of the other pages.

The seven symbols were repeated again, written down the page in a straight line. Beside each was an intricate jagged line drawn all the way to the edge of the page. At first glance, they looked like readings from an EKG machine that had malfunctioned and gone erratic.

Sound waves, he realized.

"Rando?" came Miller's voice from the radio on Rand's belt.

The single word exploded through the silence, startling Rand. It seemed unnaturally loud—much louder than it should've been. Miller's voice bounced around the chamber, reverberating off the walls. Rand winced and pressed his fingers into his ears as the amplified sound hurt his ear drums. He waited for what seemed like entire minutes for the single word spoken from his radio to fade away, as if the sound were trapped and insulated by the round chamber.

A dull ache lingered in this ears—similar to the feeling he got whenever he rocked out to music a bit too loud while driving.

"The fuck?" he whispered.

Thefuck-thefuck-thefuck-thefuck-thefuck-fuck-fuck...

Rand's whispered words reverberated up to the vault-like ceiling so clearly Rand could nearly follow its path.

He realized that since he hadn't responded to Miller, his friend would try to contact him again. Rand didn't want another jarring explosion of sound, so he twisted the radio's knob and turned it off.

Sorry to make you worry, Rand thought. *The acoustics in here are a bit much.*

He eyed the phonograph nearest to him once again. Rand wondered what James Herron had wanted to listen to so intensely that he needed to build an entire room specifically for it. Given the demonic symbols labeling the wavelengths on the back of the room's blueprint, Rand figured it wasn't good.

And I don't think I want to find out, Rand thought as he turned toward the door.

It slammed shut.

28

The sound of the heavy stone door slamming into place rang throughout the chamber and up the vaulted, conical roof. The sound produced an uncomfortable heaviness in Rand's head. Rand pressed his hands to his ears again, waiting for the noise to subside.

Once it did, Rand pushed against the door. It didn't budge.

A prickly, crawling feeling crept over Rand's flesh. Something about the energy in the room had changed—he was no longer alone.

Akhubel, he thought.

Rand turned and put his back to the door. He lifted his flashlight, then shone it directly across the cavern-like chamber.

Akhubel had appeared on the opposite side of the room.

The demon still chose to use the apparition of an

elderly man. His wrinkled, grey flesh was of similar color to the room's stone walls.

Rand was about to speak, but quickly clenched his jaw when he remembered how unpleasant sounds were in this particular room.

Then it dawned on him. With the door held closed behind him and no way to escape, he was completely vulnerable to the noise.

There was motion on the edges of the flashlight beam, so Rand pivoted his light. The records on all seven phonographs had started spinning by themselves, likely moved by Akhubel's power. The seven needles shifted in unison, poised over the records.

No, Rand thought. He swung his light back to where Akhubel had been standing, but the demon vanished.

The seven needles dropped onto the records at the same time.

And Rand was enveloped by an otherworldly cacophony.

Dark chanting. Dissonant notes. Screeching. Pulsing.

Each phonograph assaulted Rand with something different. Together, they formed a twisted discord, and the reverberation of the chamber amplified it all to unbearable volumes.

The instant and severe pain in Rand's head forced him to his knees, where he pushed his hands against his ears, but the noises were too loud. No matter how much he tried to shield himself, they filled his head.

His brain was an overfilled balloon, ready to pop. Powerful vibrations flowed through his body, unnatural pulses that felt as if they were rearranging his insides.

Dizzy. Nauseous. His throat burned as he screamed—which he couldn't even hear.

The sounds weren't going to stop, yet he wouldn't be able to bear it much longer.

The cross.

The aural assault was so intense that the singular thought only flashed through Rand's mind for a moment.

He tore his hand away from his ear and yanked the cross from where it dangled from his belt loop. Sharp pain ripped through his uncovered ear drum. He fumbled the cross at first, almost dropping it.

Not knowing what else to do, Rand lifted the cross between him and one of the phonographs. The device fell backwards from its stone foundation as if pushed by invisible hands.

It works, he thought.

Rand traced a semicircle in the air with the cross, pointing it at each of the phonographs. They fell from their perches one by one, silencing a piece of the evil symphony as they did.

When the last one fell, the final sound waves bounced around the stone walls and domed ceiling above until they faded.

Rand had no way of knowing if true silence had returned to the room, since his brain echoed with remnants of the horrible music as if it were trapped inside. His ears rang, and the room spun rapidly as dizziness took him. The balance in his inner ear were completely thrown off. He tipped sideways, falling from his knees and onto his side, then rolled over and vomited.

Something trickled from his right ear. He wiped at it and his fingers came away wet and sticky. Blood.

Darkness closed in around the edges of his vision. The pain in his head was so great Rand didn't even try to fight it. He let his world go black.

29

"Rando?" Miller spoke into the radio as he paced around the living room of the caretaker's house.

He chewed his lip while waiting for a response. Nothing.

Anxiety bristled within him. He tried to keep himself from assuming the worst.

I'll finish what I was reading, Miller thought, *and then if I still haven't heard from Rando, that's when I'll start worrying.*

Miller sat back down on the sofa and opened his laptop again. He hadn't had a chance to dig into the next post from Arthur Briggs before Rand had asked him to get in touch with Tessa.

Miller reread the post's first line.

'I've discovered a new breed of demon. I call them the Lords of Hell.'

Miller didn't even want to think about the possibility of a "new breed of demon." He was still terrified of the ones he'd already encountered. But everything Arthur

Briggs had written so far had rung true to Miller, so he knew he had to read on.

I've been speculating about a different type of demon for many years. Every now and then I meet people who tell me about their encounters with demons who exhibit behaviors that don't quite match what I'm used to.

They are far more intelligent.

Far more cunning.

Far more deadly.

Most demons delight in causing trauma and destruction, intent on psychologically breaking down their victims over time. Not these entities.

These beings are much more organized and calculated—the opposite of their aforementioned counterparts. They don't like chaos. Rather, they exhibit a complex pattern of behavior that is more akin to ritual.

At first I thought these particular demons were just the high-ranking ones in hell, but there's something else strange about them that I can't quite put my finger on.

Due to their deliberate nature, these demons are not simply attracted to locations where there is an abundance of negative energy, as most demons are. They must be summoned.

From what I can tell, summoning them is a very compli-cated process and I wouldn't dare post it here, even if I did fully understand how to do it. This means they are brought into our realm very carefully and intentionally by individuals who seek to work with them and benefit from their power.

For these demons, human possession is not the goal. They seem to prefer their incorporeal form and work alongside the people who called upon them. They wreak havoc by cooperating with the person who summoned them, lending him or her their supernatural power so that the summoner might achieve their goals in the material world. As I'm sure you can imagine, these goals are rarely benevolent. Anyone who'd take the time to learn the precise technique of summoning a powerful demon, and then proceed to do so, does not have anyone's best interest in mind other than their own.

No one I spoke to who'd encountered these entities was able to photograph them, but they were often able to record them. None spoke in English. The few samples I've heard were of ancient languages, the most common being Aramaic and Sumerian.'

Miller looked up from the computer. Shindael was known to speak Sumerian.

'Given the patterns I was uncovering, I slowly began to realize there was a breed of demon that I knew nothing about. Even after my lifetime of work, they'd managed to keep themselves well-hidden.'

Miller reread that part again. *A lifetime of work.* If Arthur Briggs had truly put in a lifetime of work, then that meant he could have even more experience than Rand.

'If these creatures existed, I needed to know. Mankind deserved to know.

According to the accounts I heard, one thing these demons had in common was that they all, at some point, claimed to originate from Mesopotamia. This makes sense because this region is the Cradle of Civilization—the origins of humanity here on Earth. As we all know, these eternal beings have been attacking our ancestors from the very beginning.

It's been some time since I've posted here. That's because I've been away searching for answers. In order to track down information on this new breed of demon, I knew I needed to get my own boots on the ground.

Throughout the last year or so, I've traveled widely throughout the regions and small towns in southern Iraq and Iran. I went to every mosque from Tikrit to Shiraz (I won't even get into the dicey border crossing, where I nearly died) to interview the Imams in the local mosques. These gentlemen were very kind and welcoming, but when I asked them about these entities, they balked.

However, I did find a few Imams who would speak to me on the subject. It was almost always the older ones who seemed to no longer fear these supernatural entities.

An Imam named Abdul had kept numerous handwritten records over the years of the townspeople who came to him claiming to be haunted by a Djinn (the word for demons in that part of that world). I asked his permission to copy them, and he said that I could. It took my interpreter a long time, but he transcribed the document's text onto a simple website here.'

The word "here" was a hyperlink.

'It will take even more time to have these documents translated into English. Until then, I hope you can read Arabic.

More pieces came together as I continued to search. In short, it all seems to be linked to an ancient child-sacrifice cult that existed in the region thousands, perhaps tens of thousands of years before. Some of the Imams told me that, even though they're rare, a few sects of this cult remain today. From time to time, the local police will uncover one of these sects and arrest the members. Curiously, these arrests never make headlines.

Abdul also informed me that people he'd spoken to who'd seen a Djinn almost always reported that the entity they saw looked very similar to one of the cult leaders who'd been arrested. I'm speculating here, but I wonder if these demons, when they appear, choose to resemble the person who summoned them...

I'm currently back home in Rose Grove and it seems I've gone as far as I can with this investigation for now. The origins of these entities and their human devotees are still mysterious, but I'll resume research when and if I can.

Although it seems this child-sacrifice cult has more or less faded into history, the entities associated with this group still remain. I have no idea how many of them there are, but some knowledgeable sources I've spoken to speculate it's less than ten. That would mean these are truly unique demons that have been set apart for some nefarious purpose. This is why I have tentatively dubbed them the Lords of Hell—because that's exactly what they are. Superior to all except the devil himself.

What their ultimate purpose is, I can't yet say. Maybe I'll never learn the entire truth. But I'll keep digging.'

Only after he finished reading did Miller realize his entire body had grown tense. His heart was racing, and his mouth had gone dry.

It could all be bullshit, Miller reminded himself, but in his gut he knew it wasn't. Something about the no-nonsense way Arthur Briggs recounted his tale resonated as authentic.

Not only had Briggs been doing this work longer than Rand, he seemed willing to push further than Rand would likely be willing to go. The areas of the world Briggs spoke about were dangerous and unstable due to war and unrest, yet the man had traveled there regardless to find the information he sought.

The post was once again followed by several replies.

'You're a legend, Briggs.'

'Keep up the good work!'

'Anyone on here who can post an English translation of Briggs's site?'

Miller scrolled back up and clicked the link Arthur Briggs had provided. The website that loaded was plain and contained only text and pictures. As Briggs had said, it was all in flowing, Arabic script.

Miller scrolled through, looking at the few pictures—drawings—that broke up the text. A sketch of a ritualistic scene caught Miller's eye. Several adult-sized silhouettes surrounded what appeared to be a small child lying flat on their back, a dark shadow hovering just above them.

Miller shivered.

Another drawing depicted two people—one laid on their back, hands and legs bound while the other stood over them, a knife raised high above his head, ready to deliver a killing blow. A shadowed figure stood next to the man with the knife, as if supervising.

Or encouraging him, Miller thought.

The browser software had dropped down a small window in the upper-right corner of the screen. It read, "Arabic detected. Translate?"

Miller clicked "Yes."

The text shifted all at once, but not to English. Instead, the Arabic script turned into symbols that Miller had never seen before. They were formed with straight lines and sharp, angular corners. Miller felt a sense of revulsion bubble up within him.

A demonic language, he realized. From a technical perspective, his computer shouldn't have been able to display those symbols, yet it had anyway. Miller clicked away from the website as fast as he could.

The forum had a direct message function. Miller clicked to send one to the user "AB." Next to the username, the website indicated Arthur Briggs's last log in was the same date as his most recent post about the Lords of Hell—over a year ago.

He probably won't get this, Miller thought. *It's still worth a shot.*

He began to type.

'Hi, AB. I hope this message finds you well. I read about your investigation of a new type of demon tied to a child-sacrifice cult. My friend and I have encountered a peculiar entity whose name sounds like it originated from the region you mentioned. Even if there's no correlation, we'd still be very interested in speaking with you about this. Please message me back as soon as you get this. You can also call me.'

Miller typed his phone number and sent the message, and the forum software confirmed delivery.

He eyed the radio beside his computer. It remained silent. Miller wanted to tell Rand about what he'd discovered, but now wasn't the right time.

Find a way out of there first, Rando, he thought. *And hurry.*

30

Libby pressed the gas. The highway she was on was a bit too windy and narrow for the speed she was going, and there were no streetlights either. She could only see what was just in front of her in the range of her car's headlights.

Her destination grew closer on her phone's GPS. The black-and-white checkered-flag indicator flashed, as if beckoning her. There, she'd find Miller and find out what was going on—and how she could help.

Red and blue lights flashed behind her. The police cruiser merged onto the highway, appearing from a hidden place just off the side of the road.

"Shit," Libby whispered. She could almost hear her father's yelling and cursing—he hated speed traps like this.

She slowed and pulled off onto the side of the high-way. The police cruiser followed.

His white headlights were so bright Libby could only

make out a hefty silhouette approaching her in the night. She rolled down her window.

"Evening." Now that the officer was closer, Libby could see him better. He was quite a large man, both tall and broad, and he wore a tan police uniform.

"Hey," Libby said.

"Any idea how fast you were going?"

"No, sir." Libby had gotten out of a fair share of speeding tickets in the relatively short amount of time she'd been driving. She hoped this would end the same way.

"License and registration." The officer held out his hand.

Libby's hopes started to fade—this guy seemed very by the book. She reached for the vehicle's paperwork in the glove box and took her license from her wallet in her purse. She passed them both through the window.

The officer used his flashlight to study her license. Libby watched as his stony expression melted away into what seemed more like trepidation. He shone the light at her, and Libby squinted. "Libby Casey?" He said her name as if he somehow recognized her.

"Yes... sir."

The officer pointed his light back at the license. Although he continued to stare at it, Libby could tell he was thinking about something else entirely. He then seemed to come to a decision and thrust her documents back through the window, and Libby took them. "Have a nice night." He returned to his vehicle, walking twice as fast as when he'd first approached.

Libby watched him go in the rearview mirror, confused. The officer had almost seemed *afraid* of her.

This has something to do with Dad, Libby thought. She couldn't quite explain *how* she knew. She just did. The officer had been ready to throw the book at her—right up until he'd learned her name.

Libby waited for the officer to drive away, but all he did was linger.

I can't believe I'm about to do this, Libby thought as she got out of her car and walked toward the red and blue flashing lights. Her friends would call her crazy for pushing her luck like that when a cop had already decided to let her go, but this situation was a lot more complicated than a speeding ticket.

The police officer was looking down at his lap when Libby approached. He hadn't noticed her. She knocked on the window, visibly startling him. He hesitated before rolling the window down, as if trying to decide if he even wanted to speak to her at all. When he finally did roll the window down, it was only a crack. "I said you're free to go, ma'am."

"Thank you. But I just needed to ask... it seemed like you recognized my name. Have you seen my dad?"

He slowly shook his head. "I'm sorry, ma'am. I can't help you."

With that, he put his cruiser into drive and pulled away. Libby had to take a large step backward to save her toes from being run over. The officer made a wide U-turn on the highway, then started back the way he came. His red and blue lights turned off, and soon he vanished into the dark distance.

It seemed like he *was the one afraid of* me, Libby thought. *Dad, what have you gotten yourself into this time?*

31

There was pleasant music.

Rand's eyelids fluttered open. Motion. He clenched his eyes shut, then opened them again to focus his vision. He caught the briefest glimpse of what he thought were feet exiting the room, the door closing behind them.

Rand then remembered where he was.

His head felt like it was full of pressure, his brain unpleasantly numb. Sharp pain sliced through the inner portions of both his ears.

Rand brought his hands to both sides of his head. He found half-dried streams of blood on his cheeks and neck which had flowed from his ears.

He forced himself to sit up. When he did, a biting wave coursed through his skull. His brain felt like it had come loose inside his skull and jostled around with every move he made.

Although his ears were numb, he could still hear the

music. It was soft and beautiful. After what he'd just endured, it was almost restorative.

He searched for the source. One of the fallen phonographs had been returned to the rock platform nearest the door, record spinning beneath the needle. The other six still lay on the floor, broken from when the cross's power had pushed them onto the floor.

Someone was just in here, Rand thought. He *hadn't* imagined those feet leaving through the door. *Who was that?* As far as he knew, besides Akhubel, he was alone inside the Herron House. His brain was still too battered to come up with any ideas.

The cross lay on the stone floor next to a puddle of his own vomit.

It saved me, Rand realized. He scooped it up and held it in his hands. Whatever power was imbued within had been enough to combat the hellish symphony.

He tried to stand, but the dizziness returned. He lowered himself back to the floor and closed his eyes, waiting for the spinning to pass. It didn't, and the nausea crept back in.

Something is seriously wrong in my head, he realized. Whatever Akhubel had done to him was too much. This wasn't just going to fade. He'd sustained a serious injury.

As Rand lingered on the floor, he caught himself fixated on the music. He surprised himself—he assumed he would've preferred total silence to give his ears a break, but as he focused on the music coming from the single phonograph, he thought he started to feel better.

There were no instruments, as far as he could tell. It sounded like a chorus of voices singing together in perfect harmony. Rand had never before heard anything so beautiful—maybe because it was in stark contrast to what he'd just endured.

Another idea came to him. The cross had showed him the way earlier, and then it had protected him from the sounds.

Can it heal me?

Rand lifted the cross and touched it to the right side of his head. Almost instantly, the heavy numbness in his right ear faded. The ringing silenced. His dizziness partially resolved. He then touched the cross to his left ear and the same thing happened. Rand wiped his hands against his cheek and neck—the blood that had flowed from his ears had disappeared.

The white-eyed girl definitely *left some kind of power behind in this,* he thought as he looked at the cross in awe. He'd desperately wished for a tool like this ever since he'd begun fighting the supernatural all those years ago. *Next time I run into Akhubel, I'll see what it'll do to him.*

Rand returned to his feet without stumbling again. He approached the single record player and lifted the needle from the spinning disc. The music stopped and silence returned to the chamber.

Whoever had set up the music for him had left through the door that had previously been held closed by Akhubel. Rand tried the latch and it opened.

Thank you, whoever you are, Rand thought.

Whoever it was, though, was gone. The rock corridor leading away from the chamber was empty.

The radio, Rand remembered. It wasn't clipped to his waist. He searched around the room, and luckily found where it had landed. The front panel had come dislodged, exposing the wires beneath.

Please don't be broken, Rand thought as he carried the radio back into the stone corridor. He tried to push the panel back into place, but it didn't hold. He pressed the button on the side and spoke into it. "Miller? Can you hear me?"

No static. No beeps or sounds when he twisted the knob on the top.

He was now completely cut off from the outside world.

Rand let the radio fall the ground and it landed with a loud clatter. There was no point in continuing to carry it with him. Miller would freak out now that he couldn't communicate with him, but there was nothing he could do about that now.

Rand pressed onward, his resolve to find James Herron's office rekindled.

32

L ibby followed the GPS on her phone to a shabby, run-down motel. The building was horseshoe-shaped, surrounding a dark asphalt parking lot. A crude wooden sign had been erected at the front that read "Beau Ridge Rose Motel." The place immediately gave Libby sketchy vibes.

Miller's yellow truck was one of the few cars in the lot. She was in the right place.

She parked beside the truck and lifted her phone to call Miller. A red neon sign that read "VACANCY" flickered in a window nearby.

Miller answered quickly. "Hey Libby."

"Hey."

"So… what's up?" Miller sounded guarded and awkward. Libby knew it was because he was preparing himself to pretend like he and her dad weren't on a case.

"I'm here at the motel," she said, getting straight the point.

Miller was silent for several long moments. "What motel?"

He sounded totally disingenuous—Miller had never been a good liar. "The Beau Rose whatever. I'm parked right by your truck. Which room are you and my dad in?"

Miller let out a grunt—it was a sound he often made when he stood up after sitting for a long time. "What are you doing? You shouldn't have come."

"Well I did, and I'm here to help with the case."

"How…"

"I overheard your phone call with my mom and I know Dad's in some kind of trouble. And you checked into this motel on that stupid app no one but you uses anymore. Congratulations, you're the new king here."

"Uh… oh."

Libby could practically hear Miller kicking himself for that.

Harsh sounds came through the phone as Miller fumbled around. Libby assumed he was walking toward the motel-room window to see for himself if she was actually there or not. She scanned the upper row of rooms, waiting for one of the curtains to be pulled away and Miller to appear. He didn't. She shifted her gaze to the first floor of rooms. None of those curtains moved, either.

The only motion came from a figure leaning against the wall next to a first-floor room, the nearby door ajar. He or she was cast in shadow. Only the orange glow of a cigarette was visible. Libby got the feeling the person was watching her.

"So come on, which room are y'all in?"

"We're not at the motel, Libby," Miller said.

She felt herself deflate. It then occurred to her that only Miller's truck was in the lot. He and her dad must've each brought their own car, but the orange Jeep wasn't anywhere to be found.

Shit, she thought. *And he probably won't tell me where they are right now.*

"Where are y'all, then?" she pressed.

"Libby…"

"Just tell me. I'm already here."

"You *really* shouldn't have come. Does your mom know?"

"Of course she doesn't. I'm here to help Dad and it's *my* decision."

"You being here will only make your dad's job that much harder. The situation tonight has already… had some hiccups. You should go back home."

"Miller, I'm not going home."

Miller sighed. "Look, I'm kind of in the middle of something. If you won't go home, then just let yourself into our room and wait for me to call you back."

He's brushing me off, she thought. She knew Miller wasn't actually planning to call her back.

"It's room seventeen on the second floor," Miller went on. "The lock doesn't work. Just jiggle the doorknob and you'll be able to get in. Go up there and *stay put.* I'll call you later."

"You'd better. If you don't, I *will* keep blowing up your phone until you tell me where I can meet you." Libby hung up on him.

Cursing under her breath, she got out of her car and locked it. The late-night chill was sharp against her arms and legs. Libby started toward the metal stairway that led up to the motel's second floor, pretending she didn't feel the lingering eyes of the smoking person in the shadows.

"You must be Randolph Casey's daughter."

Libby froze when she heard her father's name. She didn't like surprises when her father was on a case—especially one that "had some hiccups" according to Miller.

The woman stepped out of the shadows and into the strong beams of the mounted floodlights that illuminated the parking lot. She took one last drag of her cigarette, the orange tip flaring before she tossed the butt to the pavement with a lazy drop of her arm and snubbed it out with the toe of her leopard-patterned shoe.

As she neared, Libby saw that the woman didn't look anything like what she would've thought would be the motel's normal clientele. She was very pretty and had shoulder-length blonde hair. She wore a form-fitting, pink V-neck shirt and dark blue jeans that looked brand new.

"I'm Miranda Herron," she said, holding out her had. The remaining smoke from her final drag wafted from her mouth and dissipated above her head. "My husband and I are the ones who hired your father."

Libby shook Miranda's hand, though she was still caught off guard by the whole interaction. "How did you know who I was?"

Libby had been hesitant to confirm her identity to this stranger, but it also occurred to her that Miranda might be able to tell her where her dad was.

Miranda smirked. "He talked a lot about you."

Libby had a hard time believing that. Her dad rarely talked about her extensively with his clients, especially these days when he was actively trying to prevent Libby from getting involved with his cases. And even if he *had* talked about her, he surely hadn't gone into details about what she looked like or what kind of car she drove.

The only thing Libby could guess was that she'd given herself away by parking so close to Miller's truck despite there being plenty of space in the near-empty lot. That might have suggested to Miranda that Libby knew Miller.

Miranda's eyes narrowed. "How old are you?"

Libby cleared her throat. "Sixteen."

"Do you usually go with your dad on these types of cases?"

Libby cleared her throat. "I do," she said, doing her best to sound confident—as if her father hadn't run off to work this particular case without telling her. "I help him a lot, actually."

"That's nice." Miranda seemed unimpressed, despite Libby's efforts to sound strong.

Libby could definitely make out the tiredness behind Miranda's beauty. Bags had formed underneath her eyes, and the lids slightly drooped. Her body seemed rigid from holding a simmering tension. Libby had seen this look in her father's past clients who'd also suffered supernatural situations.

Regardless, she sensed this was her moment to ask. "Do you happen to know where my dad is right now?"

It feels ridiculous asking that after pumping myself up as Dad's ever-reliable assistant, Libby couldn't help but think.

"He's at my father-in-law's old house," Miranda said flippantly, apparently unaware Libby had just tried and failed to pry the same information from Miller.

"Right, but… where is it?"

"My husband told us to stay put here for now," Miranda said.

"Us?" Libby's eyes shot to the door Miranda had been standing beside as she'd smoked her cigarette. Yellow light glowed in the nearby window.

Miranda gestured over her shoulder. "My nine-year-old daughter's here with me."

"Oh." Libby's heart sank. Supernatural situations were frightening for everyone involved, but she had learned from her dad that young children were often far more affected and traumatized. Demonic spirits usually targeted young children first before ever revealing their presence to the adults.

"To be honest, it's frustrating being told to stay here." Miranda rolled her eyes. "The 'big boys' want to handle everything by themselves, as usual."

Libby certainly related to Miranda on that level. She also noted that the woman had dodged her question regarding the house's location.

"Come on." Miranda started walking toward her room. "We'll let them do what they do. Meanwhile, you and I can keep each other company."

Miranda disappeared into her motel room, though she left the door open as if she assumed that Libby would follow.

Libby hesitated as she considered her options. She hadn't come all the way here to idly pass the time with Miranda Herron. However, she *also* hadn't come to sit in her dad and Miller's motel room by herself. Libby could see on Miranda's face how much they'd all been through. Perhaps one simple way she could help with the case—

until she could meet up with her dad and Miller—was to take the client's mind off the situation for a little bit.

When Rand had been helping Georgia Collins, Libby had befriended the girl for that exact reason, and they were still friends to that day.

I'll keep her company just for a little while, Libby thought. *Then I'll find a way to get to that house.*

33

The hallway abruptly widened and dead-ended into a wall with a set of double doors. Rand scanned the wall with his flashlight. It was covered with writing, the letters appearing as if they'd been scrawled by a trembling hand.

An Absence of God.

Hardened Heart.

Forehead Sign.

Son of Sin.

A Satanic Mark.

"Here we go," Rand whispered to himself. "I think I know where I am..."

He'd passed the page numerous times earlier as he'd skimmed through the sketchbook searching for clues as to where he was within the mansion. Rand flipped the pages quickly—he remembered the one he was looking for was somewhere toward the end.

He found it. The top of the page was simply labeled "Chapel."

"After all this, James, why would Akhubel make you build a chapel?" Rand whispered.

But if the writings on the chapel's exterior wall were any indication, Rand already had a good idea of what he'd find inside.

He pushed open the doors and entered a room that could have rivaled some of the largest churches he'd ever seen. Even in the meager light, Rand could tell that James had directed his contractors to build a full-sized sanctuary. However, the interior was unlike anything that would be found in a normal church.

The altar on the far side of the room contained a large wooden cross that had been flipped upside down. To the right was a line of statues and sculptures of Jesus, all of which had been vandalized. Distorted pentagrams had been gouged into the walls—all different sizes and shapes, with the lengths of some points longer than others. Some were incomplete, lacking the final line that would have enclosed the star.

Bible verses had been written on the walls and then subsequently scratched out. However, Rand could still make out some of the passages beneath the frantic lines.

Rand shone his light on the floor. The number 3 had been drawn backwards all across the hardwood. Rand knew that the reversed three was meant to mock the Trinity—something demons gleefully did any time they got the chance.

James was told to build a chapel and then desecrate it, Rand thought. He assumed Akhubel's intention had been to further separate James's soul from anything holy. *And it worked.*

Rand heard soft sobbing from somewhere in the darkness. He tensed. After being alone inside the mansion all night, the sound of another chilled him. Rand lifted his flashlight with a slow, steady hand.

A woman sat in the front-left pew, shoulders trembling as she cried. She wore a tattered blue dress—the same as the one worn by the body that had fallen through the ceiling.

"It's you," Rand whispered.

The woman's sobbing ceased. She slowly turned her head and faced Rand. Only a small amount of remaining hair framed her long face. Her eyes were fully white and without pupils. She appeared gaunt with sunken cheeks.

She rose from the pew and ambled toward him. Her flesh was white with deep-purple bruises and red marks. Her feet were bare and dirty, and Rand realized he somehow recognized them.

She was the one I saw walking away, Rand thought.

She came to stand a few feet away from him. She seemed to study Rand.

"You put that music on for me to help me wake up," Rand said. "Thank you."

The woman didn't respond.

"You're Kendra Herron."

Something seemed to change on the woman's face, as if she'd been struck by a distant memory—as if she'd suddenly been reminded of her own name.

Jackson had said that after he'd discovered his mother was dead, James had claimed he'd already had her buried.

That wasn't true at all.

"This dangerous place collapsed on you. Then your husband just left you in here."

It made sense to Rand that Kendra Herron's spirit still

lingered inside the Herron House. She'd died tragically and unnecessarily because of James Herron's crazed actions, then her body had just been left to rot.

"You're the ghost that the caretakers see," Rand said. Kendra continued to watch him with a blank stare. "Is this where your spirit is drawn to?" Rand took another cursory glance around with his flashlight. There seemed to be no part of the chapel that hadn't been profaned. He imagined Kendra's lost soul seeking any kind of light or goodness within the depths of the Herron House. It made sense that she'd choose to come here even though all that had once been holy had been ruined.

Rand took the cross from his belt, and Kendra's blank eyes immediately latched on to it, drawn to the power within. "This cross was once destroyed, but then it was restored by the power of an angel. Maybe it can restore this place for you."

Rand went to the row of Jesus statues that lined the wall. The first had been decapitated. "You guided me and you've protected me," he whispered as he lifted the cross toward the statue's body. "Can you reverse the evil that was done here?"

The statue's severed head, which lay on the floor at Rand's feet, floated up by itself, reattached to the neck, and became whole again.

"Of course you can." He turned and looked at Kendra. The woman did not react, though she continued to watch him with interest. "I'll make things right for you here," he said to her. "To thank you for what you did for me."

Rand moved to the next statue in line. Jesus was depicted standing upright in a white robe, palms outstretched. While this one had retained its head, there were holes stabbed into the chest and torso, as if someone had jabbed at it with a crowbar.

Rand brought the cross near the wounds. The specks of broken marble that had once filled those holes rose from the floor and returned to where they'd come from, packed in tight and sealed like new.

He went to work on the walls. He waved the cross along them, and as he did the blasphemies, crude drawings, and demonic symbols faded away into nothing. Even the gashes in the maroon paint smoothed over, leaving it like new.

Rand walked up and down the pews, waving the cross over the torn fabric in the cushions. The white stuffing that had been ripped through the seams pulled back inside the lining and the holes closed themselves up.

Kendra's eyes tracked him as he strode throughout the chapel, like a painting whose eyes seemed to watch you no matter where you stood.

Rand crouched and brought the cross near the dark stains and reversed 3s on the carpet—they shrank and then vanished.

As Rand cleansed the chapel, a new energy flooded through him, confidence that he hadn't felt since he'd entered the Herron House. He'd seen the cross's power three times now over the course of the night. He felt unstoppable.

And he knew *exactly* what he was going to do the next time he saw Akhubel.

Rand went to the chapel's altar—the only thing left for him to address. The large, upside-down crucifix leaned against the wall. Rand knew it was too heavy to lift.

His own cross had no such limitations. When he

waved it near its reversed companion, the crucifix hovered in the air as if weightless and flipped right-side up. It no longer leaned against the wall, but rather balanced upright, supported with some force invisible to Rand.

He returned to where Kendra's spirit waited. "That's a lot better, don't you think? This chapel is now like it used to be. How you remember it. And it won't be desecrated again."

But Kendra's spirit still seemed unsettled. Unsatisfied.

"Did I miss something?" Rand asked.

Kendra turned toward the altar, and Rand followed her gaze. Nearby the heavy cross that now stood right-side up was a table, and upon it was a thick and heavy tome.

Rand hadn't noticed it before. When he approached, he saw that it was a Bible. He opened the leather-bound cover to a random page. The text within had been scrawled over with demonic symbols. Rand flipped through more pages. The entire Bible had been over-written by hand, translated into the evil language. Rand could hardly think of a more blasphemous thing to do.

How long did this take you, James? he thought.

Rand closed the Bible and pressed his cross against the front cover. He left it there for several long moments before taking it away again. When he opened the Bible and flipped through the pages, the demonic symbols were gone. The original text had been restored.

"That should do it," Rand said as he returned to Kendra once again. She didn't respond, but Rand sensed a change in her—a subtle shift in her energy that told him she was pleased. "I'm truly sorry for what happened to you." He was surprised by the tears that formed in the corners of his eyes. "I came to help your son and to end the evil that was invited here to harm your family. But first I need to find James's office. Can you tell me the way?"

Kendra's emaciated and battered face gave no indication as to what she was thinking. Rand started to wonder if she might refuse.

Maybe she thinks it's too dangerous for me to proceed, Rand thought. *Especially after what happened to her.*

A click and a creak came from behind him. Rand looked over his right shoulder to find a section of the chapel's wall had opened by itself and swung inward on hinges—a hidden door that he hadn't noticed before.

I never would've found that on my own, he thought.

He turned back to Kendra. "Thank—"

The woman's spirit started walking toward the passage, then passed through it.

"So you'll *show* me the way," he whispered.

With that, Rand followed the ghost into another dark and narrow corridor.

34

—————

The motel room was uncomfortably stuffy inside, a sharp contrast to the chilly night. The heat rose from the rattling window unit near the door.

On the far side of the room was a young girl with long blonde hair. She sat at the motel room's only table, purple crayon moving fast over her coloring book. She looked up and studied Libby when she came in.

"Does your dad let you drink, Libby?" Miranda asked.

A miniature cooler rested on the table between the two twin beds. A bottle of white wine stood out from the ice. Without waiting for an answer, Miranda poured some into two plastic motel cups and handed one to Libby.

"I sometimes steal beer out of his fridge," Libby said as she accepted the cup. "I'm sure he notices the empty bottles in the recycling bin, but I don't think he cares."

"Well, either way, I think we've both earned the right to some wine tonight. Cheers."

Libby tapped her plastic cup against Miranda's. She

had a feeling this woman didn't need extenuating circumstances like a haunting to help herself to a glass of wine.

"Have a seat," Miranda said, gesturing toward the empty chair across from where her daughter colored. It was the only other chair in the cramped room.

Libby sat, and Miranda settled onto the edge of the bed.

"My name's Carmen," the girl said, looking up from her coloring book again.

Libby smiled. "I'm Libby."

"Are you friends with my mom?"

"I am now. And my dad and your dad are working together."

"Do you want to color too?"

"Sure," Libby said, setting her plastic cup on the table. Carmen pushed her box of crayons and a second coloring book that she wasn't using toward Libby. "Thank you."

Libby cast a glance over her shoulder at Miranda just in time to catch the woman toss a pill to the back of her throat. She took a sip of wine, then tilted her head back to swallow it.

Libby frowned. She understood the stressful nature of nights like the one they were all currently enduring. Still, it wasn't the best idea to numb yourself.

I'll have to get the location of her father-in-law's house out of her before she's too far gone, Libby thought.

However, while Libby hadn't been thrilled to spend time with Miranda Herron, she had softened to the idea of being at the motel now that she'd met Carmen. The young girl was likely distressed over the supernatural situation afflicting her family. Libby couldn't help but wonder what terrible things the girl had witnessed before her parents had reached out for help.

Libby opened the coloring book and found a blank page filled with cartoon animals having a birthday party. She picked up a red crayon and started shading in the picture. As she did, she glanced across the table. Carmen was putting the finishing touches on a picture of a family of ducks by the lake.

"You're a very good artist," Libby said, and she meant it. All the colors matched and the girl had meticulously stayed within the lines.

"Thank you," Carmen said, smiling.

A few minutes passed. Libby had given the cartoon bear on her page a red birthday hat with yellow polka dots.

"I'm going to step out for a minute," Libby heard from across the room.

She looked over her shoulder. Miranda stood at the motel door, fresh cigarette dangling from her lips. She held her wine in one hand and a lighter in the other.

"Okay," Libby said.

Miranda went outside, leaving the door ajar.

Libby turned back to her picture. She had a feeling that Miranda was thinking she'd scored a free babysitter. Libby figured she'd have to get out of there sooner rather than later so she didn't risk getting stuck.

"How are you doing?" Libby asked Carmen as she picked up a green crayon and resumed coloring.

"I'm good," Carmen replied, and she sounded... cheerful. Libby had hoped to find out how the young girl was dealing with the haunting, but it seemed she'd have to be a bit more clear. But Carmen asked Libby a question first.

"Does your dad work for my dad? Because my dad's the boss of a lot of people."

"No, he doesn't," Libby said. "He's only helping your dad with something for a little while."

"Oh. What does your dad do? Mine owns a business."

"My dad…" Libby paused her coloring as she thought. "He helps make things go back to normal."

Carmen's brow furrowed. It seemed to Libby she didn't understand.

"Have you been scared?" Libby asked, redirecting the conversation.

Carmen looked up from her picture. "Scared of what?"

"Scared of the strange things that are happening in your grandpa's house." Libby had to assume that was where the haunting was. Miranda had mentioned Rand was at her father-in-law's house.

Carmen looked confused. "Sometimes I'm afraid of the closet in my room at Grandpa's house. But if I sleep with the light on in there, then I can see that nothing's inside. Grandpa told me to do that whenever I sleep over." She returned her attention to her coloring.

That *definitely* wasn't the response Libby had expected. From everything her dad had taught her, if there was a demonic entity in the home, it very likely would've revealed itself to Carmen first.

Maybe she doesn't spend a lot of time there, Libby thought. Although the girl had just said she spent the night over there, and even had her own bedroom at her grandfather's house. That would've been a prime opportunity for the demon to come after Carmen. When demons became attached to houses and began making their presence known, they often targeted the young children that lived in the home first. Children were easy targets, because they hadn't yet developed a full understanding about what should be real and possible in the world.

Libby remembered that many of her dad's clients said their supernatural trouble had begun soon after his or her youngest child claimed to have a new imaginary friend.

"So you haven't seen or heard anything strange lately?" Libby asked.

Carmen thought about it for a second, then shrugged. "Nope."

It made very little sense to Libby that Miranda Herron and her husband had experienced the demon before Carmen. She couldn't ever remember her dad having a case like that before.

Or maybe she's talking about her other grandfather, Libby realized.

The motel door opened again and Miranda returned. She brought with her the thick stench of cigarette smoke.

"I need to… run a quick errand," Miranda announced, glancing worriedly at her watch, as if she were late for something.

"Oh." Libby was taken aback.

It's very late, she thought. *Where could she possibly have to go?*

"Can you please keep an eye on Carmen for me? I'll be right back."

"Well—"

Miranda went to her daughter and kissed her head. "You'll be good for Miss Libby, won't you?"

"Yeah," Carmen said.

Libby realized Miranda wasn't giving her an opportunity to say no. She twisted in her chair as Miranda walked toward the door. "But I need—"

"I won't be long."

Without waiting for a response, Miranda left the motel room and closed the door behind her.

Libby got up from the table and went to the window. She pulled the curtain aside to see Miranda climb into the only other car in the parking lot. She started the engine and drove away. Libby wondered how much wine she'd already drunk, and also what kind of pill she'd taken.

Libby sighed. There was no way she'd be able to leave Carmen all alone in that sketchy place. She was stuck until Miranda returned.

I just hope she was actually telling the truth about coming back soon.

35

R and followed the ghost of Kendra Herron through a series of corridors that had been painted completely black. He kept his light on the walls as he strode past numerous demonic symbols carved into the plaster. There were also jagged lines that looked as if they'd been made by fingernails, all in sets of three.

Kendra proceeded through the black hallways, apparently unperturbed by the markings on the walls.

These corridors were not straightforward. From what Rand could tell, they zigzagged, abruptly changed direction at a sharp angle, and seemed to lead them in a direction they'd already come. Other corridors intersected, creating options for which way to go. Had Rand been alone, he'd have agonized over each decision, but Kendra proceeded forth without hesitation.

Rand flipped through the sketchbook, trying to get a reference for where he was. His surroundings didn't match any of the blueprints. *I'd never find my way through here if I was by myself,* he thought.

Rand could've sworn they'd passed the same symbols scratched into the wall more than once. It gave him the impression that they were going around in circles. Regardless, he chose to have faith that Kendra Herron was leading him where he'd asked her to take him.

The black hallway eventually opened into a wide, circular room where the roof slanted in to form a cone. Across the room was a set of double doors, the only way left to go.

Something was written on the door. At first Rand thought it was more demonic symbols, but then realized they were English letters turned upside down. The writing was large, and the phrase extended beyond the doors and onto the walls on either side. Rand had to step back to see it fully. He tilted his head to put the upside-down words into perspective.

As for me and my house, we will serve the Lord.

Rand had encountered that Bible verse earlier in the night. He flipped the sketchbook over to the blueprint of the office drawing that had spurred his decision to venture deeper into the Herron House. The same verse had been scrawled in a messy hand along the line that denoted the office's front wall.

"We're here," Rand said as he approached the double doors ahead. Once he neared, however, he paused and looked over his shoulder. Kendra had not followed.

She fears it, Rand realized. *Just like Jackson.*

Rand went to stand next to her. "You've helped me a lot tonight. Thank you."

Kendra did not respond or react. In a way, Rand got

the impression she was imploring him to reconsider entering her husband's office.

"You've been trapped here for a very long time," Rand said. "Would you like to go home?"

Over the years, Rand had encountered plenty of spirits who'd been trapped in the world of the living, bound there by tragedy or some unfinished business. In Kendra Herron's case, perhaps it was both. Regardless, there was no need for her linger there any longer. All she needed now was to be shown the way.

Rand took the cross from his belt and held it up in the space between him and Kendra. Kendra's eyes fixated on it like a pair of magnets.

"There is a bright light above you," Rand said. "Look for it."

Kendra craned her head upward and seemed to catch sight of something over her head—something Rand could not see, but knew was there.

"This is the way home. This is where you belong now. This is where you can finally find peace. I want you to go toward that light now, Kendra."

Kendra tore her eyes away from the ceiling and fixed them upon Rand again. They were wide and unsure.

"You don't need to worry about me, I'll be fine. You've done enough. You've endured more than you should have. And now it's time for you to rest."

Kendra softened, then returned her attention up above. A moment later her body floated up toward the ceiling. Then it faded from view and was gone.

Rand couldn't help but smile. It was always a pleasure guiding lost souls to the afterlife.

The poignant moment was over too quickly. Rand had

to return his attention back to the matter at hand. He faced the double doors once again. He'd come this far, and now he needed to learn if there really was a hidden passage inside James Herron's office that would lead him out of the mansion.

36

Miller stared out the window near the front
door and into the pitch-black night.

For what felt like the hundredth time in
the last hour, he brought the radio to his mouth and
pressed the button. "Rando. Can you hear me?"

No response came.

Miller sighed. No matter how much he didn't want to
admit the truth, he knew it was pointless to continue like
that. Something had happened either to Rand or the
radio. Maybe even both. Communication was cut off and
it wasn't coming back. He needed a new plan.

"What's wrong?"

Miller's entire body jolted, startled by the sudden
voice behind him.

"Whoa, easy," Jackson said, though Miller's heart was
racing.

Miller took a breath to steady his spiked nerves. "I
can't get in touch with Rando over the radio anymore."

"Oh." Jackson seemed more confused than concerned.

"We need to do something. And soon."

Jackson looked away as he considered Miller's words. "Like what?"

"Call the police." Miller knew it was a risky decision, but he needed to err on the side of caution.

Jackson studied Miller as he considered the suggestion. "I thought he told us to wait."

"We were, but that was when the radio still worked. Now we can't be sure about what's happening in the mansion."

"Right…"

Miller got the impression Jackson didn't want to call the police. In fact, Miller was starting to feel like Jackson was merely letting him say his piece without seriously considering what was *actually* being said.

Jackson pivoted on his heel and started to leave the room.

Miller surprised himself with the sudden flare of anger that rose up in him. "Where are you going?" he demanded. Jackson paused and faced Miller again. "I don't think you fully understand what's going on here. The man you hired is in *danger*."

"Why are you speaking to me like that?" Jackson did not seem pleased.

He's probably not used to hearing people talk to him like that, Miller thought. "Because you've been acting weird ever since we came back to the caretaker's house."

Jackson's eyes narrowed. "What are you trying to say?"

"You know what I'm saying. What the hell have you been doing upstairs all this time?" Miller demanded. His anger had burst, and now it was flowing free. "You said you were looking for someone to help Rand get out of the mansion, but you've come up with *nothing,* and to be honest, you don't even seem to be trying."

Jackson darkened. "You want to call the police? Fine. Go ahead." He then brushed past Miller and opened the front door.

"Where are you going?"

Jackson didn't answer as he walked out onto the porch.

Miller followed. "You can't leave."

Jackson paused halfway to his car. "Are you going to stop me?"

Miller said nothing. He only glared at Jackson.

"That's what I thought."

With that, Jackson Herron climbed into his car, started the engine, and drove away.

MILLER WAS STUNNED. *Jackson just abandoned us here.*

He understood that supernatural situations were a lot to handle, especially for someone who had never experienced them before, but the last thing Miller had thought Jackson would do was run away.

Miller felt completely overwhelmed. The entire situation seemed to be unraveling around him. It had been too long since he'd heard from Rand. Jackson had fled. Libby was also poking around when she'd never meant to be there.

Libby, Miller remembered. It had been some time since he'd spoken to her as well.

He took out his phone and called her. She answered on the first ring. "Hey."

"Are you okay?"

"Yeah. What about you? You sound... scared."

Miller took a slow breath. "I'm fine. Are you still at the motel?"

"Yeah. I met Miranda Herron."

Miller blinked a few times. "Jackson's wife?"

"I guess so? She never mentioned her husband's name." Libby paused. "You didn't know Miranda and her daughter were here?"

"No. They're at the same motel?"

"Yeah. I'm in their room right now."

Miller guessed that perhaps Jackson had been on the phone with his wife this whole time. But why? She couldn't possibly be that much help in getting Rand out of the mansion. "Has she been on the phone?"

"She actually left."

"What do you mean?"

"She said she needed to step out, and she asked me to keep an eye on her daughter until she came back."

Maybe Jackson left to check on his family? Miller thought. *Why didn't he just say so?*

Still, Miller sensed something was off. "I'll tell you again—you should go home."

"I'm stuck now," Libby said. "I can't just leave this little girl by herself."

Miller lowered his phone so Libby wouldn't hear his deep sigh of frustration. *Enough is enough,* he thought. "Let me call you back." He hung up without waiting for a Libby to reply.

Then he immediately called the police.

"Nine-one-one, what's your emergency?"

Miller opened his mouth to speak, but realized all of a

sudden he had *no* idea how to articulate his emergency. At least, not in a way that would make sense to the operator.

"Hello?"

"I need help," was all he could think to say.

"What's your location?"

"Beau Ridge," Miller said. "At the Herron House."

The operator didn't respond. Miller started to think they'd been disconnected.

"One moment, sir," she finally said. The line went blank as it clicked over, sounding like he was being transferred.

What's this all about?

The call reconnected. This time it was a man who spoke. "It's under control, Mr. Herron."

Miller was taken aback. *We were right about Jackson and the local police.*

Miller wondered if Jackson had already called about their situation. If it were "under control," then why hadn't anyone shown up? Why hadn't Jackson told Miller he'd called?

"Sir?"

Something about this isn't right, Miller thought.

The man on the line whispered to someone else beside him, but Miller couldn't make out what he said. "This *is* Mr. Herron, right?" he asked into the phone. His voice had taken on a darker tone.

Miller hung up.

37

The office's double doors were on a track that allowed them to slide open. Rand tried to separate them, but they only moved an inch.

Not locked, just stuck, he thought.

Rand set the flashlight and sketchbook down, then dug his fingers into the small space he'd created where the two doors met. Once he got enough of a grip, he tried to pull them apart, but the doors resisted. The track they were connected to was either broken or rigid with age and disuse.

Something in the mechanics of the door's track cracked and clunked, as if he'd pushed something too hard and it had snapped—the doors gave way and separated a few inches. It was enough.

Rand dusted off his hands before picking up the flashlight and sketchbook from where he'd set them near his feet. He turned his body sideways so he'd fit and slid through the space he'd created between the sliding doors.

He entered into yet another pitch-dark room. Rand

didn't need light in order to *feel* the heaviness that permeated within.

There's some bad *energy in here,* he thought.

That kind of energy could come from numerous things. Perhaps evil things had been done inside that room. Maybe evil thoughts and plans were devised. Dark rituals and magic being performed were also a possibility. From what Rand had learned of James Herron, any and all of those things were likely. Jackson had said his father had sequestered himself in his office most often. With so much time inside this one room over the years, James Herron could've gotten up to any number of things.

Rand used his light to scan the room he'd just entered. Like the mansion's entrance hall, the floor was black-and-white checkered tile. A wide and grand mahogany desk was in the middle of the room, a chair tucked underneath. Bookshelves lined both sides of the room, reaching to a high ceiling. The room itself was two stories tall—a balcony supported by two pillars overlooked the main part of the office. Rand did not see any stairs that would allow him to access that upper level.

To Rand's left was a smaller table with a chess board. A single leather chair was nearby, covered in dust. Rand went closer and studied the board, which looked like it had been abandoned mid-game. Most of the pieces stood to the side of the board, captured and out of play. Strings of spider webs wrapped around the pieces and connected them like rope bridges.

Fan of chess, James? Rand thought. He imagined the man sitting alone for hours, playing for both sides.

Upon further investigation, Rand realized the game *hadn't* been abandoned—it was finished. The white king was in checkmate. The piece stood alone and vulnerable, unable to move into a square that wasn't in the path of a black rook, queen, or bishop.

Rand pivoted his flashlight toward the right side of the office.

The floor-to-ceiling bookshelves were just as James's blueprints indicated. Books of all shapes and sizes filled the shelves—there was no wasted space.

Bingo, Rand thought. His gut had a nervous twist as he realized this was the moment of truth: when he discovered whether he'd come all this way through the mansion only to encounter a dead end. There was a chance that what he'd interpreted as a secret passage wasn't that at all.

Rand crossed the room and laid the book of blueprints on the corner of James's desk. He once again studied the drawing of the office to verify the location of the suspiciously shaded section of wall he'd found earlier.

Rand positioned his flashlight on the edge of the desk to light up the bookshelves, then went to the spot that he guessed corresponded with the drawing. He gripped the dusty spines of a few books and pulled them from the shelves, letting them fall to the floor. The shelves had a full wooden back, preventing him from seeing what was behind. They weren't a single unit, but rather smaller ones lined up flush against each other.

Good, that should make this easier, Rand thought. *Sorry, James, but I'm about to make a mess...*

Rand found the center of the shelf he thought was likely blocking the passage and tossed more books from it to give himself room to grip. He clamped both hands on the shelf and pulled. It budged. Rand gave it some more muscle, clenching his core and leaning back. He'd done plenty of barbell rows in the gym over the years, and it seemed this was when he would learn if he'd pushed himself hard enough in those workouts.

The shelf rocked. Books from higher up fell, dropping to the floor on either side of Rand. The rough spine of a heavy volume clipped his right shoulder.

Rand rocked the shelf farther. Finally, he felt it tip toward him. He sidestepped from beneath it as the shelf toppled forward, slamming into the floor with a *thud* that echoed off the high walls.

Rand retrieved his flashlight from the desk. He waved his free hand through the air, doing his best to clear away the thick cloud of dust and dirt that had shot up from the toppling shelf.

He aimed the light toward the wall he'd uncovered. Now that the shelf was gone, he'd revealed an arched passageway in the wall that led to a narrow tunnel.

38

"**F**uck yes!" Rand pumped his fist in victory. He wished his radio hadn't been broken, so he could tell Miller the good news.

The passage dipped in only a few feet before making a sharp turn to the right and continuing onward.

There was now a pile of books scattered around Rand's feet. Some had landed face up and open.

Long ago, a girlfriend had once told Rand that you could learn a lot about a person based on their bookshelves. Rand realized this was likely his best chance to learn the truth of what had led James Herron to become demonically oppressed all those years ago. Perhaps he'd also find the reason why Akhubel had gained such a powerful hold over the Herron House.

Rand retrieved the flashlight from his desk and knelt among the books on the floor. He picked them up one at a time and at random, holding them underneath the beam of light.

The State of Louisiana: A History

The Rise of Fossil Fuels

The books were dusty and aged. Some had broken bindings, with pages sliding out from between their covers. Rand felt like he was knee deep in a bargain book bin, rifling through tomes that had been out of print for a long time.

Pisces to Aquarius: The Transition of the Age

Rand paused. Jackson had told him that his father had become interested in astrology in his later years. That now seemed like an understatement—the man had dedicated the central room of his mansion to the zodiacal wheel.

But why? Rand thought. *What does the demonic have to do with astrology?*

He opened the book and flipped through the pages, which were densely packed with text. Many passages had been underlined with black ink. Notes scrawled in James Herron's handwriting were in the margins of nearly every page.

You read this cover to cover, Rand thought.

The text was occasionally broken up by diagrams, including star charts that resembled the one Tessa had given him. Next to some of the diagrams, James had drawn additional charts of his own.

This book was completely different from Tessa's astrology materials, which Rand had only briefly perused. Tessa's books had bright colors and pictures of people meditating and lotus flowers. It was definitely a vibe that Rand considered "out there," yet that resonated perfectly with what Tessa was hoping to get out of it.

This book of James's, though, was presented as a serious work, perhaps even scientific. Rand flipped to the copyright page in the front. It had been published in 1935.

The two-page spread just beyond the copyright page displayed a diagram of the entire zodiacal wheel, including the symbols for each of the twelve constellations. Rand could see how this drawing could've served as the inspiration for the central room in the Herron House. But as Rand studied it, he sensed something was off.

It was reversed, he thought. In the room James had dedicated to the zodiacal wheel, he'd swapped the order of the constellations. *But why would Akhubel make you invert the zodiac?*

There was a considerable amount of handwriting on the back of the page with the complete zodiacal wheel. Rand flipped it to find it almost completely filled with demonic symbols drawn in James's scrawled handwriting.

Rand remembered the Bible from the desecrated chapel. He closed the book, then took the cross from where it hung in his belt loop and pressed it against the cover. After letting it rest there for a few moments, Rand turned to the page again. As with the Bible, the demonic language had been translated.

A Prayer to the Stars

The constant watchers over all the ages of Mankind.

From the moment, to the hour, the day, the week, the month, the year.

The decade.

The century.

The millennia.

The age.

The Great Year, when the wheel has turned again.

Stars above, ever present through the ages of Man.

Aries. Taurus. Gemini. Cancer. Leo. Virgo. Libra. Scorpio. Sagittarius. Capricorn. Aquarius. Pisces.

Only your timeless light can protect us from a timeless evil.

"Little bit of an amateur poet, weren't you, James?" Rand muttered. He wasn't quite sure what James had been trying to communicate here, but it had clearly been important to the man. So important that the demon had made him write these words in a demonic language so they'd never be read by another human.

Rand tore the pages from the book, folded them up, then took his Bible from his jacket pocket. He tucked the torn pages into the back cover of the Bible before returning it to his pocket.

I'll look at this more closely later, he thought.

Rand set the astrology book aside. He wished he could take the whole thing with him to review more closely later, but between the flashlight and sketchbook, his hands were full.

He looked at few more books.

Chess Masters of the 19th Century

Investment Strategies of the Wealthy

The Silk Road: A Retrospective

Cymatics: The Study of Frequency and Vibration

Rand paused. It was another book that didn't quite fit with the rest of James's interests. That, and Rand had never heard the word "Cymatics" before.

He opened the book to the table of contents. This volume was also filled with small-print text with the occasional diagram of sound waves. Rand flipped through some pages, focusing on the underlined passages that had most interested James Herron.

It is strongly suspected that knowledge of sound and

frequency was understood by our distant ancestors. Structures and monuments of the ancient world have demonstrated cymatic properties that have healing effects on humans. One such example is the Great Pyramid of Giza. More modern instances include the cathedrals of Europe, whose structures were perfectly designed for visitors to fully experience the Gregorian chants within.

Perhaps the greatest cymatic achievement of the ancient world is the Hypogeum in Malta, an underground temple made entirely of rock. Its precise construction allows sounds to vibrate at 111 hertz, considered by many to be a holy frequency.

"If this is what you were going for, James, then you definitely fucked it up," Rand whispered. He shivered as he thought about the cave-like room and what the acoustics within had done to him. There was nothing holy about the sounds that had left Rand completely incapacitated.

It then occurred to him that if there were healing frequencies of sound, then there must also be destructive ones.

That room was built that way intentionally, Rand thought. It seemed James was interested in healing frequencies, but Akhubel had driven him to invert all that he'd learned.

Another book in the pile caught Rand's eye. When it had fallen from the shelf, it had landed face up and open. The page was completely filled with James's handwriting —by that point, Rand could recognize it anywhere. He picked it up and took a closer look. The book was actually a journal, and the pages were as densely filled as the other books in James's eclectic collection.

I bet there's some good information in here, Rand realized. He flipped the book over and checked the spine. It was labeled June 1989. *I wonder if he has any that are more recent.*

Rand stepped over the mess he'd made and approached the next bookshelf over that still stood. He used his light to check the labels on the spines.

Sagittarius 2013. Capricorn 2013.

He followed the book spines along the shelves. All of them were journals with similar labels on their spines. The most recent was marked Pisces 2016.

Rand didn't know where in the year Pisces fell, but he remembered Jackson had told him they'd eventually had James removed from the mansion and placed in a nursing home after his supposed dementia had gotten too debilitating.

The empty space between the journal labeled Pisces 2016 and the bookend on the shelf left just enough room for one more journal.

He wouldn't shelve his most recent one if he wasn't finished writing in it, Rand thought. He pivoted and shone the light toward the desk again. *It would probably be there.*

Rand walked over and pulled out the high-backed leather chair. It was covered in a thick layer of dust. He wiped the seat with his palm, then brushed that dust off onto his jeans before lowering himself into the chair, which was still surprisingly comfortable.

Rand started with the bottom-right drawer, which glided open smoothly on its hinges. It was empty. He closed it and opened the next drawer above. The only thing inside was an orange, wrinkled envelope. When Rand picked it up, he felt something inside. Several things, actually—small and lightweight.

Rand flipped the envelope over. The front contained

writing, though the messy scrawl wasn't English. It was demonic symbols.

Rand hesitated at first, but then opened the envelope's flap and dumped the contents onto the desk. Polaroid photographs fell out. He grabbed one and shone his light on it.

It was a wedding photo. Although they were many years younger, Rand recognized Jackson and Miranda.

He wasn't sure what he expected to find inside the envelope, but it *definitely* wasn't this. Rand grabbed the next picture, then the next, then a fourth. All were wedding pictures. In one, Miranda was sitting in a chair while Jackson stood behind her awkwardly, hand on her shoulder. In another, they were embracing each other.

There was only one picture of Miranda with someone other than her new husband. She stood beside a man whose firm and powerful eyes seemed to gaze directly at Rand. While Miranda smiled, this man smirked—the two of them had an almost identical shape to their mouths.

This is her dad, Rand thought. He wanted to set the photo down, but found he couldn't. Rand's eyes were transfixed on the man, as if he was being drawn into the glossy gaze against his will. *Hell of a father-in-law, Jackson.*

As Rand stared at the rigid man, a sense of familiarity rose. He wracked his brain, trying to think of where he might have seen him before, but came up empty.

Rand made himself put the picture down—despite the bizarre feeling that the man wasn't finished connecting with him yet.

In another picture, Jackson stood with another man in a suit. The pair had the same facial structure and similar eyes.

James.

Neither Jackson nor his father smiled. The picture looked as if it had been forced.

None of the pictures featured anyone else. No guests. No other family members. There weren't even any pictures of the venue.

Small ceremony, Rand thought. *Why? Don't wealthy people drop big bucks for their weddings?*

Rand shone the light on the envelope again. The hellish scrawl made him shiver. *Why write this over pictures of your own son's wedding?* Rand wondered. *Is it supposed to be some kind of curse?*

Invoking demons to curse people was definitely possible, but Rand knew it was a far-more-intricate process than simply drawing symbols on an envelope and shoving pictures inside. Besides, James had included a picture of himself. Why would he want to curse himself?

Rand returned the pictures to the envelope and put it back into the drawer.

"What else do you have in here, James?" he whispered as he continued searching through the desk.

He opened the top middle drawer. Inside he found yet another journal with a black leather cover. Beside it was an uncapped fountain pen, the ink having run dry long ago. Thick papers, folded into squares, were tucked behind the back cover. The spine was labeled Taurus 2016.

Now this *must be his most recent one.*

The spine gave a light pop and crack as Rand opened the journal. He turned to the first page, and it took Rand a few seconds to realize what he was looking at—James Herron had attempted to draw a self-portrait. It wasn't half bad, either. The drawing greatly resembled the man Rand had seen in the wedding pictures. He was framed within what Rand assumed was a large mirror.

Rand turned the page to find almost the exact same drawing. Another self-portrait was on the page after that.

Rand flipped through the journal faster. The quality of the drawings improved as he progressed. Eventually, James had grown beyond needing to look in the mirror and had begun skillfully drawing pictures of himself from the perspective of an onlooker. In these drawings, he always wore the same suit. His facial expression was unchanged—somber and pained.

After at least a hundred pages, the series of matching self portraits ended halfway through the journal. Rand arrived at a final chilling picture that was very different from the rest—James had drawn himself laying in an open casket.

The drawing had the viewer standing at James's feet, looking down at him from above. His arms were crossed over his chest and his eyes were closed. Although dead, his face still held the same darkened expression as the drawings of when he was alive.

Bit grim, don't you think, James? Rand thought as he flipped the page, eager to tear his eyes away from the image.

The next page was also a drawing, but not a self portrait. It spanned the entire spread within the note-book. Three silhouettes stood around a fourth, smaller one in the center of the scene, drawn near where the pages attached to the journal's spine. Rand wasn't sure if it was meant to be a child or someone in the background of the scene, appearing farther away. Several spiraling patterns emanated from the smaller figure.

Although the details were sparse, the scene seemed to be ritualistic. Rand wondered if James himself had participated in such things or if this image was merely from his imagination. He hoped the latter, but by then, very little would've surprised him.

Rand turned the page to find another drawing. Though he initially thought it was another self-portrait of James Herron, Rand slowly realized it wasn't. He brought his flashlight closer to the page... and drew in a sharp intake of breath.

The black hair. The stubbled cheeks. The angle of the jaw was spot on.

It was him. James Herron had drawn *him*.

"Impossible," Rand whispered.

The expression in the eyes matched the previous self portraits of James Herron. Rand appeared despondent and distant. He even wore a jacket, a black V-neck, and jeans. It was the same outfit he had on at *that* moment.

He knew about me, Rand thought. *He knew I'd be here.* His pulse pumped in his ears. *No. Akhubel* told *him I'd be here.*

More pages remained in the journal and he was afraid to turn them. But he knew he had to.

When he did, he found another drawing of himself that was nearly identical the first one on the page before. The only difference was that his name had been written below in James's unmistakable scrawl.

Randolph Casey.

Rand flipped the pages faster and faster. The entire

back half of the journal had been dedicated to James Herron drawing Rand over and over again.

Rand turned the final page and found a different sketch of himself. He laid supine in a casket, hands crossed over his chest. A different caption was written below.

Randolph Casey must die and this house is his tomb.

39

R and used his feet to shove the chair away from the desk and the journal. He stood as bile rose in his throat. He had to take some steadying breaths to keep from being sick.

"What the hell..."

His mind raced as he tried to put it all together. James obviously had foreknowledge of him being inside the mansion. The only place he could've learned that was from Akhubel—which meant Akhubel had planned this night for *years*.

"You must journey through the darkness," the demon had told him earlier.

The only thing left from the desk that Rand hadn't yet investigated were the folded papers that had been tucked inside the back cover of the journal. His hand reached for them, as if involuntarily. Half of his mind told him to leave it be, while the other half considered that maybe the folded papers held the final piece that drew everything together.

When Rand touched them, he noticed they had the same thick, high-quality texture as the paper in the sketchbook he'd carried with him all night. He unfolded the first one.

It was another blueprint drawing labeled "OFFICE FLOOR 2." The top of the page was frilled from having been ripped from a spiral binding.

Rand looked up and over his shoulder. The landing for the office's second story was overhead, held up by two thick pillars.

He turned his attention back to the drawing. As with the office's first floor, more bookshelves lined the walls of the second. Another space behind a portion of the shelves had been shaded darker than the rest. Beside it, James had written "TR."

Another passage, Rand thought. *Except this one is up there.*

He unfolded the second paper to find another floor plan.

Rand's breath caught. This new drawing made it clear what "TR" stood for. The top of this drawing was labeled "Throne Room."

"Well shit," Rand muttered as he scooped up his flashlight and brought it closer.

James had included far more details on this particular blueprint than any other Rand had seen that night. Designs for a magic circle had been drawn to take up most of the space on the room's floor. Within it were concentric circles and two straight lines that intersected in the middle. James had noted the circumference of each circle to the sixth decimal place. He'd also noted the exact locations of where candles should be placed with precise measurements of mere inches between them. It resembled the magic circle that had been in the mansion's tower. The two might even have been identical.

On the side of the chamber, opposite the entrance, James had sketched what appeared to be a throne situated across from the north-facing part of the magic circle. Within the throne was a familiar symbol: the sideways and circled letter A—the same one that had appeared within the magic circle in the tower and on the back of Jackson's business card.

A small square, barely visible, was drawn between the magic circle and the throne, but James hadn't denoted what it was.

Rand leaned back in the chair and considered what he'd just seen. *This throne room was meant to be used to worship Akhubel,* he thought.

Rand stood from the chair and aimed his light at the landing above. He then scanned the rest of the office, searching more closely for the stairs that would lead him up. He hadn't seen any when he'd first entered the office, and he still couldn't find any even after checking more carefully.

It must only be accessible from another part of the mansion, Rand thought. That seemed to be a curious and inconvenient design, but far from unusual given everything else he'd come across that night.

Rand's beam of light landed on a wooden ladder that leaned against the tallest bookshelf in the office. It would've been the only way to reach the highest books.

He set the flashlight on the desk and lifted the ladder, which was heavier than it looked. Rand squeezed his core to stabilize himself as he carried the ladder to the space behind the desk. He leaned the top of the ladder against the edge of the balcony above, and at a spot halfway between the two pillars that supported it.

"Problem solved," he said as he picked up his flashlight again.

He climbed. The ladder wobbled with every step. On a rung halfway up, Rand felt the wood bend beneath his shoe, threatening to give way. That startled him and threw him off balance. The ladder shook. He gripped the sides of it with both hands and paused, waiting for it to settle again. From that height, to fall back onto the checkerboard floor below would've been disastrous.

Rand hoisted himself over the banister and onto the office's second floor, then leveled his flashlight. The wood floor was overlaid with a thick, red carpet. A stone hearth had been built into the far wall. Sofas and armchairs were arranged nearby with a circular table in the middle. To the right was an arched doorway that led into a dark corridor beyond.

That must be the intended way to get here, Rand thought. He put his light onto the left wall. It was lined with more bookshelves, just as the drawings he'd found in the back of the journal had indicated.

Rand went to the shelf, assuming he'd have to topple it just like the other one. *Good thing it's smaller,* he thought as he pulled some books off to make a space for him to grab. Dust and cobwebs fell with the volumes as they dropped to the floor, thudding near his feet.

After he'd cleared a space on the shelf, Rand gripped the wood and pulled backwards, hard, once again prepared to make another mess.

But this time, the shelf swung on hidden hinges, opening like a door.

A crude, wooden door was behind the shelf. Rand tried the latch and the door opened easily, as if welcoming him in. Warm, stale air wafted into his face. A pitch-black corridor lay beyond. He aimed his light inside, but the darkness seemed to swallow the beam.

Rand's skin prickled. He felt some deep instinct beckoning him to leave this room alone.

"It's never wrong to be afraid," Rand told himself. He took a steadying breath. "What matters is pushing through the fear."

"You must journey through the darkness."

Akhubel's words once again came to Rand's mind as he took his first step into the corridor.

40

The walls of the narrow corridor were built from brick and sloped into a gentle arch above. Rand had to bend his knees to avoid scraping the top of his head against the low ceiling.

The corridor continued straight ahead without any dips or turns. After what felt like many minutes of walking, the end of the corridor came into view. The room beyond was illuminated with a soft orange glow. Rand froze—light only seemed to come within the Herron House when Akhubel was present. He then remembered how the throne room's blueprint had included the candles.

Rand forced one foot in front of the other, drawing him nearer to the dimly lit chamber ahead. He clicked his flashlight off.

The chamber in which Rand emerged had a square floor and walls that inclined inward like the inside of a pyramid. The top, however, never came to a point. Instead, the walls culminated into a flattened ceiling as if the capstone of the pyramid had been severed, making the room feel jarringly incomplete. As Rand had guessed, the light came from numerous burning candles surrounding the magic circle on the floor—an exact replica of what had been represented in the blueprint. As noted in the drawing, a throne was against the far wall opposite the entrance.

Rand's skin crawled. He imagined James Herron in the center of that circle on his knees, facing the throne and worshipping the evil entity that had manipulated him into destroying himself, his family, and his home.

Something else was between the northern part of the magic circle and the throne. Although small, it looked like it had been given a prominent display. Rand remembered the tiny, unlabeled rectangle on the blueprint. Whatever this object was, it had to have been important to James, since he'd placed it between the magic circle and the throne. Perhaps it was also important to Akhubel.

Rand approached the object while making a wide berth around the circle, careful to not accidentally break the barrier with his shoe. The small, rectangular table stood at Rand's waist. A red cloth was draped over it and atop the cloth was a black cube.

Rand neared the cube slowly, curiosity piqued. A sudden tugging at his waist startled him.

The cross, still threaded through his belt loop, was *trembling.*

"What—" Rand muttered. This was the first time the cross had done that, and it had only started once he'd gotten closer to the cube. Rand took a single large, deliberate step toward the display to see what would happen.

The cross jerked away from Rand's hip, ripping his

belt loop. It zipped through the air and clattered onto the floor near the wall.

Rand stared with awe as a new fear crept in. The cross —imbued with the power of the white-eyed girl—seemed to *refuse* to be close to the simple display, as if it had a mind of its own.

Rand returned his attention to the black cube resting on the red cloth.

"What... in the fuck... are you?" he whispered.

Rand approached the display. He turned his flashlight on again and used the powerful beam to further examine the object, which was similar in size to a Rubik's cube. Although black, it was mostly transparent, resembling glass. Within the cube was another smaller cube.

'Rand.'

The girl's voice was a familiar and pleasant whisper in his mind. Although sudden, it did not startle him. He whirled around, somehow sensing that it had come from behind him.

She stood near the chamber's entrance.

41

S he looked exactly as Rand remembered—about eight years old with long and straight silver hair. She wore a plain white dress.

And her eyes were completely white.

"It's you," Rand whispered. He was so stunned by her sudden presence that he could barely get the words out.

A new sensation washed over him, one he remembered from the last time he'd seen her. He felt light. At peace. He now couldn't seem to remember where he was or why he was there. His eyes seemed incapable of seeing the room around him, intent on focusing solely on the girl. Ever since she'd first appeared at the end of his most recent case, Rand had prayed every night to meet her again.

Now that the moment had finally come, there was so much he wanted to say. So much he wanted to ask. Yet he found it difficult to speak, as if anything he said would merely be frivolous. Her very presence seemed to transcend even his deepest thoughts. Tears welled up in his eyes.

Rand didn't feel the strength leaving his legs, but apparently it did. He was suddenly on his knees. His mind raced as he was struck by the sudden fear that she might leave him. Their time together before had been so brief, and all Rand had wanted was to linger in her presence for a few minutes longer, perhaps even forever. He sensed that he needed to say something—anything—to express to her how he felt, even though he figured she already knew.

He finally found his voice again. "I'm so happy you're back." It was the only thing he could think to say. "What is your name?"

'I've been called many things over the centuries, but you can call me Tara.'

She communicated telepathically in Rand's mind. Her voice was beautiful, and it reminded him of the perfect music that had woken him in the cavern-like sound chamber earlier.

"Tara…"

In all of his cases, he'd strived so hard to learn the name of whatever demon he was facing. It was a victory when he did. All of those moments now seemed inconsequential when compared to learning the name of this angel that had been sent for him. At least… he'd always *assumed* she was an angel. Perhaps she was something else entirely, something that no mortal language had the capacity to describe.

'Your prayers have been heard. I have been with you since the night you first saw me. I have not left your side since then.'

Now the tears streamed freely down Rand's cheeks. He'd yearned to hear those simple words for so long—

especially in his darkest moments when he felt like God had abandoned him to fight the forces of hell alone.

He wondered if Tara's continuous presence had been the reason why no new cases had come to him. Or why Shindael had avoided him.

If that was true, then how had his current case found its way to him?

'You must leave this place now.'

Rand blinked away the tears that lingered in his eyes. "What?" His hopes had risen higher than they'd ever been once Tara confirmed she was his ally in the fight against demonic forces. And now she was telling him to leave.

'You cannot fight him. You will not win.'

"But… the cross you left for me. It's helped me so much." Rand then remembered how the cross had flown away from the black cube.

'My essence is in the cross. But there are forces here even greater than myself.'

"What forces?" Rand asked. As if in response, Tara's eyes began to glow a bright, pure white, and Rand knew. "Your eyes are the same as his."

'We are the same, yet not.'

The words were seemingly a contradiction, yet Rand thought he understood. If there was a hierarchy of demons, then there must be a hierarchy of angels as well.

'You are correct. As above, so below. As below, so above.'

Tara, resembling a youthful girl, was a being of light. Akhubel, with his appearance as older man, was a being of darkness. Each was an entity of opposing forces.

"If you are the same, then help me defeat him," Rand implored.

'You are not ready for this fight. Your actions have pleased

all that watch over you, but there is still much that you do not yet understand.'

Rand could scarcely believe what he was hearing. "I've never run away before."

'As always, the choice is yours. I beg you to heed my warning. The world needs you. Humanity depends on you.'

Rand did not miss the underlying suggestion of death in Tara's words. He struggled to believe he only had two options: run away or die. There was *always* a path to victory.

"Tell me what else I need to understand," Rand pleaded.

'That is not my place. It is you who must journey through the darkness.'

Rand sucked in a sharp breath at hearing Akhubel's words come from Tara. "Have I not done that already?" he asked, remembering his trek through the mansion.

Tara did not respond immediately. It seemed as if she were considering whether to answer Rand's questions.

'There is but one man who has made this journey before you.'

"Tell me who."

Tara cocked her head to the side as if she'd heard something Rand hadn't.

'He is near. I cannot linger any longer.'

"Please, no." Rand rose from his knees. "Don't go."

'Resist all temptation. Live to fight another day.'

With that, Tara vanished.

The blissful feeling brought on by the girl's presence began to abate. Rand once again became aware of the dark chamber around him, the candlelight projecting his dancing shadow onto the inclined walls. He wiped the remaining tears from his eyes.

He'd been so happy to see Tara again. But now that she'd gone, he was even more confused than he'd been before.

You cannot fight him. You will not win.

But the girl had told him that she'd been with him since the night they'd met. She'd even left behind the imbued cross that had been invaluable to him.

The events of the night came to mind. When he'd met Akhubel in the tower for the first time, the demon had only spoken to him from a distance. In the room dedicated to the zodiac, Akhubel had communicated through the radio. When he'd appeared in the chamber with the horrible, deafening music, Akhubel had once again kept his distance, relying on the overbearing sound to harm Rand.

He can't get close to me, Rand thought. *Because Tara has been with me the whole time.* It all made sense to him now.

But if that was true, then why was Tara telling him to flee? Why did she think he couldn't defeat Akhubel?

There should be no demon I can't destroy, Rand thought. He remembered how Tara, in their first encounter, had merely touched the demon and caused him to explode into black slime. Akhubel had even confirmed that entities like him could, in fact, be killed.

He glanced at the floor by the wall where the imbued cross had landed. Since discovering its power, he'd planned to use the cross against Akhubel the next time he had the opportunity. Because it was filled with Tara's essence, it was surely a valuable weapon against him, or any demon for that matter.

Maybe this is part of having faith, Rand thought. No matter how sure he was that he could defeat Akhubel, perhaps it was wiser to heed the words of his guardian angel and leave the Herron House altogether—and to do that before it was too late.

However… he once again found his gaze drawn to the black cube on its display. Due to the prominent location James had given it, Rand figured it was a key piece as to what had happened to the man all those years ago.

I'll take it with me, Rand thought. He could study it later to hopefully learn why it had been so important to James Herron. If he were to obey Tara's warning and flee, then at least he wouldn't be leaving empty handed.

Rand grabbed the black cube and lifted it from the table. It was unnaturally cold against his palm.

Dark laughter echoed off the walls of the chamber, a sound of evil glee that chilled Rand's bones.

His surroundings blurred… and then the chamber around him vanished.

42

————

When clarity returned, Rand's surroundings had changed. The dark chamber was gone. He now stood in a completely different room, one that seemed vaguely familiar.

Square. Pillars surrounding the edges of the room. A grand staircase that led to the second floor.

The Herron House entrance hall, Rand realized.

But it was... different. A chandelier hung from the ceiling, filling the room with light. A fine, hardwood floor was beneath Rand's feet instead of the black-and-white checkerboard pattern.

I'm seeing the room as it was before, he thought. *I'm seeing the past.*

Rand was very familiar with time distortion. It often happened as a side effect of being in the presence of dark energy—and that cube he'd touched was most certainly *filled* with it.

Thinking of the cube reminded Rand to look down at

his hands. He no longer held it. It had not come with him into the past.

A middle-aged man wearing a blue suit walked into the entrance hall from an arched doorway at the side of the room. Rand instantly recognized James Herron from his drawings and photographs.

Although Rand was right in front of him, James was unaware of his presence. Rand was merely a visitor in this timeline, an invisible spectator.

James wore blue slacks and a white shirt, long sleeves rolled to his elbows. His blue suit coat was draped over this shoulder. He rolled one sleeve down and quickly fastened a cuff link in place with practiced fingers. He did the same with the other sleeve before taking his coat from his shoulder, throwing it on, and buttoning it closed. He adjusted his necktie at his collar. All the while, he wore a worried expression.

A young boy sprinted down the staircase. He wore navy shorts and a grey sweater vest with a school logo monogrammed on the breast. His running slowed when he spotted James. "Are you leaving?" he asked.

"Go to the dinner table, Jackson," James said. Rand thought the man did a remarkable job of pushing away his worried expression for the sake of his son. "I'll be there in a few minutes."

The young Jackson continued through the arched doorway James had come through. He almost bumped into an approaching woman wearing a blue dress and a white apron.

Kendra, Rand realized. He was struck by her beauty—especially after having seen the decomposed apparition of her earlier.

"James?" She wiped her hands on her apron as she neared. "Is it urgent? Dinner's ready."

James plastered on a quick smile, choosing to hide his worry from Kendra as well. "I'll only be a moment."

That didn't seem to comfort Kendra. "Isn't it unusual for Bernard to visit in the evening?"

"I'm sure everything's fine," James said. Rand could hear the doubt behind James's tone. If Kendra picked up on it, she made no comment. James leaned in and kissed his wife on the cheek. "Go ahead and start dinner without me."

James left Kendra, went to the mansion's front door, and opened it. Rand found himself envious of James in that moment—he'd desperately tried to open that same door in the present, yet it had remained held closed by Akhubel's power. The windows on either side of the door had no bars. This period of the past must have been before James Herron became oppressed.

Rand followed James onto the mansion's front porch. There was a reason he was there and witnessing what had been an important moment in the life of James Herron—a memory embedded deep within the black cube Rand had touched.

It was late evening. The clouds reflected the orange light cast by the setting sun. A black car idled near the gate Rand had passed through in the present era. A man leaned against the car, smoking a cigarette and admiring the sunset. Rand assumed he was the chauffeur.

A tall, broad-shouldered man strode up the inclined path toward the mansion's front porch. He was sharply dressed in a fine black suit. Although it was after hours, Rand figured James must've felt it was important to present himself well to this visitor—probably why he'd rushed to put his suit back on before meeting the man outside.

The man smiled at James as he neared, but James did not return the pleasantry.

This man seemed familiar to Rand, and by the time he made it to the porch, it came to him. Rand had seen him in the wedding pictures in James's office. He was Miranda Herron's father.

"Evening, James," the man said, offering his hand. James shook it unenthusiastically.

"My family has a strict dinner time, Bernard," James said. "*All* of my business matters are confined to working hours. You know this."

"My apologies," Bernard said, smile unfaltering. "I never mean to intrude, but I was in the neighborhood and knew we were overdue for a chat."

"I figured I'd be hearing from you soon," James said. "Just not *this* soon."

"Good news travels fast, James," Bernard said, his smile returning. "Surely you didn't think crossing the net-worth milestone you've just achieved would go unnoticed."

"They're numbers on paper, Bernard," James said. "The true value is what I bring to my clients."

"Right, right," Bernard said, voice trailing off and smile waning. Rand could tell the man didn't quite agree with James's perspective. "I remember when I'd first accomplished what you've done now. Seems so long ago."

"It was easy for you to make the amount of money you did after you abandoned the ideals your company was built on, just to accept a few lucrative contracts from the U.S. military."

A dark expression crossed Bernard's face. He continued on regardless. "My partners and I always knew you'd reach this point. They'd like to meet with you."

"I'm not interested in meeting your friends. I'm also not interested in what you're involved in. My work, company, and family don't need help from you or your partners."

To Rand, James's words almost sounded rehearsed, as if he'd known for a while he'd be having this discussion.

Bernard took a breath and glanced to the side, as if carefully considering his next statement. "I'm aware you already know this, but when you get to a certain level— which you've recently achieved—things change."

"What you mean is that with money comes power," James cut in.

"I prefer to call it *influence*."

"Call it whatever you want," James said. "That isn't my place. My place is here, with my company, doing the work that I love to serve my clients."

"Right, right," Bernard said. "But you need to understand that you are a great man with the potential to influence the *world*. Surely there are some changes you would like to see that would make the world a better place. What if I told you that now you have the chance to not only see these changes, but to drive them forth yourself?"

"I've said before that I'm not interested in politics or running for any office."

"I'm not talking about *politics*," Bernard said. He spat the word as if it disgusted him. "Leave the politics for the politicians. I'm talking about—" his hand formed a fist in front of his chest, an unconscious outlet for the passion that had welled within him. "—when you amass a fortune like the ones we have, people notice. You and I have more money than the governments of many countries, and we'll only keep acquiring more. Those who possess this get noticed by certain people in charge..."

"People in charge," James repeated. "You mean elected officials. Governments. Why are you saying this isn't about politics?"

Bernard loosened his fist and let his arm drop to his side. He blinked rapidly as he started thinking again, likely searching for a new angle. Rand wondered why Bernard was so persistent when James Herron hadn't budged at all.

"Let me put it in terms you'll understand," Bernard continued. "I know you love chess, so imagine a chess board." Bernard gestured with his hands, demonstrating where an invisible chess board would hover between them. "You have the pieces that make up your army. Each piece has different abilities, movements, and power, depending on their rank, right? Pawns are just that—the pawns. Then there are the knights, and the bishops, and so on. Their job is to checkmate the enemy king while protecting their own. If the pieces were alive, I'd imagine the king would have a pretty big head on his shoulders, wouldn't he? Because as far as he knows, the game is all about him.

"But what can't either the white *or* the black king see? They can't see the people who are *actually* playing the game. The chess masters. The ones who aren't on the board at all." Bernard took a step closer to James, and his full foot of height on the smaller man became even more prominent. "I'm telling you that you've earned your way off the board. No more pawns. No more knights. No more kings who think they're in charge. You can be above it *all*."

"At what cost?" James challenged.

"You're worried about the price?"

"Not the price, Bernard," James said. "The cost. At what *cost* do you get to leave the chess board?"

"A simple one, actually," Bernard said.

The front door opened and Kendra emerged, holding something wrapped in a cloth towel.

"Mrs. Herron! Good evening." Bernard's false smile quickly returned.

"I… didn't mean to interrupt," Kendra said softly.

"You're not interrupting at all."

"This is for Clara. Homemade banana bread." Kendra offered the towel-wrapped dessert.

"Oh, thank you very much," Bernard said, accepting the gift. "It smells incredible. Clara and I will enjoy this later tonight."

Kendra gave a wan smile as her eyes darted between the two men. She seemed to sense the tension. "I'll just…" She walked backwards into the house and closed the door behind her.

When she was gone, Bernard turned back to James. "Such a lovely lady, your wife. Remember that your decision—or indecision—affects her as well."

"I've heard quite enough," James said, voice firm. "Bernard, I think it's time for you to go."

Bernard's face fell. For the first time, he seemed truly sad. "Please trust me, James. As your friend, I'm *imploring* you to understand that this is a ship you want to board before it sails away."

James only shrugged his shoulders and let them drop.

"I don't know what else to tell you, Bernard. 'As for me and my house, we shall serve the Lord.' "

Bernard's eyes softened as his gaze fell to the ground. Rand could see that he'd reached the end and had accepted his failure.

"I don't think it's necessary for you to return here ever again," James added. His voice was a low, and it definitely wasn't a suggestion.

"I see," Bernard said. "In that case… may I offer you a parting gift?"

"I don't need—"

Bernard dug his free hand into his suit jacket pocket and withdrew a small object wrapped in a red silk cloth. Rand's eyes fixated on it as Bernard handed it to James.

"Farewell, my friend." With that, Bernard descended the front porch steps and returned to where his chauffeur waited by the car. James watched the vehicle drive away until it was out of sight, as if ensuring the man was leaving his property for good.

Only then did James turn his attention back to the silk-wrapped object in his hand.

"Don't, James." Rand couldn't stop the words from tumbling out his mouth, even though he knew he was powerless to influence the past.

James used his other hand to peel the cloth away, revealing the black cube beneath. He looked at it curiously for a few moments, the dangling red cloth still between the cube and his palm. Then James picked it up with his other hand, touching it directly for the first time.

Rand's surroundings faded once again.

43

To Libby, it felt like Miranda Herron had been gone forever.

Carmen was asleep on top of the covers on the twin bed farthest from the door. Twenty minutes after her mother had left, the girl said she was sleepy, and Libby had encouraged her to lie down. Carmen began softly snoring a few minutes later.

With Carmen asleep, it gave Libby's mind time to run wild with possible explanations as to where Miranda had gone for so long.

For what seemed like the hundredth time, Libby went to the motel-room window and pulled the curtain aside to see if there was any sign of Miranda's car.

Libby heard her phone buzz.

Must be Miller, she thought. *He actually* did *keep his word and call me back.*

Libby walked to where she'd left her phone on the table. No one was calling, yet the faint vibrating persisted.

Libby followed the sound and found another phone

tucked halfway under the bedspread of the unoccupied twin bed.

Miranda had forgotten her phone. The caller ID simply read "BB."

Despite worrying about Miranda, Libby opted to not answer the call.

She obviously isn't with whoever's calling anyway, she thought. Libby tucked the phone back where she'd found it.

The vibrating stopped, and the call likely went to voicemail. But then BB called again a moment later.

Something's going on, Libby thought.

Again, she chose not to answer.

But what if Miranda is calling from wherever she is? Trying to get in touch with me? Libby brushed the idea away. Whoever was calling was a saved number. *Unless she met up with a friend and is using their phone?*

Or maybe it was something else that was none of her business. Libby knew well that it only meant one thing when she got hit up late at night.

BB ended the call. Then promptly called back a third time.

Libby huffed and snatched up Miranda's phone, then brought it to her ear. "Hello?"

Light static came through from the other end.

Her stomach lurched. She'd picked up those garbled phone calls before. They almost always happened when her dad was on a case. Demons often communicated through technology, often distorting the signal as they did.

"Who is this?" The voice was a man—definitely human

—which should've been a relief, but it wasn't because of the intense, accusatory tone.

"Um…"

If she answered truthfully, she'd have a lot of explaining to do about why she was there. But she couldn't pretend to be Miranda. The caller obviously knew Miranda's voice well.

"Who *is* this?" He was irritated now. Libby had a feeling that she'd made things worse by answering the phone.

A second later, the caller hung up.

Libby returned the phone to where it had been. She resolved to not answer it again no matter who called.

She gasped when the motel door opened abruptly.

Miranda rushed into the room, once again accompanied by the thick scent of cigarette smoke.

She paused when she saw Libby. "Oh. You're still here."

"You asked me to stay…"

Miranda nodded, apparently only now remembering. "Right, I did. Thank you."

Libby studied the woman. Something seemed off. Had she drank more? Taken another pill?

"I think I left my phone somewhere in here. Have you seen it?"

"I thought I heard something buzzing on the bed."

Miranda went to the side of the bed and fished her phone from the sheets. She scrolled through something, then tensed.

Libby's heart beat faster. If Miranda looked closely enough, she'd see that Libby had answered one of the calls.

Miranda tapped her screen and brought the phone to

her ear. She went back through the open motel door and lingered just outside the room. She remained outside for several moments as she spoke.

"Okay," she finally said. Libby could tell Miranda was trying to keep her voice low. "Yes, Daddy." She hung up.

Daddy? Libby thought.

Miranda's shoulders relaxed as she took a deep breath. She then returned to the room and went to Carmen's bedside and shook her daughter's shoulder.

"Carmen. Wake up," she whispered.

Carmen stirred, then sat up and rubbed at her eyes. A portion of her hair was matted from she'd slept on it.

"Come sit over here for Mama." Miranda urged Carmen out of the bed and walked her to the chair where'd sat when coloring earlier. Her half-finished pictures were still there. "Sit right here, baby."

Miranda took a silver thermos from her purse, uncapped it, and set it down on the table in front of Carmen. "And drink this for me, okay?"

"What is it?" Carmen asked sleepily. Libby was wondering the same thing.

"It's good for you. Just drink it for me, please."

"Does it taste bad?"

"No."

Carmen picked up the thermos, sniffed it, then took a single sip. She didn't seem to find it offensive.

"See? Be a big girl and finish it."

Carmen raised the thermos again and took several more swallows. Miranda stood over her and supervised, as if she were administering medication.

"What is that?" Libby asked.

"I think you should go," Miranda told Libby.

"Is everything okay?"

"Thank you for keeping an eye on Carmen while I was gone. You must be tired, so you should go get some sleep."

Carmen set the empty thermos down on the table with a clank, then wiped her mouth.

"Good girl, thank you so much," Miranda said, checking the bottom of the container to make sure Carmen had drank it all.

"Mama, what's going on?" Carmen asked.

Miranda smoothed the matted bits of her daughter's bedhead. "Nothing, baby. It's going to be okay."

"*What's* going to be okay?" Libby asked more forcefully.

Now Miranda glared at her. It seemed she'd suddenly lost all her patience at once.

"It's time," a deep, masculine voice came from the motel-room door.

Libby hadn't seen him arrive. A very tall, broad-shouldered man stood at the doorway. He appeared to be in his sixties, but Libby had a feeling he was much older than he looked. He wore a charcoal-colored suit and his short grey hair was neatly combed to the side.

The man's hard eyes fell on Libby now. She could tell he hadn't been expecting her to be there.

"Who is she?" the man asked Miranda.

Libby recognized his voice from the phone call she'd answered.

"She's Randolph Casey's daughter," Miranda said.

Libby blinked with surprise. For some reason she couldn't quite explain, it unsettled her that the man knew she was Rand Casey's daughter.

"I see." He was visibly displeased. There was also

another look in his eyes, one that Libby couldn't quite place. To her it almost seemed like... recognition. But how?

"Do you know my dad?" Libby asked.

"Word gets around."

Libby suddenly remembered Carmen. Why hadn't the young girl reacted at all when her grandfather had arrived? When Libby finally tore her gaze from the imposing man, she saw that Carmen's head hung forward. She'd fallen back asleep.

That happened fast, Libby thought. Almost *too* fast.

"I believe I asked you to leave," Miranda said.

It was a sedative, Libby realized. Apprehension crawled through Libby. *Miranda gave her daughter a sedative.*

"Miranda is right. Leave now." The man's harsh tone carried with it the hint of threat.

Libby stiffened. She'd thought she was doing a good thing by keeping a young girl company, but realized now there was a lot more going on here that she didn't understand. She was in over her head.

Maybe Dad was right, she couldn't help but think. *Maybe I shouldn't have come.*

As much as she didn't want to leave Carmen, Libby found herself walking toward the motel-room door, her insides twisting more and more with each step she took closer to the towering man.

He stood aside and allowed Libby to leave, then slammed the door behind her.

A NEW CAR was in the motel parking lot—a premium-sized black SUV. The driver, passenger, and one of the back doors were all wide open, and the yellow cabin light was on, as if prepped for a quick departure.

Libby ducked around the corner of the motel wall adjacent to Miranda's room. There was no way she was going to leave the situation alone after what she'd just witnessed.

Who the hell sedates their own daughter? she thought. Carmen was definitely in some sort of danger.

Libby's eyes went to the rear bumper of the car. There was no license plate.

Who is this guy? Libby thought. *How can he drive around in an illegal car?*

A minute later, the motel-room door opened again. Yellow light from inside streamed onto the dark parking lot.

Libby peeked around the corner from where she hid.

Miranda carried Carmen toward the car. She placed her carefully into the backseat and buckled her seatbelt. The girl's head drooped forward, still asleep.

Miranda returned to the motel room. Her father was speaking, and although he tried to be quiet, his powerful voice carried.

"You shouldn't have let her come in here."

"I'm sorry," Miranda said. She sounded on the verge of crying. "Do you want me to... bring her back?"

Bring me back? Libby thought. *For what?*

"We don't have time. Casey is the only one who matters."

"Right. Everything should be ready," Miranda said.

They're going to wherever Dad is, Libby realized.

The rectangle of light on the asphalt shrank as

someone closed the motel door. The conversation became too muffled for Libby to make out anymore.

There was some kind of plan happening, and it sounded like it involved her dad.

"Casey is the only one who matters."

Since these people had sedated their own daughter and granddaughter without blinking an eye, Libby had to assume they had foul intentions for her father. And she was the only one who knew.

Libby made her decision in the moment.

She came out from around the corner where she'd hidden. The door to the motel room was only open a crack, blocking her from view. She climbed into the back-seat of the SUV, slid beside where Carmen slept, and scrambled over the seat backs and into the trunk.

There, she flattened herself so she wouldn't be seen.

And waited.

44

The candlelit chamber materialized around Rand. A cold weight was in his hand—he once again held the black cube. Rand blinked several times as he tried to organize the thoughts that were crashing through his head.

It hadn't been James Herron's fault at all that Akhubel had entered his home. He'd been *cursed*.

Cursed by Miranda Herron's father.

All because James had refused to join him.

Bernard hadn't been clear about who or what he'd wanted James to join, but James seemed to know—or at least knew enough to be confident in refusing.

The implications of it all slowly crept into Rand's mind.

Jackson would be relieved to hear that none of this had been his father's fault—that he hadn't actually invited the demon into his home. But did Miranda Herron have any idea what her father had done?

Surely not, Rand thought, although he caught his quick reaction. He hardly knew the woman.

If Miranda didn't know what her father had done, she likely wouldn't take it well when Rand told her the truth. He assumed she'd reject the idea outright and refuse to accept it, and Rand couldn't blame her for that.

Even further, Rand wondered how Miranda had gone on to marry the son of the man her father had cursed. He recalled the wedding pictures in James's desk drawer. Bernard had been present at the ceremony, which had taken place many years after the conversation Rand witnessed. Why would Bernard allow his daughter to marry into a family that he himself had cursed?

It was all a tangled web. The more Rand thought about it, the fuzzier it all became.

Enough, he told himself. *I won't get to the truth on my own. I need more information.*

He'd confront both Jackson and Miranda and find out what they knew about Miranda's father and what the man might've been involved in. That would be both a difficult and uncomfortable conversation, but he'd worry about that when the time came. For now, he had to refocus on his primary goal—getting the hell out of the Herron House.

A heavy feeling of dread crept into Rand's bones, and he tensed. He then had the strong sensation that someone was behind him. He turned.

Akhubel sat upon the throne.

Rand felt like he was suddenly seeing the demon with new eyes. Throughout the night, he'd chosen to appear as a tall, elderly man with broad shoulders. The resemblance was now uncanny.

"Bernard," Rand said.

"No. It is very unwise to confuse me with my master."

A sickening feeling settled into the pit of Rand's stomach. *How does a mortal get a powerful demon to call him master?* Rand thought. He'd never heard of that before. He wondered if Akhubel's choice to resemble Bernard was some sort of tribute to the man.

Rand was acutely aware that he was very much alone with the demon in the darkest depths of the Herron House. There was nowhere left for him to go—the throne room was a dead end. It was very possible he'd have to fight his way out.

"You cannot fight him. You will not win." Tara's words once again sprung to mind.

"Wise words from the girl," Akhubel said. He must've read Rand's thoughts. "So go ahead and flee. It does not matter now. You won't get far."

Anger surged inside of Rand. "I don't need to run away. I've fought and defeated monsters like you before."

"Not like me," Akhubel said. He sounded gravely serious. "Listen to the girl. Feel free to take that with you. It's a gift from me to you."

Rand remembered the cube that he still held.

James Herron was cursed as soon as he touched it, Rand thought. *And now I've touched it too.*

Rand's frustration got the better of him. He reared back and threw the black cube toward Akhubel as hard as he could. The demon vanished just in time. The cube struck the back of the throne, and whatever power it contained broke the top portion of the throne, blasting pieces away from the chair's body.

The cube clattered to the floor. Although it had felt like glass, it did not break.

Akhubel rematerialized onto the throne. "I'd advise you not to be so reckless. That artifact is quite powerful."

Rand glanced to where his cross still lay on the floor. He remembered the plan he'd had for the next time he encountered Akhubel. Now would be his chance.

"You did not heed my warning earlier when I told you that your friend was in danger. Now it is too late for you to help him."

Akhubel had told Rand the same thing after their conversation in the tower. He'd rushed downstairs only to discover that Miller was fine. But it had been several hours since his radio was destroyed, so he had no way of knowing what Miller was up to now. "Leave Miller alone. This is all between you and me."

"It isn't only between you and me, Randolph. There is much that you do not yet understand."

Rand clenched his jaw. More of Tara's words had come from Akhubel's mouth. Rand was starting to understand what the girl had meant when she'd said they were somehow linked.

As above, so below.

"Your friend is not alone," Akhubel went on. "It seems now your daughter will also share his fate."

Rand felt his rage stir. That was impossible—Libby had no idea where he even was.

He opened his mouth to refute Akhubel's threat, but the demon vanished before Rand could say anything.

Rand had reached a tipping point. Now that Akhubel had mentioned Libby, he'd lost all interest in spending any more time within the Herron House, poking around

James's secret rooms and belongings while trying to learn what had happened to him all those years ago. Enough was enough. Rand knew he had to get out of there and make sure Miller and Libby were safe.

Is this why Tara told me to leave? he wondered.

Rand scooped up the cross from the floor. He glanced to where the black cube lay near the foot of the broken throne. He'd initially wanted to bring it with him, but now that he knew the cube was cursed, he'd changed his mind.

He turned his back on both the throne and the black cube and hurried out of the chamber.

45

R and did not linger when he emerged from the throne room. He rushed down the ladder to the first floor of the office, nearly toppling it over in his haste. Then he bounded into the secret passageway he'd uncovered earlier.

Rand used his flashlight to illuminate the way forward. The narrow walls were only wide enough to allow one relatively small man to pass through, and the stone that made up the floor and walls hadn't been smoothed. Portions of it protruded into Rand's path, tripping him up if they were low and banging against his arms and shoulders if they were high.

Despite the obstacles, Rand did not slow down. Libby and Miller were the only things on his mind now, driving him forward. Banging and scraping against the outcroppings in the stone didn't hurt him—at least not yet. He'd feel the pain when his adrenaline subsided, but that was a problem for later.

The passage ahead narrowed considerably, and Rand

grunted as he forced his body through the tight space. The rock felt like it was squeezing him, as if it were alive and trying to trap him. If he got stuck, he'd likely never be found. Rand had heard stories of cave explorers getting lodged between rocks in the depths of the dark chasms they'd ventured into, only to be found long after they'd perished.

The floor suddenly disappeared from beneath him—he'd inadvertently stepped out into empty air. His insides lurched the same way they did when he had dreams where he was falling. Rand lashed out with his hands, but only found empty air as tumbled over a ledge he hadn't seen.

He landed hard onto stone, kicking up a plume of dust at the same time. The flashlight sprung from his grip, and pain jolted through his wrists and knees.

Rand rolled onto his back, groaning. He reached to the side and retrieved his flashlight, then shone the light to where he'd fallen from. Sure enough, the portion of the tunnel he'd been in moments before had abruptly ended with a sharp drop-off.

The pain from his fall lingered, but he forced himself to stand. He scanned his surroundings with his light. This new section he'd tumbled into was thankfully wider.

The light revealed something unexpected on Rand's left: bars. There was a cage built into the stone wall.

Rand caught the briefest glimpse of what lay on the other side of the cage before quickly tearing the light away to remove it from view. He hesitated to shine the light in that direction again to confirm what he thought he'd seen.

He finally forced himself to point the light toward the

cage once again. There was a large prison cell built deep into the wall. The floor beyond the bars wasn't visible beneath the dozens of skeletons that covered it. Many of them still wore their hard hats and work boots.

Rand recalled hearing tales of kings and emperors who'd ordered the people who'd built their tombs killed and buried within them so that their secrets would never be revealed.

Rand tore himself away from the cell and quickened his pace through the passage. As he went, his light revealed even more cells built into the walls, all filled with human remains. Some of the skeletons reached their arms through the bars as if begging Rand to take them with him. He broke into a jog, eager to be away from the death that pervaded the tunnel.

Rand came to another drop-off, but this time he noticed it before he fell. He shone the light over the edge. It was higher than the first, but not by much. Rand jumped down and landed hard on his feet, knees bending into a deep squat.

He straightened and surveyed his new surroundings. The crude stone walls and floor had ended. He was now in a new corridor, and he recognized the cream-colored wallpaper adorned with twisting, spiraling vines.

I've been here before. That means I'm close...

The flashlight beam caught the shape of a prominent arched doorway up ahead. His heart pounded at the thought of finally emerging from the decrepit labyrinth.

But when Rand passed through the doorway, he emerged right back into the Herron House entrance hall.

"What the..." he whispered. All his hopes of escape came crashing down.

46

R and slowly traced his flashlight throughout the room, hoping and praying that the light would reveal something different, but it didn't. The checkerboard floor sprawled beneath him. The mansion's front door was on his left, the grand staircase to his right. The black bag he'd left behind still lay in the center of the room.

After all that... I ended up right back where I started...

His chest heaved as his breathing turned to desperate pants. He tried to calm himself, but he knew he was losing it.

Rand went to the front door and tried to open it, just in case something had changed. It didn't budge.

Randolph Casey must die and this house is his tomb.

The words from James's journal sprung unbidden to his mind.

I was never meant to get out of here, he thought. *Akhubel has me sealed inside.*

Rand realized just how easy it had been for Akhubel. The demon had simply slammed the door shut, sealed it, and that was that. Barely any effort needed. The handful of days it would take for him to slowly wither away would be mere entertainment for Akhubel as he gleefully watched from the shadows.

Rage borne by hopelessness bloomed inside him. Rand stormed to the center of the entrance hall. "Akhubel!" he shouted, and his voice echoed off the high walls. If this house was truly meant to be his tomb, then he refused to sit around and wait for the end to come. "*Akhubel!*"

Rand heard a latch giving way, followed by a loud creak. He remembered that sound from the very beginning of the night.

He turned to find the mansion's front door slowing swinging open.

He thought he would've felt relief, but his experience didn't allow it. Adrenaline coursed through him, putting him on guard.

Rand leveled his flashlight to see who had finally opened the door.

Jackson Herron strode into the entrance hall. He lifted his hand to block out the bright light. "Can you put that thing down?"

"Jackson," Rand said.

Jackson lowered his hand and squinted into the flashlight's white beam. "Listen. We need to talk."

"Where's Miller?" Rand hated how his voice trembled. He suddenly became aware of the flashlight's thick, sturdy design, as if the device had subtly communicated to him that it'd make a decent weapon.

Something heavy pressed onto Rand's shoulder. Gripped it. He slowly turned to find a large, grey hand with mottled flesh.

47

Numbness coursed through Rand's body. It started in his right shoulder where he was held and flowed throughout him. When it reached his hand, he lost the feeling in his fingers and the flashlight fell from his grip, clattering onto the floor.

Within seconds, he'd lost almost all sensation within him—so when Akhubel forced him to walk, Rand had no choice but to obey. He worked hard to resist, to pull away from the demon, but Rand had lost all control of his own body.

But he's not supposed to be able to touch me, Rand thought. He'd wanted to protest out loud, yet he couldn't move his mouth to speak. He remembered that he'd touched the cursed black cube. He wondered if doing that had driven away whatever protection Tara had been giving him.

Rand was led to the entrance of the tower on the second floor. He couldn't feel his legs or his feet, yet he did not stumble as Akhubel guided him up the spiraling stone steps.

He's taking me back to where it all started, Rand thought.

They came to the room where he'd first met Akhubel. The candles that surrounded the magic circle on the floor were burning once again, filling the room with dim, flickering light. Akhubel compelled Rand to lay supine on the floor, his torso in the center of the circle.

Jackson appeared in Rand's line of sight, having followed them upstairs. He went to the table against the wall and took from it several lengths of rope. He used one to tie Rand's wrist to the metal clasp embedded into the stone Rand had tripped on earlier. Jackson did the same with Rand's other wrist and both ankles, giving each rope a final tug to secure them.

After Rand was tied down, Akhubel took his hand away. With the demon's touch gone, the numbness faded and sensation returned to Rand's arms and legs. He struggled against the ropes, but he was firmly held in place.

"J-Jackson," Rand blurted once he'd regained control of his throat and mouth and could speak again.

Jackson Herron looked down at Rand with a forlorn expression behind his eyes.

He's being coerced into this, he realized.

"I can help you."

"You really can't," Jackson said. He stood to Rand's left, Akhubel to his right. Both looked down on him.

"Just stop and think about this for a minute." The words fell fast and desperate from Rand's mouth. All the while, his entire body was tense, arms and legs pulling hard at the ropes that bound him, just in case one of them gave way. Sweat broke out over his chest and forehead.

"I've had my entire life to think about this night." Jackson's response was calm, almost meditative.

"It wasn't your father's fault. He didn't do this to your family. Bernard did."

Jackson's cool demeanor cracked for a moment upon hearing the name—just enough for Rand to notice.

"I know what happened that day," Rand pressed. "Bernard wanted your father to join him in something. James refused because he was trying to *protect* you all. But Bernard cursed him by giving him a little black cube. That curse brought *him*." Rand jabbed his head toward Akhubel.

Jackson was silent for several moments, his face expressionless. "You're not telling me anything new," he finally said.

A hollowness formed in Rand's chest as the remaining shreds of hope slipped away. "So you already knew what your father-in-law was about when you married Miranda."

"Refusing Bernard Bale's generous offer was the worst thing my father ever did," Jackson said. "I refuse to end up like he did."

"Jackson, you don't want to do this. Making deals with demons is *never* what it seems. I can help you get out of this."

Rand was well aware that Akhubel could permanently shut him up whenever he wanted. Yet the demon allowed him to keep speaking and appeared unaffected—as if everything Rand said merely amused him.

"You can't," Jackson said. "And you won't."

"They *lie*, Jackson. They deceive."

"Maybe that describes the spirits you've met, Randolph," Jackson said. "But Akhubel is very different. He's been serving the Bale family for generations. Because of him, the Bales are some of the most powerful, wealthy, and influential people in the world."

Rand's eyes darted back and forth between Jackson and Akhubel as he tried to fully comprehend what he'd just heard, but he couldn't. How was what Jackson had said even possible?

"The Bales? I've never even heard—"

"No, you've never heard of the Bales, and neither has anyone else," Jackson said. "That's all by design, because real power is unseen."

A heavy dread crept into Rand's heart when he recalled what Bernard and James had spoken about. "What... what exactly are the Bales involved in? Governments and politics?"

"You're starting to understand. Now you see why you cannot help me. You're merely a college professor pretending to be a demonologist in your spare time. You run to the rescue when teenagers play with Ouija boards, and that makes you feel like you're doing God's work." Jackson smirked. "But you have no idea about what's going on over your head. There are some very sophisticated and organized people who know *far* more than you. There is knowledge so ancient and occult that it's only handed down to a chosen few. Truths that your chubby sidekick will never find in his internet searches.

"These people know how to use this knowledge against the masses, and they do. With the help of spirits like Akhubel, these are the people who control everything and everyone on the entire planet. They decide who gets elected. They decide who wins wars. They decide which nations rise and which ones collapse. Yet no one has a clue these powerful people even exist." Jackson leaned in closer. "You have *no idea* about what you think you're saving me from. Or even the reality of the very world you live in."

Rand wracked his brain for anything to refute what Jackson had said. But all of Rand's thoughts seemed to mute. He didn't want to believe anything he'd just been told. It was too grand. Too widespread. Impossible.

But was it? Rand could scarcely imagine what an extremely wealthy man like Bernard Bale could accomplish when he had the cooperation of demonic entities lending him their supernatural powers.

"And you intend to join them," Rand said.

"Marriage into the Bale family does not mean acceptance." Jackson sounded like he was reciting a statement he'd been told numerous times to ensure he never forgot it. "Acceptance is earned."

It suddenly occurred to Rand that by Bernard marrying his daughter to Jackson—the only surviving member of the Herron family—Bernard had effectively absorbed James Herron's empire, perhaps doubling Bernard's wealth in a single move.

An old-world strategy used in the modern day, Rand thought.

"I've waited many years for this night," Jackson said. "When Bernard told me it was finally time, I was more than ready—and pleased to hear that my final test was quite simple: locate an enemy of the Bale family's spiritual allies and bring him to my father's house."

Rand began to understand his role in all of this. Given his current circumstance, he had a good idea of the purpose he was to serve.

"You could've just killed me as soon as I'd stepped inside," Rand said.

"I thought Akhubel would when you came up to the tower earlier. But I now see that these matters are never straightforward. Everything is a ritual. There is always a careful process."

"You must journey through the darkness," Rand remembered. *It was all one big ritual.*

"Your mother's spirit was trapped in here all along, you know." It was the last thing Rand could think of to appeal to Jackson's empathy, if any remained. Sure enough, Jackson's face seemed to soften. "I met her deep inside the mansion, and I set her free. She didn't deserve the torment Bernard inflicted on your family. Does that help you see what kind of people you're dealing with?"

Akhubel watched Jackson. Rand got the feeling the demon was allowing him a chance to change Jackson's mind—to see if the man would remain committed.

"You're right," Jackson said. "She *didn't* deserve what happened to her. So I thank you for that. But again, this is all so much larger than her, or any of us."

Jackson walked away from Rand's side and retrieved something from the table on the other side of the room. He returned holding a knife.

Rand struggled against his restraints when he saw the blade. The ropes bit into the flesh of his wrists and ankles, but it was clear he wouldn't escape. "Jackson, please!"

"You seem like a nice guy, and in another life we probably could've been friends," Jackson said. "I've never done anything like this before, so I'm just going to get this over with." Jackson knelt beside Rand and Akhubel did the same, mirroring Jackson's movements exactly, as if they were one in the same. "Let's move this out of the way first." He then stuck his hand into Rand's interior jacket pocket—the right one that he usually kept empty.

What's he—

When Jackson withdrew his hand, he held the black cube in his palm.

Rand stared at it with wide eyes. "Impossible. I left it—"

"It doesn't matter where you leave it," Jackson said. "Once you touch it, it stays with you." He set the cube on the floor beside him.

Jackson then gripped the knife with both his hands. Both the blade and hilt appeared to be made of dark, glass-like material, resembling the black cube. He lifted the knife high above his head, arms outstretched, then he started chanting in a hellish language. The words resembled what Rand had heard when he'd been trapped inside the room filled with record players.

"Don't do this!" Rand shrieked. But Jackson didn't seem to hear him.

Akhubel stared down at Rand, no hint of emotion on his stony face. If the demon was pleased that Rand's death was coming, he didn't show it.

Libby. Tessa. Miller. Tara. Rand saw them all in that moment. He hoped they would be okay. Perhaps they'd even be better off without him, as he'd often wondered.

Jackson's chanting ceased. In the next moment, he brought the blade down with all his might.

48

Bernard and Miranda rode mostly in silence.

Libby did her best to keep her breathing shallow, fearful any noise would give her away.

She inched her hand toward her pocket and pulled out her cell phone. She quickly turned it to silent so it wouldn't make any sound. Then she sent Miller a text message.

On the way to wherever you are. Hiding in the backseat.

"Are you okay?" Bernard asked. Miranda didn't respond, but she must have nodded. "Are you sure?"

"I have to be," Miranda replied, though she sounded despondent. "This has been coming for nine years. I've had that long to prepare."

Prepare for what? Libby thought.

"Dedication will always be rewarded," Bernard said. "Some matters can be unpleasant, but this has always been about something much bigger than ourselves."

Libby had been so focused on the conversation that she hadn't noticed Miller's response appear on her phone.

In whose backseat? What's going on?

Libby reread what she'd sent Miller. She'd typed it in such a frenzy that she now realized it hadn't given him much information.

The car slowed. "This orange Jeep must belong to Randolph Casey," Bernard said.

"Casey's partner should still be there, according to Jackson," Miranda said.

"Well. Let's find out."

Miller texted again.

Are you okay?

Libby didn't have time to explain everything, so she typed and sent what she could.

I THINK YOU NEED TO HIDE.

MILLER'S STOMACH felt like it was caving in on itself.

I THINK YOU NEED TO HIDE.

Headlights flashed just outside the window.

His eyes darted around the room, looking for somewhere to hide. He rushed out of the living room and into the small, adjacent sitting room.

Outside, car doors opened and closed.

The only place Miller could go from there was up the stairs. He hated to retreat further into a corner, but it was his only option.

The front door opened and closed.

The second floor of the caretaker's home was more like a loft. An open door led to bedroom, and another went to a bathroom, but it was a small door on the far side of the room that caught Miller's eye. He rushed over and found a closet filled with coats.

Voices came from downstairs.

He was out of time, so he went inside and closed the door gently behind him.

Although muffled from inside the closet, Miller could make out two voices—a man and woman.

Miller's phone buzzed, seeming much louder than it actually was now that he needed to be totally silent. A nervous chill gripped his heart as he fumbled it out of his pocket and switched it to silent mode.

The buzz had come from another text from Libby.

I've gotten out of the car. I'm hiding outside until they leave.

Good, Miller thought. Now he could only hope they didn't find *him.*

Footsteps grew louder as someone came up the stairs. Miller could feel their presence a mere handful of steps away from where he hid, separated only by a flimsy door.

"Is he up there?" called a woman from downstairs.

"I'm looking." The voice of the man was deep and powerful.

"He's here somewhere. He wouldn't leave his computer."

Miller winced. In his desperation, he'd left all his stuff laid out on the coffee table in the living room. Even if he had remembered, though, he wouldn't have had time to pack it all up.

Slow footsteps moved around the room, shuffling things around.

Stupid closet, Miller chastised himself. *It's obviously the first place to look.*

He stepped backward away from the door—as if that

would make a difference. His heel brushed against something on the floor.

Miller looked down, but the complete darkness of the closet didn't allow him to see. He lifted his phone and turned on the flashlight.

It took everything within him to stifle the scream that tried to erupt from his throat.

The man looked to be about sixty years old, wearing old blue jeans and white t-shirt. He was propped upright against the back wall of the closet, head tilted to the side. A thick rope still dangled from his neck, which was purple and black. His legs were outstretched—the man's shoes had been what Miller had nearly stepped on.

The current caretaker, Miller thought. The man didn't look like he'd been dead for long. *Jackson must've done this before we arrived.*

"We have to check up on Jackson," the woman shouted from downstairs.

"I'm aware," the man said, terse and annoyed.

Miller clenched his eyes, silently urging the man to give up the search. *Yes, please leave, you're late for something, just go.*

The footsteps settled just on the other side of the closet door and lingered there for several long moments, as if the man were considering whether to check or not.

Miller held his breath and waited for the door to swing open.

It didn't. Instead, the man spoke.

"I've never had much patience for cowards."

The words came slow and menacing. Any remaining illusion Miller had that he was actually hiding from the man evaporated.

"There are things that I must see to tonight that are far greater than you. But rest assured, I'll catch up with you soon."

Miller's body trembled. His lungs burned from his held breath.

The footsteps faded down the stairs.

Miller waited until there was total silence before letting his breath go, panting as if he'd been underwater for too long.

"Miller!" someone shrieked from the first floor—and he recognized this voice.

He bounded from the closet, cool air brushing against his sweaty face. He rushed downstairs.

"Miller?" Libby called again.

Miller rounded the corner into the living room and nearly face-planted right into her.

She threw her arms around him and squeezed him tighter than he'd anticipated, pressing the air from his lungs. "You're okay. They didn't find you?"

"Um." Now wasn't the time to share what he'd been told, nor what he'd discovered in the upstairs closet. He didn't need to worry her any more than she already was. "They don't know you're here, do they?"

"No."

"Where did they go?"

"They got back in the car and went that way." She pointed. Miller knew it was the direction of the Herron House.

"You shouldn't have come here," Miller said. "That was very—"

"Well I'm here *now*, aren't I?" Libby snapped.

"Someone had to tell you those weirdos were about to show up."

Miller shut his mouth. Libby was right. If she hadn't warned him, he'd have been sitting right there in living room when they'd barged in. The man had let him go—albeit with a threat to find him later—but would the woman have shown less mercy?

"Where's Dad?"

"As far as I know, he's still inside the mansion."

"And that's where *they're* going?" Miller nodded. "Then we have to help him." Libby tugged on Miller's arms, pulling him toward the door.

"Libby, wait. I think you should—"

Libby rounded on him. "Are you serious? I'm not leaving! My dad's in danger and we're the only ones who can help him. Come on!"

Miller realized there was nothing he could say that would dissuade Libby from rushing to the mansion. He was either going with her, or she was going alone. He set his jaw and mustered up the last bit of courage he had remaining after a *very* long night.

It was time for him to return to the Herron House.

49

R and clenched his eyes shut.

He waited for pain, but none came.

Perhaps that meant it was all over.

He opened his eyes to find Jackson and Akhubel still kneeling over him.

The demon's arm was outstretched over Rand's chest, palm facing up. Jackson's knife had stabbed through it, and he was still gripping the hilt.

Jackson looked as confused as Rand felt. He let go of the knife and cast Akhubel a questioning look.

Abraham and Isaac, Rand remembered. *An angel stayed Abraham's hand at the last moment...*

"I don't understand," Jackson said. For the first time, he looked fearful. "I thought this was what you wanted."

"You've done well," Akhubel said. His pierced hand still lingered over Rand. "It is time for your true test."

Jackson's shoulders slumped. Beads of sweat had formed at his temples. He swallowed heavily before saying, "What is it?"

"Now that I know you are willing to perform sacrifices when called upon to do so, you must offer the *true* sacrifice." Akhubel lowered his outstretched arm and returned it to his side. The black knife remained embedded in his palm.

Jackson gestured toward Rand. "It isn't him? I thought—"

"As you said, everything is a ritual."

Jackson's face fell at hearing his own words repeated back to him.

"Do you see now?" Rand blurted out. "Nothing about this is going to be what you think. Let me go and I can help you."

Jackson didn't seem to hear Rand at all. His jaw clenched, and resolve seemed to return to his body. "Tell me what I need to do."

"There is only one sacrifice that is acceptable to me and to my masters."

"Tell me," Jackson demanded.

"Youth. Innocence. Purity."

Akhubel's meaning seemed to dawn on Jackson at the same time as Rand. "A child."

"It is the only way."

"Come on, man," Rand pleaded. "This is too much!"

Jackson clenched his fists as they hung at his sides. Rand could tell he was trying to force himself to stay the course, but the fear was evident behind his eyes. "Tell me who, and I will do it."

"Jackson, no!" Rand shouted.

Akhubel did not respond. The demon held Jackson's gaze with a blank, emotionless stare.

"Tell me *who!*" Jackson's outburst told Rand that the

man was slipping. If he didn't keep up his focus, then he was in danger of backing out of the whole thing.

"A child of your own blood," Akhubel finally said.

Those were the words that finally did it—Jackson's facade of strength finally failed. His lip trembled and he hung his head. A few moments later he began to sob.

Carmen, Rand thought. He'd only seen the girl once when the Herrons had brought her along to his classroom. She'd sat quietly at the back of the room, coloring while Jackson and Miranda had spun him a web of lies.

Akhubel did not take his glowing eyes off the broken man, studying him, as if waiting to see if this final line would be the one Jackson refused to cross.

Jackson tried to take in a deep breath to steady himself, but it was broken up into many desperate gasps. "Miranda knew about this?" His voice was small and weak.

"Since the day Bernard agreed to let you marry her."

Jackson clenched his eyes. Tears streamed down both his cheeks.

Long moments stretched on, and the only sound that filled the chamber was Jackson's sobs.

But every moment that passed was another where Jackson had not yet refused.

"Jackson," Rand said, trying to keep his voice gentle, "this is too far."

"Shut up," Jackson snapped. He stood from where he knelt and turned his back on both Rand and Akhubel. He slumped toward the stone wall and leaned onto it with both his palms, head hung between his outstretched arms. His shoulders shook as he cried.

"She knew all along," Jackson whispered to himself. "How could she…"

Akhubel continued to peer at Jackson. The demon seemed unbothered by Jackson's reaction. Rand figured Akhubel cared little for what Jackson felt—all that mattered in the end was what he chose to do.

"The true sacrifice," Akhubel had said. Rand realized that Jackson sacrificing a man he'd met only a few days before was easy compared to his own daughter.

"Let me go and I can help you out of this," Rand said to Jackson's back. He had very little confidence that was actually true, but he had to try. This was no longer just about him. The life of a young girl was now at stake. "You're better than this, Jackson. You *can't* do this. You know in your heart that this is wrong."

Once again, Akhubel made no attempt to stop Rand from speaking. His desperate pleas only tested Jackson further. Rand was no longer the only one having his entire worldview turned upside down that night.

Jackson's crying finally abated. His body grew rigid. He wiped at his cheeks and nose, then pivoted to face Akhubel once again. His eyes were puffy, yet a darkness had settled within them. "I will do it. There is no other way."

"Jackson, don't do this," Rand said. From Jackson's perspective, it was true—there *was* no other way. He was in too deep, and if he failed to complete the ritual that night, Rand figured the consequences would be dire. It came down to either Carmen's life or his own.

Rand understood well what any other father would choose. But the family Jackson had married into was clearly far from ordinary.

"Come with me," Akhubel said.

Akhubel rose and walked away from where Rand lay bound to the floor. He approached the stone stairs that led higher up in the tower.

"Wait," Jackson said.

The demon paused, then turned to face Jackson. He fixed the man with his glowing glare as if daring him to say that he'd changed his mind.

"Untie me," Rand said. If Jackson was about to refuse, Rand needed to be free. He'd have to help defend him against what Akhubel might do.

Jackson returned to Rand's side, yet he kept his attention on Akhubel. "I would like to request that you allow me to finish him."

"What are you doing?" Rand's whole body tensed again.

Akhubel's eyes seemed to narrow with suspicion. "I've told you, Randolph Casey is not an acceptable sacrifice."

"I know," Jackson said. "I apologize for my weakness earlier. It was unacceptable. I came here tonight to demonstrate that I am fully committed to the Bale family and to you. Randolph Casey has been your enemy for a long time, right? Allow me the honor of putting an end to him."

"Jackson…" A numb hopelessness settled in Rand's stomach.

The man wore a stony expression as Akhubel silently considered the request.

Akhubel shifted his attention toward the chamber's entrance. "What say you?"

Rand lifted his head to follow Akhubel's gaze, and his breath caught in his throat.

Shindael was there.

It had been many months since Rand had last seen his demonic nemesis, but he looked just as Rand remembered —a nondescript face with pale blue flesh, as if he'd been frozen. His small black eyes were affixed to Rand.

Dark despair slithered through Rand's chest. He couldn't possibly imagine how things could get worse for him.

'You were to be given to me.'

Shindael's whispered voice filled Rand's mind.

The pieces were slowly falling into place. Akhubel preventing Jackson from killing Rand did not mean that he'd be set free. Rather, he was to be turned over to Shindael.

'Let the man do as he wishes. But keep Randolph's heart intact.'

Without missing a beat, Akhubel returned to Rand's right side. He extended his palm, offering the black knife to Jackson. Jackson gripped the hilt and pulled it from Akhubel's hand. The demon appeared to feel no pain from its extraction.

Jackson pressed the knife against Rand's left thigh. He felt the coldness of the blade even through the denim of his jeans. His femoral artery was just underneath. Like the jugular in the neck, it would bleed freely once severed.

"Please," Rand whispered. It was the only word he had left. But deep down, he knew begging would be wasting what little breath he had remaining.

It felt like a bee sting on his thigh, a sharp burst of pain that came and went. Next came the trickle of warm, wet blood against his leg.

In that moment, tears filled Rand's eyes. He once again

thought of his family and friends. They'd likely never know what had happened to him that night.

"We must proceed," Akhubel said.

Jackson gave Rand one last look before walking away from him.

Rand gazed up at the dark stone of the chamber's ceiling. Part of him wanted to lift his head again to see if Shindael was still there, watching him bleed out, but there didn't seem to be any point. He didn't want the demon to be the last thing he saw.

Rand's entire body went limp, as if it wanted to give him a few moments of peace at the end. It felt as if it were emptying itself of everything—breath, life, and even his soul. All of it seemed to be flooding out from his leg and onto the floor. Darkness closed in around the edges of his vision.

The written words of James Herron were the last thing that came to his mind.

Randolph Casey must die and this house is his tomb.

50

The steps leading up the Herron House's porch took the breath from Miller's lungs the same way they had when he'd first climbed them at the beginning of the night. His gasps came out as warm clouds of vapor in the chilled night.

But his breath caught in his throat when he reached the porch and saw that the mansion's front door was wide open.

Libby charged toward the mansion's entrance and the darkness beyond. She stopped when she noticed Miller was no longer beside her. "Why are you stopping?"

"The door."

"What about it?"

"It's… open." Miller allowed himself a brief moment of hope that Rand had found a way to open the door and escape. But deep down he knew that if Rand had gotten the door open, he would've come straight to Miller.

They *opened it*, Miller thought. *It was sealed closed until* they *were ready to get in.*

"What are you waiting for?" Libby demanded.

Miller knew Libby wouldn't understand why he was so shocked, and he didn't have time to explain. Together they entered the front door, like walking into a gaping mouth that swallowed them both.

Miller's eyes were immediately drawn to the beam of white light coming from Rand's flashlight. It lay on the floor next to the staircase.

This isn't good, he thought as he approached it. *Rando must've come back here, but I don't think he would've left this behind...* Miller picked up the light.

"Which way?" Libby asked, frantic.

Miller pointed the flashlight up the stairs that led to the second floor. "Up." He couldn't say why, but something in his gut pulled him in that direction. "To the tower."

Libby took the steps two at a time and Miller followed.

"This place is huge," Libby said as she gazed down the second-floor corridor which was shrouded in shadows. "How are we going to—"

"There." Miller aimed the light at a large arched doorway to the right. Just beyond it were spiral stone stairs. Miller figured they led to the tower where Rand had gone at the beginning of the night.

"Are you sure?" Libby asked. Despite her eagerness to find her dad, even she seemed put off by the idea of climbing those stairs.

Miller didn't respond—he just started climbing, and Libby followed. The stairs spiraled round and round the tower's body until they came to another arched doorway that led to circular chamber.

Miller froze when he saw what was inside. *Oh...*

Although numerous candles provided only a dim light, it was enough. A large portion of the circular room's floor was covered in a smooth, undisturbed layer of blood.

Rand lay supine in the middle, his wrists and ankles tied to metal clasps embedded into the floor. He was completely still.

Miller heard Libby coming up the stairs behind him. He wanted to intercept her so she wouldn't see what he'd discovered. But he was so stunned that he couldn't react quickly enough.

Libby appeared beside him, peering into the chamber.

She broke. Began to cry. She tried to speak, but the words only came out as pinched whispers. She walked into the room, her steps leaving footprints in her father's blood. She knelt beside him and reached out to him with trembling hands. She touched his face. His eyes were closed. Libby bent over and pressed her face against her father's motionless chest. Her shoulders heaved as she sobbed.

We have to get out of here. Miller couldn't articulate where the sudden thought had come from. Probably from a self-preservation instinct deep within him. Whoever had done this to Rand was likely still nearby, and they would have no qualms about doing the same to him and Libby.

Miller went to Libby and laid his hands on her shoulders as gently as he could. In that moment, he felt what Libby must've felt: a strong urge to be close to Rand, even though he wasn't really there anymore. But there simply wasn't time for that.

"Libby," he whispered. "We have to leave."

Libby only gripped her dad's body tighter. Her fingers clawed into his arms, as if refusing to let go.

Miller realized he was going to have to force her. He hated himself for not giving the girl time to say goodbye, but he knew it was necessary. Every second they lingered lowered their chances of making it out of the mansion.

Now that he was closer, he saw that the greatest concentration of blood was near Rand's left thigh. A deep gash was barely visible amidst the dark red.

"We can't stay." Miller squeezed Libby's shoulders slightly and pulled her toward him. "There are some very evil people here right now."

"I don't want to leave him!" she shrieked through her tears.

"We're coming back for him, I promise," Miller said. "But right now—"

"You go, then! I'm staying."

A fresh wave of bawling burst from her as she buried her face into the space between Rand's face and shoulder.

Miller understood he wouldn't be able to reason with her. She wasn't going to hear any logic in that moment.

He noticed something on the floor. It was so covered in blood that Miller wasn't sure what it was, but he knew it was out of place. He picked it up, and it left behind a cross-shaped outline of the floor underneath the layer of blood. He held the simple wooden cross in both hands. The blood that coated it made his palms sticky.

The cross from Rand's last case, Miller thought. Before they'd lost communication between their radios, Rand had told him the cross had aided him somehow.

He noticed that Libby was looking at him now. Her

face was pinched and red, eyes and cheeks wet. Her gaze fell to the bloody cross. "What's that?"

"Your dad's cross. It was on the floor next to him."

"The broken one put back together by the girl with white eyes?" Libby asked. She knew the story from that night just as well as he did.

"Yes. The last time I spoke to your dad, he told me he'd discovered the girl was somehow connected to it."

Libby blinked a few times as she stared at the bloody cross. Then she snatched it away from Miller and turned her attention to her father's lifeless body. She quickly swiped at the tears from her cheeks. "He said he believed the girl he saw that night was an angel."

Miller realized what she was thinking. "He told me the same thing."

Libby looked at the wound on Rand's thigh. "If that's true..."

51

A magnificent display spread out before him. It seemed to expand in all directions, and he sensed it was infinite. Brilliant lights—yellow, orange, and red—swirled like vapor in between countless stars. The stars and the colors twisted into a spiral, much like the images of galaxies he'd seen on television.

Rand didn't remember waking up there. He didn't remember arriving. He didn't even remember becoming aware. He was just... there. He wasn't sure if he was standing up or laying down. Perhaps he was floating.

Maybe it didn't matter if he was standing or laying or floating. He got the impression that those concepts weren't important here. That the only thing that mattered in this place was simply *being*.

He looked down at himself. His body wasn't as he remembered. He appeared to be made of white light. For some reason, Rand wasn't alarmed by that.

I'm an apparition. It was the first thought that came to him. He looked exactly like the demons he'd faced when they chose to appear, except their manifested bodies were black.

Someone else was there with him. Rand knew her.

"Tara?"

His voice sounded vague, very unlike what he was used to. Once again, this alteration to his physical form didn't alarm him. He actually found that he *preferred* it.

"Hello, Rand." Again, the girl's voice was soft and soothing, almost like music.

"Where am I?"

"I know it can be frightening to go through this, but it is necessary."

Rand only stared at her. He didn't feel afraid at all. In fact, he couldn't remember the last time he'd felt such a complete *absence* of fear.

"I'm not afraid," Rand said.

"Good."

"I'm..." He searched his mind for a word to describe the pleasant emptiness he was experiencing. "Comfortable." But even that didn't do it justice.

"I'm glad, but you cannot stay here for long," Tara said. "You must make a decision. The choice is yours and yours alone."

"What choice?"

A thought entered Rand's mind so suddenly it felt as if it had been implanted there by Tara.

Go on or return?

That was his choice. But what did it mean?

"Go on to where?" Rand asked. "Return to where?"

"The choice is yours," Tara repeated. "But there is someone who would like to meet you first."

Her gaze shifted to focus on something behind Rand.

He turned. An elderly gentleman had joined them. He wore a blue suit, hands clasped behind his back. He had greying hair and a heavily lined face.

"James Herron."

The man nodded. "It's good to finally meet you."

Seeing James brought on a sudden deluge of memories from Rand's experiences in the man's home. They all appeared into his mind at once, and he wondered how he could've possibly forgotten them.

Rand looked back to where Tara had been, but she was gone.

When he returned his attention to James Herron, the man was suddenly much closer. Rand was not startled by his sudden closeness, however, but comforted.

"You've been through so much," James said. "Not just in my home, but even before."

More images flashed through Rand's mind. Georgia Collins in the hospital, possessed by Karax. Deckard Arcan, eyes glowing red from the evil spirit that had been within him. He even received images of things he hadn't been present for, but had only heard about —the two demonic children on Stacy Thompson's doorstep, and Libby tied up in Deckard's mansion's attic.

In all of those events from the past, even the ones he hadn't personally witnessed, Rand understood there was one thing that drew them all together: him.

He'd worked hard to save them, and he'd been success-ful. But their trauma from those horrific experiences would remain with them all for the rest of their lives, buried deep within. Rand could never save them from that no matter how hard he tried.

Another memory came to him—Tessa telling him they'd all be better off without him.

"They *are* better off without me," he said, responding to the memory out loud.

"I thought the same thing," James said. "But is it true? I'm gone, yet my son still suffers."

His son? Jackson Herron, Rand finally remembered. With the recollection of Jackson came the memory of the last thing he'd experienced before appearing here—wherever "here" was.

Once again, Rand had no reaction to the memory. To him, in that moment, it was merely a neutral event that had occurred.

"I made a choice," James said. "I chose to ignore the darkness that threatened my family. I thought that if I ignored it, it would go away. I was very wrong. My son made a choice as well. He chose to embrace that same darkness."

Rand would've thought James might be saddened by that, but he was starting to realize the emotions he was accustomed to didn't seem to have a place here.

"For years, I had visions of you in my dreams and nightmares," James went on. "I knew that one day you'd come."

"And that I'd die in your home," Rand said.

"And you did," James said as if he were pleased with himself for being right, even it meant Rand had lost his life. But Rand felt no offense. Something about his own demise seemed negligible in the grand scheme of things.

"How did you know?" Rand asked.

"Time is not linear as it is experienced in the physical realm. You already know this."

Rand remembered the times he'd experienced the past. He wondered what he was seeing now. The future? Somehow it felt separate from any sense of time he'd ever known.

"If I'm already here," Rand said, "then I may as well just…"

"Stay?" James said. "That's certainly one option. It's nice here, isn't it? There's nothing at all to worry about."

Rand understood what James meant. Even though he'd had flashes of memories from his previous cases—memories that usually kept him awake at night, paralyzed with guilt—he felt nothing this time. It seemed as if those negative emotions *couldn't* exist here.

"That, and it's nice to be unified with something greater." James turned and faced the spiraling clusters of stars and colors in the distance. "You feel the way you do, Rand, because you are home. This is where we all come from. You see it from a distance every single night, yet you pay it no mind. Look." James pointed. "There's Aries and Taurus. Gemini, Cancer, Leo." His finger moved just slightly as he listed off the houses of the zodiac. Rand tried to see what James was pointing at, but the specific constellations were lost within the billions of other stars, visible only to James's practiced eye. "Virgo. Libra. Scorpio. Sagittarius. Capricorn. Aquarius. Pisces."

"Why are these stars so important to you, James?" Rand asked. He looked at the older man, taking his gaze away from the spiraling clusters. "You read and wrote about them. Studied them. Built a room dedicated to them in the center of your home. Why?"

James met Rand's gaze. "Because they are constant. For

that reason, I trust them. They offer both guidance and protection from the darkness."

That confused Rand. "What about God?"

James only smirked. "The sun will rise in one of the twelve Houses for two thousand, one hundred and sixty years before passing to the next, bringing with it a new age. The sun will have traveled through all twelve Houses after twenty-six thousand years, and then repeat it all over again. In that time, generations are born and then die. Civilizations rise and then fall. Religions come and go. But that wheel of stars will remain through it all, cycling through the ages, watching over all of mankind. Because they have seen everything, there is great power and wisdom written in those stars."

Rand struggled to make sense of what James was telling him. It all sounded very similar to what Tessa spoke about when she brought up her new interest in astrology. Rand had only ridiculed her for it, yet he wondered now if he'd been wrong to have done so.

James seemed to sense Rand's confusion. "You'll understand before long. Trust me."

More memories came to Rand. Libby, his daughter. Miller, his best friend. Even Tessa, who he still had a great fondness for despite all that had happened between them.

"They need me," Rand said.

"They do," James said. "But as Tara said, their needs and desires—even their fates—do not matter here in this moment. All that matters is your choice."

James's words reminded Rand of something he wondered about often—why *him*? Why had *he* been the one that had gotten caught up in fighting the supernatural? Billions of people would live their entire lives never having a single brush with the spiritual realm. Why couldn't he have been one of them?

Why hadn't he been allowed to *choose*?

Rand then understood what he was there to do.

He could go on, and then he'd never have to worry about another demonic entity ever again. He intuitively knew that evil spirits would never be allowed anywhere near this place—his home.

Or he could return, and step fully into the mission he'd been given.

A mission given by who? God? Tara? The entire cluster of swirling galaxies that lay before him?

A mission given to myself by me, Rand thought. Because if he chose to return and continue his fight, he could finally accept that his life had been chosen by *him*. No longer would he feel that someone else had chosen it for him. He could accept it.

"I choose to return," Rand said.

James didn't react. He only said, "I knew you would."

"How?"

James smirked. "So strange how easily we forget things we've just learned."

Rand considered that for a moment, then remembered. "Because time is not linear. You can see it all at once." As Rand looked at James, he got the impression that the man knew exactly how the rest of his life would play out now that he'd decided to return. "But I still have so many questions." Rand looked around to see if Tara had reappeared, but she had not. Many of those questions he'd wanted to specifically ask her.

"I know," James said. "But now is not the time. It isn't

good to linger here any longer than necessary. Action must be taken in another place."

James Herron faded away. The spiraling galaxies dissipated.

Rand intuitively sensed that once he'd made his choice to return, he no longer belonged there.

He was needed elsewhere.

52

Libby held out the cross and gently placed it against the open wound on her father's thigh.

Then, she waited.

Miller saw Libby's chest heave as her breathing became more frantic. Miller was experiencing his own ebb and flow of optimism. It had spiked when he'd found the cross, but now with every second that passed, it crashed lower and lower.

"Please," Libby whispered. "You were there for him once. Help him now."

Miller couldn't bear it anymore. He'd allowed himself to have hope, but now he had to face reality. Rand Casey was gone, and he and Libby were in danger. They had to get out of the mansion before it was too late. "Libby, that's enough. We have to—"

The cross began to glow with a clear, white light, so bright Miller had to look away. Libby gasped.

The blood on the floor began to move and shift. The

puddle that had covered half the floor grew smaller and smaller.

"The blood..." Miller said.

"It's going back *in*," Libby said, pointing. Sure enough, Miller saw that the blood was flowing back into the gash in Rand's thigh, as if pulled there by the glowing cross Libby held against the open wound. It was like watching a video in reverse.

"Miller, it's working!" Libby shrieked. New tears had come to her eyes.

Not only was Miller in awe of what he was seeing, but also by what he was feeling. As soon as the white light emanated from the cross, an overpowering comfort came over him. All feelings of guilt and grief upon seeing his friend's corpse immediately left him. His feelings of fear and needing to defend himself were also gone. All that remained was a gentle peace that seemed ready to persist forever.

Is this how Rand felt in the presence of the white-eyed girl?

The last of the blood on the floor returned to Rand's body. As soon as it did, Rand Casey's eyes shot open and he took in a huge gulp of air, as if he'd been holding his breath underwater and had just broken the surface. The cross's brilliant glow ceased.

"Dad!" Libby shrieked. She hugged him as best she could while he was still tied to the floor.

Miller's mouth dangled open, spellbound by what he'd just witnessed.

Rand's eyes blinked rapidly as he looked around the room, confused.

"Libby?"

"I'm here," she said.

Rand's eyes then settled on Miller. "What…"

Now that the cross's brilliant light had faded, the feelings it had chased away started to return. Once again, Miller understood that they weren't safe.

Despite the miracle, it was too soon to celebrate.

Miller sprung into action. He dug his hand into his jeans and removed the pocketknife he always carried with him. As he did, he noted that even the blood that had stained his palms from when he'd picked up the cross was gone.

Miller opened the blade and got to work sawing the ropes that bound Rand.

"What's happening?" Rand asked.

"Don't worry, buddy, we're getting you out of here," Miller said. His knife cut through the first rope and Rand's right hand was free. He started moving his arm in circles, loosening up his shoulder. Miller got to work on the left.

Libby stood back to give Miller more space to work. Tears still filled her eyes, but they were different from before.

Once freed, Rand got to his feet. He wobbled, then caught his balance.

"Was I…" Rand's eyes darted between Miller and Libby. Miller could see the memories returning to him. His brow furrowed. "Libby, what are you doing here?"

"I'll tell you everything later," Miller said. "But we need to get out of here *right now.*"

He took hold of Libby's shoulders and ushered her toward the door. She went with him, but both stopped short when they realized that Rand wasn't following.

"Rando!" Miller snapped. "Come on!"

Rand's gaze remained focused on the staircase on the far side of the circular room, which Miller assumed led even higher in the tower—and the opposite way they needed to go.

Miller went to his friend, grabbed his arm and pulled. "I told you I'd explain later, but right now we need—"

Rand shook his arm loose from Miller's grasp. Miller was shocked by Rand's strength, given that he'd been completely dead just a minute before.

"Rando—"

Rand turned away from the stairs and gave Miller his attention. He wore an expression that Miller couldn't quite read.

"You can leave," Rand finally said. "But I have to go up."

He extended his open palm toward Libby. She hesitated for a moment, but ultimately returned the cross to Rand. He slid it through his belt loop, like he was sheathing a sword.

Miller had no idea what was up those stairs, and he had a feeling Rand wasn't quite sure either.

"But—"

"I made a choice," Rand said. "Now I have to do what I promised I would."

53

Rand's leg muscles strained as he bounded up the stone stairs two at a time, ascending the steep incline. He panted for breath.

He didn't know what he'd find at the top of those stairs. That should have frightened him, especially given everything that had happened so far that night. But ultimately it didn't *matter* what was up there. He'd made his choice, so it was his job to face it, regardless of what it was.

The stairs ended at an arched threshold with no door attached. The chamber within was circular, mirroring the one downstairs Rand had just come from. A domed ceiling of glass capped the room. Through it, he could see the star-filled night sky. Like James Herron's office, the chamber had a second floor with spiral steps running along the wall to a landing above. Thick pillars rose from floor to ceiling. As below, the room was dimly lit by burning candles in sconces along the walls.

Rand climbed the smaller steps to the chamber's second floor—then stopped short.

Carmen Herron lay on the floor, arms and hands outstretched, her blonde hair splayed. Akhubel leaned over her, supported by his hands and knees. His vile mouth gaped open like a black pit. Soft spirals of light rose from the girl's sleeping body, twisting into the air before being abruptly sucked down Akhubel's throat.

He's consuming her, Rand thought. He remembered the drawing in James Herron's journal.

Rand didn't know what the spirals of light coming from Carmen's body were. Perhaps they were her energy, or life force, or maybe even her soul. Whatever they were, Rand understood that Akhubel was *feeding*.

And that he had to stop it.

Rand advanced toward the demon and the girl. Even as he neared, Akhubel didn't seem to notice his approach —he was too preoccupied with the girl. Rand tightened his grip on the cross and raised it over his head, ready to stab Akhubel with the holy symbol.

Someone slammed into Rand from his left, tackling him. He went down hard, and the cross clattered away.

Jackson Herron stood over him. His eyes were wide, frantic. "How... You're dead."

"I was. But I can't stay dead if I still have your mess to clean up."

Rand returned to his feet. Despite the sudden activity that had happened beside him, Akhubel still did not acknowledge either of them. Apparently the demon could only focus on what he was doing until it was done. Carmen appeared very white and sickly, and Rand understood he didn't have much time.

"I'm taking the girl away from here," Rand said.

All of Jackson's surprise at seeing Rand alive had now been replaced with a desperate glare, though Jackson said nothing.

Rand took a step toward where his cross had landed.

Jackson lunged at him again, yet this time Rand was ready. Jackson gripped handfuls of Rand's jacket sleeves to wrestle him to the ground, but Rand resisted. He got low and pushed his shoulder into Jackson's stomach, intending to scoop him off his feet and drop him onto his back.

But Jackson didn't go down. He was stronger.

Rand felt a sharp elbow to his spine, followed by Jackson's knee slamming into his stomach and forcing the air from his lungs.

In that moment of stunned pain, Jackson grabbed Rand and pulled him away from Akhubel and toward the chamber's stone wall. He then thrust Rand against a door, which burst open behind him.

Rand tumbled out onto the tower's balcony. He scrambled back to his feet, but Jackson was upon him again, swiftly kicking him in the chest. Sharp pain blossomed, possibly from a broken rib.

Jackson forced Rand against the balcony's stone railing, which bit into his lower back. He took a punch to the jaw, another to the cheek. He felt warm blood trickle from his nose.

A third came, but Rand ducked and slipped away from his cornered position.

"The ritual is almost complete," Jackson said. "I'm so *close*. You won't mess it up for me now."

Rand wiped at his bloody nose. Jackson stood between

him and the door that led back inside. The stone balcony wrapped entirely around the cylindrical tower. The night sky above was filled with stars.

He's just keeping me away, Rand realized.

Rand's face throbbed, as did his chest and back, while Jackson hardly looked winded. Rand knew now that Jackson was a lot stronger than him. Still, he had to push through. There was no other choice.

He clenched his fists and mustered another surge of willpower. He let out a primal, angry growl and rushed forward.

Jackson did not move to dodge or engage. Instead, he reached behind his back and withdrew from his belt the black knife he'd wielded earlier.

Rand abruptly stopped his charge as Jackson swung the knife in a wide arc, narrowly missing Rand's stomach.

Jackson advanced, swiping the blade, forcing Rand to backpedal even farther away from the door. But he realized that if he kept going, the circular balcony would eventually lead him back around.

Jackson seemed to sense his plan—the man leapt forward, knife raised, and Rand could not dodge in time. He caught Jackson's wrist in both his hands, holding the knife at bay.

Jackson leaned his body against Rand's, pressing him against the lip of the balcony again. His arms trembled as he tried to keep the knife from inching closer. He became aware that Jackson was also in position to flip him over the edge.

Rand kicked one of Jackson's ankles, sweeping the leg briefly from under him. The man's momentarily lost balance was enough. Rand took Jackson's wrist and forced the knife down, stabbing it through Jackson's own thigh.

He bellowed in pain.

Rand slipped away. Jackson collapsed to one knee, black knife buried to the hilt into the meat of his mid-thigh. Blood saturated his jeans.

Rand saw his chance. He took one step toward the door, but Jackson forced himself to stand and blocked the way yet again. He glared at Rand.

"You can't stop me with a knife through your leg," Rand said. "Just move aside."

Jackson reached into his pocket and withdrew the black cube. He wound up like a baseball player, preparing to throw it at Rand.

His breath caught.

It all happened too fast for Rand to react. Jackson hurled the cube toward Rand's feet. Upon impact, the balcony floor beneath where Rand stood broke apart under whatever dark force the cube contained, just as it had when Rand had thrown the cube at Akhubel earlier. The stone floor of the balcony split, then gave way.

And Rand fell.

54

Libby reached the top of the stairs and emerged into another circular chamber, this one with a second floor that overlooked the first.

Miller came up behind her, panting from having chased her up the stairs. "You heard your dad. We need to go."

"I'm not leaving him again." Although cold fear coursed throughout Libby's body, she knew her father still needed help.

She spotted smaller stone steps along the wall that led to the upper section of the room. Near the top was an open door, and the night sky was visible beyond.

"He must be up there," she said as she began to bolt up the stairs.

A loud commotion came from somewhere outside. It sounded like a piece of a building collapsing, followed by her father's scream.

"Dad!" Libby rushed up the stairs toward the open door.

"Libby, wait!" Miller called behind her.

But before Libby could rush through the door and onto the tower's balcony, something sickening caught her eye.

Carmen lay on the ground, unconscious, and atop her was one of the most appalling creatures Libby had ever seen.

Her eyes darted back and forth between Carmen and the door that led to the balcony. The weight of the dilemma came upon her all at once.

Miller appeared at her side. He seemed just as stunned as her by what he saw. "A child-sacrifice cult," he whispered. "The Lords of Hell."

Libby furrowed her brow. "What?" But something else caught her attention—her dad's cross on the floor on the far side of the room. It lay near one of the thick pillars that supported the domed ceiling.

He tried to stop this.

Libby rushed toward the cross, determined to finish what her father had attempted. She crouched and reached for it.

Someone appeared from behind the pillar and stomped their foot onto the cross, pinning it to the ground.

Libby craned her neck up.

Miranda Herron.

Libby's rage boiled. The woman had been in the room's shadows, *watching* as her own daughter was being feasted upon by a demon.

"Who are you sick people?" Libby straightened, glaring at Miranda and refusing to break her gaze. "How could you do this?"

"This moment has been planned for years," Miranda said. "And it will not be ruined by you *or* your father."

"Where is he?"

"My husband is taking care of him now." Miranda's eyes briefly went to the balcony door behind Libby.

"Miranda," a powerful yet familiar voice boomed from below, near the chamber's entrance. "What's all the noise up there?"

It's him, Libby thought. She felt ice in her veins.

"He's angry," Miranda said, glaring. "You and your father have crossed the wrong people tonight."

The woman then lashed out, striking Libby across the face. Libby clenched her jaw and pounced at Miranda, ready to rip her apart for what she'd done to her own daughter.

55

At the sound of the powerful voice, Miller turned toward the chamber's entrance to find a tall and broad-shouldered elderly man. Miller recognized the voice from when he'd been hiding in the closet.

The man shifted his hard gaze to Miller.

Nowhere to hide now, Miller thought. He was immediately struck by how closely the nearby demon resembled the man. He remembered what he'd read from the mysterious Arthur Briggs. *The Lords of Hell resemble the ones who summon them.*

His mind raced as he assessed the situation. Across the room, Libby sparred with Miranda, the two women clawing and wrestling with each other. Rando was likely outside on the balcony with Jackson. Miller swallowed hard when he realized what he needed to do.

He descended the steps to the chamber's first level, drawing upon every bit of courage to force himself to face the intimidating man.

Bernard glared at Miller as he neared. The man's lip gave a short curl. "I see you've decided to leave your hiding place. Just shows even cowards can sometimes surprise you."

"There's a lot you don't know about me." Miller tried to make himself sound threatening, but at no point in his life had anyone *ever* considered him threatening.

Bernard gave a mirthless chuckle. "There is *one* thing I know about. That is, the minute you intruded upon the ritual, you became a part of it."

Miller didn't fully understand what that meant, but it couldn't be good. "I refuse to be a part of it."

"You don't have the luxury to refuse," Bernard said. His amusement at Miller's show of bravery was now gone. "Get out of my way. I need to ensure my son-in-law hasn't botched things too badly." His eyes went over Miller's head to the second-floor landing, where the young girl was being given to the demon.

Although Bernard was older, Miller still sensed a dark strength within him. He wouldn't be able to prevent Bernard from passing, but he still had to do whatever he could to buy Rand more time. Miller couldn't hope to fight Bernard, but he could possibly distract him.

"It doesn't matter how powerful the Lords of Hell are," Miller said, striving to speak with authority. "With God on our side, we will *always* be stronger."

Something shifted in Bernard—his malevolent expression was replaced with a flash of concern, though it was brief. He shifted his gaze back to Miller, and Miller held the hard stare, refusing to break it first.

"You were right. There *are* some things I don't know about you. It seems you're closer to the truth than you should be." He let out a low growl. "You may have just saved yourself now that I know you're useful."

Miller blinked. *What does that mean?*

Bernard moved swiftly. He took a large step toward Miller, wrapped his large hands around his neck, and squeezed.

It had happened so fast that Miller hadn't had a single moment to defend himself. He gripped Bernard's wrists and tried to pull the man's large hands away, but his hold was too strong.

Miller felt Bernard's strength upon him, forcing him to his knees. He tried to suck in a breath, but his airway was clenched in the man's vise-like grasp.

Bernard brought his face close to Miller's. "You *will* tell me where to find Arthur Briggs."

Miller knew he should've been shocked to hear that name come from Bernard's mouth, but he was too focused on trying to breathe again.

"You've clearly been speaking with him. Where is he? Tell me now!"

Bernard released Miller's throat just enough to let him speak.

"No!"

Bernard punched Miller hard in the jaw. His body locked up from the sudden shock and he collapsed. His brain felt rattled inside in his skull, and blood trickled from his lip.

"I have ways of getting information," Bernard said as he stood over Miller. "You don't want it to come to that."

Miller had no idea where Arthur Briggs was, or how he was connected to Bernard. But he sure could play it up to buy Rand more time to save the girl.

Miller looked up at the towering man. "I'll *never* tell you."

Bernard didn't seem surprised by that response. "Very well. If that's how you want to do things…"

A sick delight settled in the older man's eyes.

56

The sinking feeling of falling gripped Rand's heart as he tumbled through empty air.

As fast as it had come, it ended with a heavy thud onto a hard surface. Rand covered his face as broken chunks of stone rained down around him, striking his legs, forearms, and torso. The impact from the fall sent pain through his entire body.

When all had settled, he uncovered his face. He'd landed on the tower's lower balcony after about a ten-foot drop. The circular balcony above was missing a chunk, destroyed by the black cube.

Rand rolled onto his side, jaw clenched, trying to will the pain away. He knew he didn't have time to lay there injured. He had to press on.

Something caught his eye among the stony rubble, reflecting the light of the moon. The black cube.

Rand figured that whatever power was within the cube could easily be turned back around onto Jackson. He grabbed it, then forced himself to stand. His aching body cried out for him to stop, but Rand refused. He limped along the balcony, powering through the pain each step caused in his knees and hips.

Rand came upon a door that led back inside the tower to the room with the magic circle. He crossed it and stumbled up the stairs once again.

When he reemerged into the tower's uppermost chamber, he saw Miller to his right, on the ground, with a broad-shouldered man standing over him. The man's back was to Rand.

Miller was bleeding from the mouth and looked frightened and helpless. From where he lay, his eyes found Rand and silently pleaded for help.

The large man looked over his shoulder at Rand, following Miller's gaze.

Bernard. Rand recognized him instantly.

Given Bernard's sudden look of surprise, Rand got the impression that Bernard somehow recognized him too.

"It's *you*," the man snarled.

Rand acted fast. Just as Jackson had done, he drew his arm back and pitched the black cube directly at Bernard Bale. The man's eyes went wide when he saw what was hurtling toward him.

The cube took him in the chest. Bernard yelped as the object's power thrust him off his feet and sent him hurtling through the air. He crashed into the chamber's stone wall and crumpled into a heap on the floor.

Rand wanted to ensure that his friend was okay, but that would have to wait. He rushed up the steps to the chamber's second floor. Akhubel was still harvesting energy from the young girl, but something else drew his attention.

Libby was entangled with Miranda Herron.

"Libby!" Rand couldn't help but shout.

Both paused and looked at him.

It was Libby who took advantage of the distraction. She gripped Miranda by the scalp with both her hands, then yanked her toward the edge of the landing. Libby shoved Miranda into the railing and the woman nearly toppled over it, flapping her arms to regain her balance. Libby didn't hesitate. She scooped Miranda's legs and sent her backwards over the edge. She shrieked as she tumbled over. Rand heard the loud thud when Miranda landed on the lower level below.

Libby didn't waste a moment. She scooped up the cross from the spot on the floor where Rand had dropped it earlier. "Dad!" she called as tossed it through the air.

Rand caught it, then approached Akhubel, holding it out toward the demon.

"In the name of the Lord Jesus Christ, I command you to release this girl and be gone from this place!"

Akhubel slowly closed his gaping mouth. He craned his neck and fixed his glowing eyes upon Rand. Despite all the commotion around him, it was the first time he'd broken his focus away from Carmen.

"Jesus has no power here," the demon snarled. "You should know that by now."

He then opened his mouth again and resumed absorbing Carmen's energy.

Libby joined Rand at his side. "Dad, do something else!"

But Rand didn't know what else to do. Commanding demons in the name of Jesus was *supposed* to work—especially when using a cross that was imbued with the power of God.

"Akhubel does not fear God."

The words came from Rand's left. Jackson leaned heavily against the doorframe that led to the balcony. The right leg of his pants was completely soaked with blood.

"Call this off," Rand ordered him.

Jackson gripped the hilt of the black knife still embedded in his thigh and gave it a sharp jerk, ripping it from his leg. He let it clatter to the stone floor, red streaks of blood landing with it. "It is done."

Rand tore his eyes away from Jackson. Both Carmen's flesh and hair had turned white—she'd been almost completely drained.

Rand wracked his brain as he looked above him through the domed, glass ceiling. Toward God and toward the heavens—where he'd chosen to return from just for this very moment.

"What am I missing?" The words were a whispered prayer.

Rand blinked and became aware of what he was looking at—the black night sky above, filled with stars.

"Dad, what are you staring at?" Libby sounded desperate.

James Herron put the stars at the center of his home, but Akhubel made him reverse the zodiac.

Rand reached into his jacket pocket and took out the Bible he'd carried with him all night. He'd used that very book to drive away many demons in the past. But now, he simply opened it to its back cover and removed the single page he'd stuffed inside. He handed the Bible and the cross to his daughter, and she took them reluctantly.

"Why are you giving these to me? Don't you need them?"

Rand unfolded the paper—the page he'd torn from James Herron's astrology book, which had the corrupted writing translated by the power of the cross.

"You fear the stars," Rand whispered.

"What?" Libby said. "Dad, what is—"

"In the name of all the ages of mankind, Akhubel, I command you to leave this place. The Age of Aries rebukes you. The Age of Taurus rebukes you."

Akhubel once again turned his attention away from Carmen.

"The Age of Gemini rebukes you. The Age of Cancer rebukes you."

Akhubel slowly stood.

"The Age of Leo rebukes you."

The demon took a step away from Carmen.

"The Age of Virgo rebukes you."

Akhubel snarled at Rand, though the demon stepped backward, as if driven by an unseen force.

"It's working!" Libby said.

"Stop that!" Jackson hobbled toward Rand, but Libby acted fast. She put herself between Jackson and her father and swiftly kicked the man in his wounded leg. He howled and crumbled into a heap on the floor.

"The Age of Libra rebukes you." Rand spoke louder now as he read from the paper. "The Age of Scorpio rebukes you. The Age of Sagittarius rebukes you. The Age of Capricorn rebukes you. The Age of Aquarius rebukes you. And the current epoch of mankind, the Age of Pisces, *rebukes you.*"

Akhubel pressed himself against the far wall, unable to

put anymore distance between himself and Rand. He curled himself into a ball as if cowering away.

Libby crouched over the young girl and gently shook her shoulders. "Carmen, wake up." She pressed her fingers into her throat. "She's alive, Dad."

Carmen stirred, then slowly opened her eyes.

"Carmen!" Libby said. But the girl still couldn't seem to get her bearings. The color slowly crept back into her skin and hair.

"What have you done?"

The familiar voice came from behind Rand. Bernard Bale and Miranda stood at the top of the stairs. Bernard appeared totally uninjured, which shocked Rand. Minutes before he'd seen how forcefully the black cube had thrown the man against the stone wall. Rand wondered if Bernard's connection with Akhubel lended him some kind of dark magic that protected him.

"It's over," Rand said. "Your ritual has failed."

Bernard glared at him. Miranda seemed frightened.

Carmen sat up and rubbed at her eyes, unaware of where she was or what had happened to her. Libby positioned herself between the girl and Akhubel, using her body to keep her from laying eyes on the creature.

"Carmen, come here," Miranda said. Carmen turned and saw her mother.

"Carmen, wait." Libby pleaded.

"Mama." Carmen rose and ran past Rand, into her mother's arms. Miranda picked her up and held her.

"It's okay, baby," she whispered to her daughter. "I'm here."

Rand felt his disgust rise. *She has no idea what her own mother has done,* he thought.

Jackson struggled to his feet, both of his blood-covered hands holding the wound in his leg. He took in the scene around him: Akhubel cowering against the wall. Carmen, still alive. His father-in-law's fury.

"Let's go," Bernard said to Miranda. He then turned and descended the steps.

"Bernard, wait," Jackson pleaded.

Miranda lingered for a few moments, giving her husband a look of pity.

"Miranda…"

Miranda ultimately turned her back on Jackson and followed her father.

"Is Daddy coming?" Carmen's pinched voice was barely audible, and Miranda did not respond.

Rand went to the edge of the landing that overlooked the chamber's first floor. He watched as Bernard and Miranda approached the arched door that would take them down the tower. Rand wanted to go after them, to seize Carmen away from them, but he knew that would be futile. He'd only barely managed a feeble victory.

Miller looked up at him from the first floor. He sat propped against the wall, lip and nose bloody from his confrontation with Bernard. He held his stomach as well. He seemed to be waiting to see what Rand would do next.

Miranda and her daughter disappeared through the door and down the stairs. Before Bernard followed, he paused and shouted over his shoulder.

"Akhubel! Finish them all!"

57

R and heard a low growl behind him. Akhubel had straightened back up at the sound of his master's command—and his strength had seemingly returned.

He then affixed his glowing eyes to Libby, who was nearest to him.

"Libby!" Rand called out.

Akhubel leapt toward Libby, mouth gaping open as if ready to bite her.

Libby didn't even have time to dodge. Akhubel moved too fast.

"No!" Rand shrieked.

Libby whirled around to face the demon.

When Akhubel was mere inches away, Libby thrust the tip of the cross toward him. It pierced him in the chest.

Akhubel wailed in pain, stumbling backwards as his grey and mottled body filled with white light. He disintegrated as the pure rays tore through him, writhing in pain until there was nothing left of him and his screams fell silent.

The cross clattered to the floor.

Libby turned toward her dad, eyes wide and frightened as if she couldn't believe what she'd just done.

Rand couldn't believe it either. He stood in stunned silence as it slowly sank in that Akhubel was gone.

Jackson was the first to move. He limped toward the door to the tower's balcony and disappeared outside.

"Jackson," Rand said, but the man ignored him.

"Go check on Miller," Rand told Libby, and she nodded. He then followed Jackson out onto the balcony.

RAND EMERGED OUTSIDE JUST as Jackson swung his good leg onto the balcony's narrow railing and climbed on top of it, dragging his injured leg up with him.

"Whoa whoa whoa," Rand said, taking a step toward Jackson, but then stopped himself. "You don't need to do that."

Jackson got his feet underneath him and slowly straightened his legs, arms outstretched to keep his balance.

"Please come down."

He only shook his head, regarding Rand with a fearful look. "You have no idea what you've done."

"I tried to tell you that I could get you out of this," Rand said. "There is *always* a way."

"But there isn't."

Rand *almost* agreed with Jackson. The man had betrayed his own father and married into a family allied with a demonic entity. He'd committed his life to Akhubel, and he'd even been willing to sacrifice his own *daughter* to the demon.

It was all unforgivable. But Rand had done his part. He'd freed the man from the evil as he'd originally promised. How Jackson Herron was ultimately held accountable for his sins was not up to Rand.

Jackson shifted a bit and flapped his arms to regain his balance, nearly toppling over the edge. Rand's stomach lurched, as if he were the one on the edge at such a height. Thankfully, Jackson managed to recenter himself.

"There *is* a way out of this." Rand tried to force his panicked voice to be calm.

"I *failed*." The word shot sharply from his mouth, laden with regret. "My family has abandoned me, as they should. Even worse than that, Akhubel is… he's…"

Dead. Jackson couldn't seem to bring himself to admit it. Rand could only wonder how that was worse than Jackson being expelled from the family.

"Please let me help you," Rand pleaded.

"If you had any sense, Randolph Casey," Jackson said, "you'd climb up here with me. Because now that you've crossed Bernard Bale, your life will never be the same again."

Those words sank deep into Rand. He already knew in that moment that Jackson Herron had spoken the unfiltered truth.

There was a disturbance in the air between Rand and Jackson, and then a black shadow appeared. Startled, Rand stepped away from it.

Impossible, Rand thought. *Akhubel's gone. Libby got him with the cross…*

A familiar, whispered voice arose telepathically inside of Rand's mind.

'He's a useless fool, but he is correct.'

The shadow then materialized into the form of another familiar entity.

Shindael.

Adrenaline jolted through Rand's body.

Over Shindael's shoulder, Jackson stared at the demon with wide eyes.

'You've made some new enemies tonight, Randolph. It will be very amusing to me to see how you might handle this.'

Rand clenched his jaw at hearing Shindael repeat Jackson's words. There was no way Rand could deny its veracity now. "Who are these people? Who is the Bale family?"

Although Shindael's face rarely betrayed emotion, Rand could've sworn he saw the hint of a smirk in the demon's black, slanted eyes.

'You will learn soon enough.'

Shindael lifted his clawed hand. As he did, a swift and invisible force thrust Jackson Herron backwards off the side of the balcony.

"No!" Rand called.

But it had happened too quickly. Jackson Herron had simply been there one moment then gone the next.

Rand heard the soft thud below.

'Before, it seemed this was a fine night for you to finally die, Randolph. But now I'm delighted to see what the Bales will do to you and your family.'

Shindael vanished just as quickly as he'd appeared, leaving Rand alone atop the Herron House tower.

58

Rand descended the stone steps. When he returned to the room where he'd died, all the candles that had once been lit were now extinguished. The magic circle on the floor had also disappeared.

It probably vanished as soon as Libby killed Akhubel, he thought.

Rand reached the bottom of the tower and approached the landing that overlooked the Herron House entrance hall. Libby and Miller stood by the mansion's open front door, waiting for him.

"Are you all right?" Miller called up to him.

"Yeah."

"And Jackson?"

Rand swallowed heavily. "Shindael… punished him."

Libby and Miller exchanged a dark look.

Rand descended the staircase and went to his daughter, where he wrapped her in a tight hug. She squeezed him back.

"You saved my life up there. Twice," he said. He kissed the top of her head.

"Maybe *now* you won't push me away when I try to help you with these things."

Rand had no idea how she'd gotten there. He hadn't even told her he was taking the case. But he'd be forever grateful that she'd come for him.

He retrieved his black bag from where he'd left it at the beginning of the night and slung it over his shoulder.

"What happens now?" Miller asked.

"We get very far away from here as fast as we can."

Rand approached the wide-open front door. He'd pursued a way out of the mansion all night, and now it lay right in front of him. He walked out onto the mansion's porch and into the chilly air. The sky had just begun to brighten into a grey morning.

"Rando, wait." Miller said as he and Libby followed Rand outside. "We have bodies. There's even another one you don't know about yet inside the caretaker's house…"

Rand swallowed. "You think Jackson killed him?"

Miller nodded.

Miller doesn't know the half of it, Rand thought as he remembered the dozens of withered bodies in the depths of the passageway leading from James Herron's office.

"I think so. I tried calling the police after we lost contact over the radio," Miller explained. "I know we aren't supposed to do that while working a case, but I didn't know what else to do at the time, and Jackson was really starting to act strange."

"I understand. What did they tell you?"

"I… don't think they're going to be much help."

Rand remembered how Jackson had talked the police

officer out of giving him a speeding ticket. At the time, Rand had assumed that had been the result of a friendly relationship with small-town law enforcement. Now that Rand knew more about the Bale family's scope of influence, he wondered if *all* the local officers had been in Jackson's pocket as well.

What about the state police? Rand wondered. *How deep does it go?*

"I still have to try," Rand said, removing his phone from his pocket. He had a single bar of signal now that he was outside of the mansion. He dialed 911 and the operator answered.

"What's your emergency?" she asked.

"I need to report a body."

"What is your location?"

"Beau Ridge, Louisiana."

The operator fell silent.

"Hello?" Rand finally said.

"One moment, sir."

The line went dull as the operator put him on hold. Light static buzzed while Rand waited. He had only called 911 a handful of times in his life, but he knew this kind of response wasn't normal.

The line connected again. "It's all under control, sir." This time it was a man who spoke.

"But there's—"

"Sir," the man cut Rand off with a tone that was not to be questioned. "It's *under control.*"

Just as I thought, Rand thought.

"Wait. Who is this?"

Rand quickly hung up on him.

"Let me guess," Miller said. "It's under control."

Libby appeared frightened as she looked between her dad and Miller.

That simple exchange told Rand all he needed to know about Jackson's—and the Bale family's—relationship with the police. Miller was right. They weren't going to be any help at all.

"Let's get the hell out of here," Rand finally said.

59

The drive away from the town of Beau Ridge began with uncomfortable silence. Exhaustion had enveloped Rand all at once. He'd been forced to dig deep all night, to be on constant alert. Now, it was finally taking its toll.

"Dad," Libby said from the backseat.

"Yeah?" Rand glanced at her in the rearview mirror.

"I know you're tired and probably don't have the energy to think about it right now, but I'm really worried about Carmen."

"So am I," Rand said. He still could barely fathom that the girl had been born and raised specifically to be a ritualistic sacrifice. Now that the ritual had been foiled, he wondered what those twisted people would do with her. "You're right. We'll need to do something. I just don't know what yet."

Rand was beginning to understand what Jackson and Shindael had told him. Before, his cases had a clear beginning and end. This time, that wasn't true at all.

But this was never a real case, he reminded himself. *This was a trap.*

The things he'd seen and learned inside the Herron House would haunt him far into the future. The Bales would not simply allow him to walk away from everything. He'd be dealing with the fallout from the night's events for a long time, perhaps the rest of his life.

Rand heard something vibrating; he thought it was his phone, but when he picked it up from where it lay in the space underneath the center console, it showed no incoming call.

Miller dug into his pocket. "Who's calling *me* so early in the morning?" He stared at the screen for a few moments without answering, perplexed.

"Who is it?" Rand asked, and he immediately heard the nervousness in his own voice.

"A number from Georgia. I think I know who this is…" Miller tapped the screen once to answer the call, then activated the speaker phone. "Hello?"

"This is Arthur Briggs." The caller's voice was gruff. He almost sounded angry.

Who? Rand knew he should be watching the road, but he couldn't tear his eyes off Miller.

"Um… Thank you for getting back to me, Mr. Bri—"

"Please tell me you didn't engage one of the Lords of Hell."

"What?" Rand whispered. *Lords of Hell?*

Miller nervously cleared his throat. "We did."

The man was silent for a few moments before he said, "That's *really* bad for you."

"But we killed him," Miller added quickly.

The man on the phone scoffed. "Don't lie to me."

"I wouldn't lie about something like this. My friend—the one I mentioned in my message to you—he recently discovered that demons could *die*. And tonight we watched a Lord of Hell die."

"No shit demons can die," the man spat. "I've known that for a long time. Your friend is clearly not very knowledgeable about the spiritual world, and neither are you."

Rand felt his anger surge toward the man—he'd just brushed aside what Rand considered to be one of the most important discoveries of his life. "Who the hell is this guy?"

"If you've killed one of the Lords of Hell, then I feel sorry for you. You've committed an act of war against all of the underworld, and now they will come for you. They will not stop."

Miller seemed quite taken aback at the man's abrupt declaration. Finally, he said, "Can you help us? That's why I reached out to you in the first place."

"This is not my fight. You stirred up this trouble. There's nothing I can do for you."

"But—"

The line went dead.

"Hello?" Miller said.

"Who the hell was that?" Rand asked.

Miller lowered his phone and sighed. "I dug up a little research on Akhubel. I didn't get a chance to tell you what I found before our radios disconnected, though."

"Where does he get off calling me an amateur?" Rand's tone was aggressive now. "He doesn't know me *or* what I've been through."

But Miller only gave Rand a somber look. "His name is

Arthur Briggs, and I think you should listen to him, Rando. He knows what he's talking about."

Rand didn't want to believe it, especially after what he'd just heard.

"You've committed an act of war against all of the underworld."

Although Rand was upset, he had to pause and admit that what Arthur Briggs had told him sounded awfully similar to Shindael's threat.

"I'll show you what I found when we get home," Miller said.

Rand gripped the steering wheel. Despite all that had happened, there was apparently still more for him to learn. There'd be no rest for him any time soon. He pressed his foot on the gas.

"I'm scared, Dad," Libby said.

Rand didn't respond. At least, not out loud.

I am too, he thought.

60

R and pulled into his driveway just as the first raindrops of the coming storm landed on his windshield. He should've been happy to finally be home, but his thoughts had raced throughout the entire drive. The guy who'd called Miller had only made things worse.

Rand would've given anything to drop Miller off at home and Libby at her mom's so he could sleep the rest of the day away, but he knew that wasn't possible. He needed Miller to help him make sense of who Arthur Briggs was, and he also still had no clue how Miller had dug him up from whatever far corners of the internet he perused.

Rand climbed out of the Jeep and went to the trunk to retrieve his bag. Miller did the same, while Libby headed toward the front door.

"You sure this Arthur Briggs guy can be trusted?" Rand asked.

"I really do think so," Miller said.

"Dad," Libby said, voice tense. She'd halted a few steps away from the front door. It was slightly ajar.

Rand knew for a fact he'd closed *and* locked it before he'd left.

He dropped his bag onto the driveway and rushed past Libby. "Wait out here."

Rand paused just outside the door. He tilted his ear toward it, trying to hear if anyone was inside. The only sound was the thunder rumbling overhead in the distance.

He pushed the door open, revealing the destruction within.

Every cabinet in the kitchen had been opened and the contents strewn about. Dishes were smashed. Pipes had been destroyed, leaving water flowing over the debris. The overhead light in his living had been pulled from the ceiling and was dangling by its wires. His television screen was smashed. The fabric of his couch had been ripped open, and the stuffing had been scattered around.

But none of that mattered to Rand. All of it could've been done by any common vandal.

Far more harrowing were the demonic symbols gouged into his walls, the dark red and black stains on his carpet, and the *very* familiar magic circle of Akhubel drawn onto his roof. Getting the precision of the circle was difficult enough when it was drawn on the floor, so to have it on the ceiling should've been impossible. Whoever had done this had help from beyond.

The star chart Tessa had given him remained on the kitchen table. It was unfolded, though Rand explicitly remembered leaving it folded up. More demonic symbols had been written over the chart, making it unreadable.

Rand had ridiculed Tessa for her interest in astrology, yet Rand could no longer deny that the power of the stars had saved his life. He didn't quite understand how, but he planned to learn. He now knew it was no small insult to see his birth chart desecrated.

"Oh no." Libby stood at the threshold of the front door. Miller was behind her.

Rand walked deeper into his house and saw the vandalism continued down the hallway. In the office his shelves and books had been torn down. Everything that had been on top of the desk—his lamp, a pile of books he'd been reading, and a few framed pictures—had been swiped off onto the floor. Next, he went into his bedroom at the end of the hall. His bed was overturned, and his clothes had been thrown from his closet.

"Dad…"

Rand returned to the hall. Libby peered into her bedroom, seeming distressed.

Her room had also been desecrated, but there was something different that wasn't in any other part of the house—a single phrase was written repeatedly across the walls in a scrawling hand.

SLAYER OF AKHUBEL

Libby looked like she was about to cry.

Rand strived to wrap his mind around it all. Clearly there was an organized group of people who were already aware of what had transpired at the Herron House. They even knew that *Libby* had been the one to kill Akhubel.

Rand remembered Jackson Herron's final words to him: *"Now that you've crossed paths with Bernard Bale, your life will never be the same again."*

"Rando, what's this?" Miller asked from the living room.

Rand exhaled sharply. He wasn't sure he could handle any more surprises.

He returned to the living room. Miller gestured toward the coffee table in front of the ruined couch, which was perhaps the only piece of furniture in Rand's entire home that had been spared. There was only one thing on top of it—something that hadn't been there before.

The black cube.

Rand had left it in the Herron House's throne room, only to have it inexplicably reappear inside his jacket pocket. He'd left it behind a second time after he'd hurled it at Bernard Bale in the tower.

It was clear to Rand now that the black cube would follow him.

"What does it all mean?" Libby asked, dejected. She'd torn herself away from staring at her wrecked bedroom and had returned to the living room.

"It means…" Rand began, but he couldn't find the words. Miller and Libby peered at him, waiting for an answer, or some sort of encouragement, or a plan.

Rand couldn't give them any of those things. He'd never felt so hopeless and vulnerable in his entire life.

"I don't know what it means," he finally said. "But I have a feeling it won't be long until we find out."

Randolph Casey will return!

To be notified as soon as he does, visit my website to sign up to my email list.

https://rockwellscott.com/free-book/

As soon as you sign up, you'll also receive a FREE gift from me—my supernatural horror novella that is not available anywhere else. You'll be able to download the book directly to your e-reading device in seconds.

HEY THERE.

Thank you for spending your valuable time reading my book, and I hope you enjoyed it.

As you may know, reviews are one of the best ways readers can support their favorite authors. They help get the word out and convince potential readers to take a chance on me.

I would like to ask that you consider leaving a review on Amazon or Goodreads. I would be very grateful, and of course, it is always valuable to me to hear what my readers think of my work.

Thank you in advance to everyone who chooses to do so, and I hope to see you back in my pages soon.

Sincerely,

- Rockwell

But it's too late. There, he finds Trevor trying to make contact with the spirit that tormented them years ago.

And Trevor refuses to leave. He is determined to cleanse the house and remove the entity. But the supernatural activity becomes too much to handle, and Jake knows they are both unprepared for the fight. Worse, the entity targets Daniel, Jake's young nephew, and wants to bring him harm. And when the intelligent haunting shows signs of demonic infestation, Jake realizes they aren't dealing with a mere ghost.

Jake attributes the evil spirit for driving his parents to an early grave. Now it wants to claim the rest of the family, and the only way Jake and Trevor will survive is to send the entity back to hell.

A Haunting in Rose Grove is a supernatural horror novel for readers who love stories about haunted houses and battles with the demonic — the truest form of evil that exists in our world.

The Gravewatcher

Every night at 3 AM, he visits the graveyard and speaks to someone who isn't there.

Eleanor has created an ideal life for herself in New York City with a career that keeps her too busy, just as she likes it. But when she receives an anonymous message that her estranged brother Dennis is dead, her fast-paced routine grinds to a halt. She rushes to Finnick, Louisiana — the small, backward town where her brother lived and temporarily settles into his creepy, turn-of-the-century house until she can figure out how he died.

But that night, Eleanor spots a young boy in the cemetery behind Dennis's house, speaking to the gravestones. When she approaches him, Eleanor's interruption of the boy's ritual sets off a chain reaction of horror she could have never prepared for. The footsteps, the voices, and the shadowy apparitions are only the beginning.

Eleanor learns that the boy, Walter, is being oppressed by a demonic entity that compels him to visit the graveyard every night. She suspects Dennis also discovered this nightly ritual and tried to stop it, and that is why he died. Because there are others in Finnick who know about Walter's involvement with the evil spirit and want it to continue, and they will do whatever it takes to stop Eleanor from ruining their carefully laid plans. Now Eleanor must finish what her brother started — to rescue the boy from the clutches of hell before he loses his soul forever.

The Gravewatcher is a supernatural horror novel for readers who love stories about haunted houses, creepy graveyards, and battles with the demonic - the truest form of evil that exists in our world.

ABOUT THE AUTHOR

Rockwell Scott is an author of supernatural horror fiction.

When not writing, he can be found working out, enjoying beer and whiskey with friends, and traveling internationally.

Feel free to get in touch!

Instagram

https://www.instagram.com/rockwellscottauthor/

Facebook
www.facebook.com/rockwellscottauthor

Twitter
@rockwell_scott

www.rockwellscott.com

rockwellscottauthor@gmail.com

Printed in Great Britain
by Amazon